About the Author

Simon Bywater's journey began in Dunstable, born into a bustling household with two broth unfolded amidst the rustic charm of a village sl Cambridgeshire. His family's diverse background was reflected in his upbringing, with a father hailing from Bengaluru (Bangalore), India, and a mother rooted in Luton, Bedfordshire.

At the age of sixteen, Simon embarked on a remarkable path by joining the Royal Marine Commandos in 1985. Over the years, he served with 40 Commando RM, traversing the globe, and facing the challenges of active service, including a significant stint in Northern Iraq during Operation Safe Haven in 1991. Simon's tenure in the Marines instilled in him a profound sense of duty and resilience that would shape his future endeavours.

Transitioning from military life, Simon embarked on a new chapter by joining Greater Manchester Police. In roles spanning Uniform and the Criminal Investigation Department (CID), he gained invaluable experience in the vibrant communities of Wythenshawe and Moss Side, South Manchester. However, Simon's roots beckoned him back to Cambridgeshire, and at the dawn of the Millennium, he returned with his family to embrace a new chapter.

Driven by an entrepreneurial spirit, Simon ventured into the realm of business, where he found success through various ventures. Yet, his ambitions extended beyond commerce. Simon's multifaceted journey saw him delve into the realm of literature, where he is currently engrossed in crafting a new book. Additionally, his dedication to public service is evident through his roles as an elected Cambridgeshire County Councillor and Huntingdonshire District Councillor, where he tirelessly advocates for his community's interests.

Beyond his professional pursuits, Simon finds solace and vitality in his personal passions. Through his diverse interests and unwavering commitment, Simon Bywater embodies a spirit of resilience, adaptability, and boundless curiosity.

"AMBITIONS FLAME"

In youth, a blazing fire did gleam,
Ambition's flame, a radiant dream.
With dreams so high and spirits bold,
I chased the stars, my story well told.

But as the years, like rivers, flowed,
That fiery passion eased and slowed.
The flame that once burned fierce and bright,
Now flickers softly in the night.

For life has tempered my wild desire,
Yet left a spark, in a smouldering fire.
I guard it well, that ember small,
For it's the essence of my all.

In getting older, I've come to see,
Ambition's form may change in me.
No longer roaring, but steady and wise,
A beacon now, 'neath older skies.

This subtle flame, I'll cherish dear,
A reminder of what brought me here.
With wisdom's grace, I'll gently tend,
The ember's glow, until the end.

Simon Bywater

By Simon Bywater

Forced Out

Honourable Retribution

Life Skills for Young People and How to Become a Decent Human Being

Verses of Life

SIMON BYWATER

PAY BACK
"When Life Costs"

First Published in 2024 by Charente Publishing

Copyright C Simon Bywater 2024

This edition printed 2024 by Amazon Books

The right of Simon Bywater to be identified as the author of this work has been asserted by him in accordance with the

Copyright, Designs, and patents acts 1988.

All rights reserved. No part of this publication may be reproduced, transmitted, or stored in a retrieval system, in any form or means, without permission in writing from the publisher, nor be otherwise circulated in any form of binding or cover other than in which it is published and without a similar condition being imposed on the subsequent purchaser.

Typesetting in Garamond

Printed by Amazon

1 Devastation

Richie trudged home, the weight of a miserable day pressing down on his shoulders like a burden too heavy to bear. As he stepped inside, the silence greeted him, amplifying the emptiness within. His heart sank further when he realised Dad was still absent, swallowed by the sterile corridors of the hospital, undergoing endless tests and treatments.

In the dimly lit lounge, Tom, engrossed in the world flashing across the Xbox screen, seemed oblivious to Richie's arrival. Amid his inner turmoil, Richie endeavoured to mend the divide, to share the worry that weighed heavily on both their hearts.

"You heard from Dad?" The words hung heavy in the air, filled with concern and longing for reassurance.

"Nah," came Tom's abrupt response, his focus solely fixated on the digital realm before him, as though escaping the weight of their reality.

Richie's longing for a genuine connection tugged at him, an ache deep within that yearned for the warmth of understanding shared between brothers. He tried to breach the gap, hoping for a flicker of acknowledgment from Tom, but his attempts were met with fleeting responses, barely more than whispers in the wind. It was as though Tom's spirit lingered elsewhere, tethered to the virtual landscape flashing across the screen, disinterested in the tangible reality around them.

Their conversation hung heavy, words evaporating into the air, leaving behind a desolate silence that echoed Richie's disappointment and the gnawing worry that clawed at his chest. His voice, laced with both sadness and concern, trailed off into the hollow space between them as he retreated into the solitude of his thoughts. The distance between brothers widened, a gulf growing with each passing moment.

Tom's obsession with the "shoot 'em up" video game had consumed him for hours, the cacophony of gunfire and alien cries drowning out their feeble attempts at connection. It was a world of vibrant pixels and adrenaline, a sanctuary where Tom sought refuge, oblivious to the potential bond waiting to be nurtured between them.

As Richie maneuvered through the room, deliberately crossing Tom's line of sight in front of the TV, a fleeting hope emerged that this disruption might prompt a real conversation. Yet, it only yielded frustration. Tom's imaginary character in the game suffered a fatal blow, and the room erupted with his outraged cry.

"Oi, get out of the way! I've just been killed because of you, idiot!" Tom's shout reverberated, accompanied by the clatter of the controller thrown in vexation.

The room crackled with tension, the once-muted emotions now thrumming palpably in the charged air. Richie stood there, caught between the ache for connection and the realisation that in this moment, the chasm between them had only grown wider.

Richie grinned as he casually tossed his rucksack onto a nearby chair, strolling away toward the kitchen. Unbeknownst to him, this minor action deeply wounded his brother. Tom had poured hours into reaching a crucial stage in the game, a temporary escape from the harshness of his reality. Discovering his efforts disregarded left him shattered, a storm of emotions brewing inside. In a surge of overwhelming devastation, Tom leaped to his feet and dashed out of the room, his words cutting through the air, "You're an idiot! I hate you!"

Disregarding Tom's exaggerated reaction, Richie sauntered into the kitchen. Once there, he retrieved a plastic snap-seal bag of weed from his trouser pocket, glancing over his shoulder to ensure Tom hadn't returned. Carefully, he tucked the bag between cookbooks in a cupboard, confident it would remain undisturbed. It was a safe hiding spot, considering no one in the house seemed likely to use those cookbooks anytime soon.

Tom dashed up the stairs, bolting into his bedroom and slamming the door shut behind him. His emotions overwhelmed him, and tears streamed down his face in uncontrollable sobs. What might seem trivial to some was, for Tom, the tipping point of a series of letdowns and feelings of abandonment by his parents.

A school tie hung at the end of his bunk bed; its knot never undone he conveniently slipped the loop over his head in a desperate attempt to startle his older brother and draw much-needed attention. He secured the other end to the bunk bed. In his young mind, the gravity of the risk was eclipsed by his raging emotions. Anger coursed through him, frustration mounting at the perceived lack of care and understanding from everyone around him. Why wasn't anyone acknowledging the turmoil in his family? Why didn't Richie seem affected by their parents' breakup? Their family unit was crumbling, compounded by the looming threat of their father's potentially fatal brain tumour.

Still sobbing, Tom clumsily grappled with the tie around his neck, his mind clouded with despair. To young Tom, life felt utterly bleak in that moment.

Richie had opened a packet of biscuits and was just making himself a cup of tea when he heard a loud dull thud from upstairs. What's that he wondered? He had heard Tom shouting, but it wasn't out of the ordinary. There had been disputes and scuffles between them over the past couple of months which was hardly surprising given the circumstances right now.

After two quick sips Richie placed his cup on the kitchen surface and wandered upstairs. Reaching the landing he opened the door to Tom's bedroom. His younger brother dangled from the end of his bunkbed, a shocking tableau that left him stunned. Toms face once lively, now bore a ghastly, pallid hue. Bloody tear drops wept from his eyes, staining his young cheeks. Tom's eyes remained fixed and staring. He was unconscious and his body motionless. In this very instant Richie felt paralysed unable to move. He was frozen in the moment of time and instinctively shouted "TOM, TOM!" There was no response.

Sprinting towards Tom's lifeless body, Richie grabbed his younger brother in a bear hug around the waist in an impulsive attempt to take the weight off the ligature. The slippery wooden floor made it hard to stand upright. Tom had also been slipping in his socks moments before in the panic to try and save himself. So much so that his socks had degloved from his feet in a desperate attempt to save his own life. Reaching up with his right arm Richie fumbled to remove the tie from the top of the bunkbed to release the tension around his brother's neck. Achieving additional strength as adrenalin raced, he lowered Tom to the floor. He was in utter panic and his heart pounded in his dry mouth. It was all happening so quickly, yet it all seemed to be happening in slow motion. "What do I do," "what do I do" he asked himself?

Richie had no first aid experience but could see his brother was not breathing. Leaving his motionless brother on the bedroom floor he raced downstairs and straight out of the front door screaming "HELP, HELP, HELP ME"!

Bill a retired council worker was just in the process of emptying his rubbish into his wheelie bin at the side of his house when he heard and then saw Richie appear in utter panic. He knew instantly there was a problem and ran towards Richie who was by now standing in the middle of the road with his head in his hands sobbing uncontrollably.

"What's up son?" came the calm measured response from Bill. Countless operational tours as a young Soldier in Northern Ireland had sapped all of Bill's excitement and adrenaline in his stage of life.

"It's my brother, it's my brother Tom!"

Bill turned to his wife who had come out of their house having heard the noise. He calmly asked her to call the Police and Ambulance services.

Bill followed Richie into the house and reached the bedroom where Toms motionless body lay on the wooden floor. "He has tried to hang himself!" Richie shouted sobbing between breaths. The enormity and gravity of the situation was now hitting Richie like an express train.

Richie stood frozen, his heart still pounding in his chest, as he watched Bill desperately attempting to resuscitate his brother. Dismay etched deeply onto Richie's face, his eyes wide with a mixture of fear and helplessness. The scene unfolded before him like a slow-motion nightmare, each moment stretching agonisingly long. He could hear his own breath catching in his throat, the intensity of his emotions threatening to overwhelm him. His hands clenched into fists at his sides, longing to reach out and do something, anything to aid in his brother's revival. Yet, all he could do was stand there, a silent witness to the struggle unfolding before him.

They both knew it was going to be a hopeless task………….

2 Tangled Loyalties

The walls of the flat seemed to close in on Richie, suffocating him with the oppressive atmosphere, his mind restless with thoughts of loyalty and survival. Jonesy, the gang leader who held his fate in his hands, had summoned Richie for a meeting.

The door swung open, revealing Jonesy's imposing figure. Dressed casually, he exuded an air of authority that demanded respect. His eyes, sharp and piercing, scanned the room, scrutinising every detail. The silence hung heavy, broken only by the sound of distant sirens and the nervous shuffling of feet.

Richie swallowed hard; his throat suddenly dry. He knew compliments from Jonesy could be a double-edged sword. They could either be a sign of approval or a prelude to a demand he couldn't refuse.

"But" Jonesy continued, his gaze narrowing, "I've heard whispers of a rival gang encroaching on our territory. Their activities are starting to affect our business. I won't tolerate such disrespect."

Richie's heart sank. He was being assessed, forced to prove his loyalty to Jonesy and protect his own interests. The city's criminal landscape was an ever-shifting chessboard, and he was a mere pawn in this game.

County line drug and exploitation gangs were the new cancer spreading out into the UK. Jonesy had honed his skills in selecting easy targets, finding his expertise more effective when preying on the most vulnerable. Jonesy was a facilitator and Richie was going to be another easy victim to add to his county line-up. Nothing over the ordinary to start with. Just make him feel confident in his company, then perhaps lending out a little bit of cash or toping up his pre-paid mobile. He knew vulnerable young people burned through mobile data.

Over time Jonesy was beginning to corner a big part of the drugs market in the town. The offside to this sort of trading was the risk of violence, threats, and intimidation. Violence and intimidation were an occupational hazard and he had learned to live with it. Jonesy had seen lots of scary moments in his life as a young dealer but if he could keep 'dodging the bullets' and stay one step ahead of his competition, he would be fine. Jonesy's little soldiers in his "county line network" were expendable. So Richie had to learn quickly or suffer the consequences.

In his teenage years, Jonesy grasped the dynamics of overseeing his territory on the streets of South Manchester, the very neighbourhood he grew up in. For countless young men in the area, navigating these streets was perceived as a crucial "rite of passage," and despite the inherent dangers, many chose to embrace it. Throughout his experiences, Jonesy encountered a considerable amount of violence and shootings, but the most harrowing episode etched in his memory occurred in a car park adjacent to the Grafham Pub, where his gang leader, including his elder brother Darnell, were ruthlessly executed.

The Grafham Pub, now replaced by a modern and upscale office block, served as the backdrop for this tragic event. The haunting memories of the unsolved executions that unfolded that night lingered vividly in Jonesy's mind. The impact was profound not only on him but also on his associate Sonny, who, after witnessing the incident, was never the same. Sonny succumbed to the allure of "the gear" and tragically lost his life to a fatal overdose, a fate that attributed to the trauma he endured that fateful night.

Since that incident, there had been countless additional shootings. A handful of Jonesy's associates had narrowly escaped dangerous situations, though such close calls were par for the course in the street dealer's relentless game of "cat and mouse." Whether it was rival gangs or the constant threat of the cops, Jonesy remained vigilant.

Despite harboring suspicions about who might have been responsible for his elder brother's death that night, nothing concrete had ever surfaced. Jonesy had come to understand that any challenge to his territory wouldn't be ignored or left unaddressed. A culture of "tit for tat" prevailed, ensuring that threats on his turf would be met with swift retaliation or retribution. Maintaining his credibility was paramount, and Jonesy knew that any display of weakness on the street would be exploited by rival gangs. In this urban jungle, one had to make it clear they were no pushover, and Jonesy was determined to assert his dominance, dealing decisively with any unwelcome interest from others on the streets.

"I need you to uncover the mastermind behind this and put an end to it," Jonesy's voice carried a gravity that allowed no room for dissent. Richie exchanged cautious glances around the room, his unspoken communication conveying the seriousness of the task. He had little choice but to accept the request; defying Jonesy was a risk they couldn't afford.

Richie's contemplation was interrupted by the buzzing of his phone. An informant's message revealed rumours about the rival gang's leader, pointing to a potential culprit. It was a lead to follow; a step closer to the truth they sought.

Richie shared the details with Jonesy, who listened attentively, his eyes reflecting a mix of satisfaction and calculation. When Richie concluded, Jonesy nodded slowly, acknowledging their success.

"You've proven your worth," Jonesy stated, his voice laced with begrudging admiration. "But remember, loyalty is a two-way street. Betray me, and you'll discover consequences far worse than you can imagine."

Richie's heart sank once again. Loyalty was a precarious tightrope he had to navigate. Bound to Jonesy, his fate was permanently entangled. In this dangerous dance, he had to tread carefully, juggling allegiances to survive in a world where trust was a rare commodity.

Richie shared a silent understanding. He had gained a reprieve, but the web of loyalty and power only grew more intricate. He knew he had to remain vigilant, forever aware that the stakes were high, and his destiny hung in the balance.

****

Later that night Richie sat alone in his dimly lit bedroom; his heart heavy with a burden that seemed impossible to shake off. The walls, once adorned with posters of his favourite bands and carefree memories, now closed in on him, suffocating him with the weight of his mistakes. The silence of the room amplified the echoes of regret that reverberated through his mind.

It all began months ago when Richie's curiosity led him down a treacherous path. In his small suburban town, boredom had become his constant companion, whispering temptation into his ear. He was drawn into the murky world of drugs, enticed by the illusion of escape from the monotony of everyday life.

Jonesy, a charismatic but dangerous figure, became Richie's gateway to this clandestine realm. What started as a casual experiment soon turned into an addiction and sense of belonging. The highs and euphoria provided temporary respite from the numbing realities of his existence. But with every promise, Richie unwittingly signed a contract with the devil, plunging himself into a cycle of dependency and debt.

Jonesy, ever the opportunist, capitalised on Richie's vulnerability. The initial kindness and camaraderie quickly transformed into a suffocating grip. Richie found himself trapped in a web of owing money to Jonesy, a debt that grew exponentially with each transaction. The consequences of defaulting were dire, a constant reminder of the risks lurking just beyond his doorstep.

3 Glimmer of Strength

Fifteen-year-old Mia slowly regained consciousness, her body feeling heavy, as if weighted down by the weight of the night before. As she struggled to push herself up, pain coursed through her body, a chilling reminder of the terror she had endured.

Fear and confusion clouded her thoughts as she pieced together fragments of memories. The night had started like any other, another shift on the county lines, transporting drugs to unfamiliar territories. But this time, something had gone horribly wrong.

The flat was a "doss house." It lacked any visual signs of the clean well-kept home she had desperately hoped and wished for as a young child. She clutched the worn sheets, her knuckles turning white. Tears welled up in her eyes as she recalled the faces of the perpetrators, the haunting echoes of their laughter. Mia's innocence had been shattered again, replaced by a lingering sense of violation and shame. Despite the warmth in the flat her whole body shivered at the thoughts.

Empty beer bottles and cups were strewn around the room on any available surface. The wooden flooring was tired, worn, scuffed, and hadn't seen a decent brush or hoover in months. Balls of fluff congregated in the corners of the room like tumbleweed from the American west.

Gently, she reached up to touch her bruised face, wincing at the tenderness. The pain was both physical and emotional, a cruel reminder of the darkness that had engulfed her. She felt trapped, suffocated by the secrets she carried, unsure of how to break free from this nightmarish existence.

As Mia peeled herself out of bed, her legs threatened to give way beneath her. She stumbled towards the bathroom, her vulnerability evident in her hesitant steps. Her fiery red hair was matted and tangled, mirroring the chaos that had consumed her life.

The sound of running water filled the bathroom as she splashed her face, the cold liquid awakening her senses. She stared at her reflection; her eyes haunted by the horrors she had experienced. But within the depths of her pain, a flicker of defiance burned inside. Following the last Police investigation after she had been attacked, she perceived a sense of everyone in the justice system was against her.

Mia wiped away the tears, determination etching itself onto her face. She refused to let this, or her life define her. No longer would she be a victim, a pawn in the twisted game of county lines. She craved freedom, a life untouched by the shadows that had consumed her.

With every ounce of strength, she could muster, Mia resolved to reclaim her power. She would no longer be silent, no longer allow herself to be a victim of circumstance. She would find a way to escape the clutches of the monsters that had violated her but first she had to battle her addiction.

As she stepped out of the bathroom, Mia's eyes landed on her phone, a device that had been both a lifeline and a tool of her enslavement. It held the contacts of the people who had used and abused her, those who had perpetuated her suffering.

Seated on the bed, Mia began contemplating her brief existence. Taken into her initial foster family at the tender age of eight, she found herself caught in the tumult of her parents' unstable relationship, revolving around her father's struggles with drug addiction, alcohol dependence, and violence. Tears welled up in her eyes, streaming down her cheeks as she grappled with the unfairness of her life. Throughout her short journey, Mia had devised her own coping mechanism, attempting to numb the pain by drowning everything out with the solace of drink and drugs.

At the age of twelve, Mia's world shattered when her birth father, Bobby, was convicted of fatally stabbing her mother, Rebecca, during a drug-fuelled and drunken domestic altercation. The devastating news reached Mia through a police officer who had arrived at her foster home, the place she called home at the time. With no other relative or next of kin to break the news, Mia was left in profound distress, feeling abandoned by the support system around her.

Her father, 'Bobby,' received a life sentence for the murder of her mother. Since that tragic event, Mia had neither spoken to nor heard from her father again. While everyone else in her life moved forward, the haunting memories of that incident lingered with Mia every day.

Mia harboured conflicting emotions for her mother—love, hatred, and an overwhelming sense of loss. Despite her mother's imperfections, Mia couldn't help but long for the woman who, flawed as she was, remained her mother.

"Why couldn't she have just sobered up and taken me away from it all, keeping us safe?" Mia pondered, grappling with the painful what-ifs.

The irreversible outcome of her parents' tumultuous relationship cast a permanent shadow over Mia's life. Her mother was gone forever, and the enduring pain of that loss weighed heavily on her. The profound absence of her mother served as a significant catalyst for Mia's struggles at such a tender age, leading her to seek solace through self-medication and inadvertently losing the battle against alcohol and drugs. This, in turn, hindered her ability to find stability in foster care placements.

Navigating school proved to be equally challenging for Mia. Her teachers failed to comprehend the depths of her experiences. "How on earth could they?" Mia questioned. Her teachers came from stable middle-class backgrounds, a world vastly different from Mia's upbringing in squalor amidst drugs, alcohol, and domestic violence. They couldn't fathom her childhood, only perceiving a disruptive young girl with anger issues and no interest in learning.

At times, Mia faced uncertainty about where she would sleep or when her next meal would come. Consequently, her commitment to completing homework for a teacher fluctuated in importance, depending on one's perspective.

During her most challenging moments, attending classes or sitting exams were the last concerns on Mia's mind. Schools and teachers, proved to be unreliable allies. Mia perceived the education system as more focused on the school's reputation based on exam results than on enhancing her life prospects. She believed that individuals in education were only valued when their outcomes affected "exam stats."

Under the supervision of the local authority, Mia found herself thrust into an unexpected encounter with locally elected councillors who aimed to include young representatives from the care system in their meetings. Initially hesitant, Mia reluctantly accepted, swayed by her social worker's encouragement. However, the councillors, clad in polished attire and exuding an aura of superiority, seemed disconnected from Mia's reality. Most of them were privileged white middle-aged women, adopting a condescending "Yummy Mummy" approach. One particularly liberal councillor, purporting to empathise with Mia's struggles as a retired head teacher, only managed to further irritate her with his arrogant demeanor.

"Fat chance he understands," Mia seethed, incensed by the obliviousness of a system that had consistently failed her. Voicing her frustration, she bluntly told the elder councillor to "Fuck off," resulting in her exclusion from any future meetings of similar nature.

A resounding knock echoed through the flat, jolting Mia back to the harsh reality of her everyday life. As she approached the front door, the silhouette of a man loomed behind the glass exterior. Pausing for a moment, Mia hesitated, uncertain of the visitor's identity. If it were someone sent by Jonesy, neglecting to answer the door to a customer could incur his wrath.

With reluctance, Mia cautiously opened the door, securing it with the rusty chain lock, and peered through the narrow gap to investigate who was there…..

4 The Ravages of War

Maxim's eyes fluttered open, and he slowly sat up, his body stiff from the unrestful night. A deep sigh escaped his lips as he gazed around the small room that had become his refuge, a place where memories intertwined with the present, where pain mingled with hope.

In his mind's eye, Maxim could still vividly recall the day that changed his life forever, the day war tore through his home city of Mariupol one of the largest cities in Ukraine. He was just a young person, innocent, and full of dreams for a future that now seemed distant and unattainable. It had been a great city to spend his early childhood in but now it had been destroyed and flattened by the Russian invaders.

The echoes of explosions and gunfire reverberated through the air as chaos engulfed the city. Fear gripped Maxim's heart as he witnessed his once peaceful neighbourhood crumble under the weight of destruction. The world he had known was being torn apart, leaving behind a trail of shattered lives and broken dreams.

In Ukraine, daily life turned into a lottery once the bombings commenced. When the shelling first erupted, the uncertainty of survival pervaded his thoughts. The looming conflict became a daily source of worry for everyone, tearing families apart because of a senseless war initiated by Russian aggressors.

Maxim's father, a respected university lecturer in Marine engineering, and his mother, a scientist, had provided the family with a comfortable life before the outbreak of war. They instilled in Maxim the values of honesty and trustworthiness. His name, Maxim, signifying "The greatest one," served as a constant reminder, although in recent times, he hadn't felt particularly 'great.'

Running through the rubble-strewn streets, Maxim searched for his family. His heart pounded in his chest as he called out their names, his voice drowned out by the cacophony of violence. Tears streamed down his face, blending with the dirt and soot that clung to his cheeks.

When the air strike hit, the explosions reverberated through Maxim's part of town, inducing an immediate sensation of nausea and weakness. Describing the experience to those who had never lived through it proved challenging. After the explosion, he remembered being paralysed by the shockwave, a surreal moment where time seemed to freeze, and the events unfolded in agonising slow motion. His limbs felt heavy, overcome by a numbness that penetrated deep into his soul. Maxim knew the bombs had struck his home.

Trudging through the remnants of what was once his home, he encountered a skeletal structure, its walls crumbling akin to his shattered hopes. The block of flats that had housed his family was no more, reduced to a crumpled mess of smouldering concrete, broken glass, and household debris strewn in disarray. Thick, lung-clogging dust hung in the air, making it difficult to open eyes or breathe. Visibility, initially reduced to arm's length, slowly improved as rays of sunlight clawed through the dissipating dust clouds.

The haunting screams from the scene of devastation continued to echo in Maxim's mind. People of all ages ran around, screaming and crying, frantically searching for loved ones amidst the shock and confusion, covered in grime, dust, and blood from their injuries. In their desperate attempts to find family members under the rubble, the severity of the situation seemed almost paralysing. Good neighbours staggered around in shock, while others bravely pulled bodies from the debris.

Amidst the chaos, Maxim noticed Adara, a family friend from the floor above their home, lying motionless in the road. Her head twisted to the side; it took Maxim moments to comprehend the horror before him. Trying to convince himself that it was not her and a horrific dream. He observed Adara's shredded clothes and the absence of both legs above her knees, surrounded by thick, clotted blood mixed with dust. Adara's wide-open eyes and blood-stained gaze cut deep into Maxim's heart, leaving an indelible mark.

The scene unfolding before him appeared unfathomable, and he grappled with the inconceivability that any rational human being could inflict such horrors upon another.

The impact of the devastation reached beyond the physical destruction, delving into the depths of Maxim's psyche. The fragments of a once familiar landscape, now reduced to ruins, mirrored the shattered remnants of his understanding of humanity. The gravity of the atrocities witnessed lingered, leaving an indelible mark on his perception of the world.

As he stood within the chaos, the weight of the surreal experience pressed upon him, challenging his ability to reconcile the reality of the brutality. It was not just the crumbling structures and debris-strewn streets; it was the shattered sense of security, the loss of trust in the fundamental goodness of humanity. The enormity of the situation weighed heavily on Maxim, his mind struggling to process the profound shift in his perception of the world and the inherent cruelty that had unraveled before his very eyes.

Dread gripped him as he maneuvered through the debris, his eyes desperately searching for any trace of his loved ones. Then, there they were. Maxim's heart sank at the heart-wrenching sight unfolding before him. His parents lay lifeless, entwined in a cruel embrace, a poignant testament to the love that had been mercilessly snatched away. Their once-vibrant features now bore the scars of terror.

Maxim crumbled his body yielding to the weight of despair as his sobs intertwined with the haunting echoes of war. In that poignant moment, his innocence shattered, replaced by a soul burdened with profound loss and anguish. The devastation that befell on his family marked a seismic shift in Maxim's life, one where the foundations of normalcy crumbled beneath the weight of tragedy.

As shells continued to land nearby, others pulled him away for his safety. Life, for Maxim, was forever altered by the irreversible destruction he witnessed. Unable to return or salvage personal possessions from the rubble that once held his cherished home, he ran for his life alongside others fleeing the shelling. The burden of guilt weighed heavy on him, knowing that survival came at the cost of abandoning the remnants of his past.

It became desperate for Maxim in the days following the bombing. Days turned into weeks as Maxim navigated the treacherous landscape of a war-torn country. Hunger gnawed at his stomach, and desperation clung to his every step. He encountered fellow survivors, forming a makeshift family bonded by tragedy and a shared desire for survival.

Before escaping Ukraine, a sagacious figure had imparted a crucial piece of advice to Maxim: always falsify his age if he aimed to navigate the challenges of life in Western Europe successfully. The rationale was clear, in European countries like the United Kingdom, being classified as a younger child rather than the young man he was would inevitably secure him more assistance and benefits.

When the chance to flee the harrowing conditions in Ukraine materialised, Maxim clung to it with unwavering determination. Armed with nothing but a small bag carrying the remnants of his shattered dreams, he embarked on a perilous journey towards the United Kingdom, a land that held the promise of a fresh start.

From that moment it all became a bit of a blur to Maxim. He was moved around to various buildings and places. Asked countless questions repeatedly. He had difficulty understanding but there always seemed to be interpreters at the end of a phone. His patience to practice English when he had been at home with his parents gave him the ability to understand.

Recalling the sage advice he received in Ukraine, Maxim adhered to his fabricated narrative about his age upon arriving in the United Kingdom. He confidently asserted to customs officers that he was merely fifteen years old. Initially met with suspicion regarding the truth of his age, Maxim was astonished that, lacking a passport, they accepted his account. To his surprise, the officers classified him as a child, prompting swift assistance from the local authority's young people's placement team within hours.

Maxim couldn't help but find it peculiar that British government agencies embraced his story without substantial scrutiny or fact-checking, given that to most, he clearly appeared in his early twenties. In an ironic twist, the social worker from the local authority, tasked with placing him in a foster care home, didn't seem much older than Maxim himself. The absurdity heightened when the first set of prospective foster parents expressed concerns about Maxim's actual age and the potential risks it posed to their own children. Despite the parents' reservations, the social workers dismissed their worries, challenging the foster father's unconscious bias. Maxim perceived their actions as gross naivety, almost laughable and negligent.

Eventually, this family decided to discontinue fostering, a tragic turn of events that made Maxim question his own ethical stance. He grappled with an overwhelming sense of guilt for exploiting the system that was aiding him, realising that his actions were taking the place of other more vulnerable children in greater need of care. Despite these moral quandaries, Maxim pushed these thoughts aside, compelled to prioritise his own survival in a cutthroat world where progress often demanded a less-than-nice approach.

The individuals he encountered had not witnessed the catastrophic explosions that obliterated entire streets, decimating anything and anyone within the blast range. Young friends from school, companions Maxim had grown up with, were extinguished before his very eyes. Families that were there one moment vanished, leaving only body parts in the next. The overwhelming horror and carnage proved too much for Maxim. He knew he had to maintain focus and avoid contemplating the broader implications where emotions threatened to overwhelm him.

After months integrating in the City of Manchester Maxim had met Jonesy while he had been spending more time away from his foster placement. Maxim had never felt settled with the allocated foster parents. It wasn't that he was ungrateful, but he struggled with his lies. He was a young man and he wanted to be out and not held back by living under the umbrella of social care. It was a bittersweet situation to be in.

Maxim never envisioned himself getting involved in dealing drugs or running errands for Jonesy. At the time, he found himself in a vulnerable situation, desperately seeking a means to survive. Observing young individuals dealing weed in the area, Maxim got the impression that, if one managed to evade the local police, it was considered acceptable and socially permissible. When he raised questions with Jonesy, he endured a brutal beating from a gang of men who not only assaulted him but also took his money. It was a cunning game of exploiting vulnerable individuals like Maxim, who found himself unable or unwilling to report the incident to the authorities.

Unbeknownst to Maxim, joining forces with Jonesy came with a steep price tag. Given the escalating debt, it became increasingly evident that he would never be able to fully repay what he owed Jonesy. He knew of other young people and asylum seekers who were in a comparable situation to himself. The girls suffered even more because not only were they being criminally exploited they were also being sexually exploited by Jonesy and his violent associates. A young girl named Mia, whom he had developed a fondness for, attempted to distance herself from Jonesy, only to suffer a severe consequence for her decision. A group of Asian men had beaten her with a baseball bat and locked her in a room without food, water, or a toilet. Three days passed before she was allowed out on the promise that she would continue to deal cocaine and pay back her fictitious debt.

    Maxim found himself unable to seek help from his social workers due to threats made by Jonesy. Unfortunately, Maxim had disclosed his true age and the fact that he had fled from local authority care to avoid a barrage of inquiries. Children's services had labelled him as "missing," leaving Maxim anxious about the potential consequences and worried about Jonesy's actions.

    So, for the time being, Maxim complied with Jonesy's directives, obediently following his wishes and instructions. He kept a low profile and hustled on the streets to maintain shelter and avoid additional complications. Fortunately, Maxim had the support and friendship of Richie to provide solace during this challenging time...

5 Call for Help

Alone in his dwelling, Neil grappled with the weight of his diagnosis, the burden pressing heavily upon him. His gaze fixated on the phone, his finger hovering over the keypad, fully aware that the impending call held the power to permanently reshape the lives of those nearest and dearest to him. With a profound breath, he initiated the dialling process for his brother Matt's number, his heart thudding relentlessly in his chest. It had been years since their last exchange, and Neil wasn't even certain if the number was still valid.

As the phone rang, Neil's thoughts raced, a cascade of shared childhood memories inundating his mind. Throughout their early years, they had maintained a close bond, offering unwavering support through the highs and lows albeit life had eventually driven them apart. Now, confronted with the harsh reality of a terminal brain tumour, Neil found himself in dire need of his brother's presence more than ever before.

Having returned from the garden, Matt was interrupted by the sound of his mobile phone ringing. The distinct ringtone, playing the familiar tune "when the going gets tough, the tough get going," stirred a multitude of memories from his past. Casting a quick glance at the display, he observed that the call hailed from an unfamiliar number in the United Kingdom. Finding it peculiar, he answered with a hint of suspicion.

"Is that you, Matt?" The voice on the other end inquired.

Uncertain of the caller's identity, Matt responded cautiously, "Yes, who is this?"

"Matt," Neil's voice trembled, carrying a blend of fear and vulnerability. "It's me, Neil."

A moment of silence hung in the air, followed by a tone of concern in Matt's voice, "Neil, what's wrong? Is everything okay?"

Neil took a deep breath, struggling to hold back tears that threatened to surface. "No, Matt, everything is not okay. I... I've been diagnosed with a terminal brain tumour."

Silence hung heavy in the air, broken only by the sound of Neil's shallow breathing. He anxiously awaited his brother's response, knowing that his words had shattered the world they had known.

A blend of shock and disbelief tinted Matt's voice as he managed to articulate his thoughts, "Neil, I... I can't even begin to imagine what you're going through. I'm so sorry."

"My business collapsed during Covid, Sarah left me, and, worst of all, my youngest boy Tommy just died in a tragic accident. I fear Richie is getting involved with drugs and gangs. I just don't know what to do or to whom to turn. I can't even manage my own health condition, and my mind is becoming foggy. I need help," Neil pleaded.

Matt took a moment to gather his thoughts. Neil, who had everything in life, had just reached out to him for help. The mention of "gangs" and "drugs" agitated Matt, and a flame of anger ignited within him.

"Are you still there, Matt?" Neil inquired.

Buying himself a little more thinking time he responded, "Look Neil, this is one hell of a phone call to get out of the blue. Can you give me time to process this, and I will call you back as soon as I can. It's just too much for me to take in right now."

"Ok thanks, it's appreciated." Neil replied anxiously.

Placing the mobile back into his shirt pocket, Matt retrieved a cold bottle of beer from the fridge before stepping out into his garden. As he savoured the refreshing beverage, his gaze wandered towards the end of his garden, lost in thought on a sunlight day in France.

His moment of introspection was interrupted by a voice, "Are you okay? Who was that on the phone?"

Nicole, a slender and attractive brunette whom Matt had started dating when purchasing his French farmhouse, was inquiring. She worked as the real estate agent "agents immobilisers" and had facilitated the sale of the house to Matt. Nicole had been drawn to Matt's amiable and courteous nature, yet she was still trying to decipher the depths of his character and the commitment he envisioned for their relationship.

Not wanting to involve Nicole in the conversation or reveal too much of his own past, Matt responded casually, "Oh, it's just some English guy asking about a price for a job."

Matt had fallen deeply in love with Nicole over the past few years but was often frightened and hesitant on how to show his true affection. He had never been good at letting his emotional guard down especially around women. During his time in the Marines, he had been raised in an environment where displaying vulnerable emotions was strongly discouraged. He became accustomed to suppressing and concealing his feelings. Expressing emotions was perceived as a vulnerability that could jeopardise not only himself but also his comrades in the intense context of combat.

Nicole was Matts alter opposite. Relaxed, trustworthy, understanding but unaware of Matts military background. Matt had wanted to keep his military service hidden in his new life in France. That way Nicole wouldn't get drawn into having conversations about war and the fighting he had been part of. It was easier this way and it helped Matt to start again, reset his life, recover, and find the much-needed closure from those dark days of war. In France, people had started embracing Matt for the person they saw him as, rather than dwelling on his past, and he was perfectly content with that.

Upon his first arrival in France following the tumultuous events in Manchester, Matt discovered a tranquil sanctuary. It was a place where he could begin to unwind, relax, decompress, and rediscover the joy of living. It was during the process of purchasing his "small holding" that he crossed paths with Nicole, who happened to be single, and an instant connection formed between them.

Nicole proved to be an exceptional cook and a crucial pillar of support for Matt when he first arrived in France as a solitary Englishman. Beyond her culinary skills, Nicole went beyond by assisting Matt in securing farming work, navigating government applications, and serving as his translator. Her invaluable help facilitated a swift and smooth transition for Matt, allowing him to settle comfortably in France. With Nicole's guidance, he gradually grasped local conversations, enhancing his ability to interact in French. This played a pivotal role in his integration, and soon he found himself warmly welcomed by the local community.

Nicole hailed from a petite French farming family situated on the outskirts of Chabanais. Her father, Bernard, had served in the French Foreign Legion, specifically during the intense conflict in Algiers throughout the 1960s. Despite his noteworthy military background, Bernard seldom broached the topic with Nicole, who, out of respect, refrained from probing into the details of his service. All she knew were glimpses, her father possessed a couple of medals commemorating his service, and on a rare occasion, he had revealed his "Kepi" cap to her when she was a young girl.

Bernard took immense pride in his service, yet he consistently sidestepped any attempts to delve into the specifics, redirecting conversations swiftly. Nicole suspected that her mother, Gabrielle, held a deeper understanding of Bernard's courageous exploits in Algiers but also opted not to broach the subject.

Months into their relationship, Nicole introduced Matt to her father at a barbecue. Initially, the introduction felt a bit tense, given the language barrier, but as the conversation unfolded, both men discovered a surprising amount of common ground. Nicole couldn't quite pinpoint it, but there was an undeniable connection between them. For Bernard, who had never had a son of his own and missed that dynamic on the farm, the bond was particularly special. The reason for their natural camaraderie eluded Nicole.

Matt's drive and eagerness to tackle challenges, no matter how daunting, endeared him to people. His passion for outdoor activities and his adeptness at farm work resonated perfectly with Bernard's lifestyle. This alignment suited Matt, and life was heading in the right direction. With no mortgage, a steady military pension, and a consistent flow of work, Matt felt like he had turned a new chapter in his life.

6 Rob

Having resided in his ground-floor maisonette for a little over a year, Rob vividly recalls the thrill he experienced when his housing officer reached out about the availability of the flat. The prospect of securing a new living space added an exciting chapter to Rob's life.

A decade ago, Rob's world crumbled in the aftermath of a harrowing motorcycle accident. It was a sunlit afternoon, the kind that beckons bikers to embrace the freedom of the road, feel the wind on their faces, and revel in the joy of the ride. Rob, lost in his thoughts, cruised along a familiar road when fate mercilessly intervened. A distracted drink driver carelessly veered into his lane, colliding head-on with his bike in a heart-stopping moment.

The impact was brutal, shattering glass, twisting metal, and propelling Rob's body through space like a ragdoll. The crash erased his memory, leaving only elusive fragments of what came before, like scattered puzzle pieces refusing to form a coherent picture.

Paramedics found Rob unconscious at the scene, his head battered and bruised. Working urgently, they stabilised him and raced him to the nearest hospital. Despite the medical team's relentless efforts to save him, the accident had inflicted a severe brain injury on Rob. In an instant, his once-vibrant mind descended into chaos. Memories, skills, and experiences became a tangled mess within his injured brain. The person he used to be became a mere spectre, trapped within a broken vessel.

Police estimated the impact at over 60 mph, resulting in catastrophic consequences for Rob. His traumatic brain injury and ensuing learning difficulties forced him to start life anew learning to eat, talk, and walk. His ability to communicate with confidence vanished, leaving him locked in a silent prison within his own mind. It was as if he were a spectator, unable to express thoughts or comprehend the world around him. His family yearned to hear his voice, to witness a glimmer of recognition in his eyes, yet each day brought only sorrow and uncertainty.

During this darkness, a glimmer of hope persisted. The human brain, with its extraordinary ability to heal and adapt, could carve out new pathways even in the face of damage. However, Rob found that his injuries had changed people's perceptions and behaviour towards him. His social circle dwindled, and he became increasingly isolated. What irked him most were the strangers who, unaware of his story, judged him with unconscious bias upon their first meeting. Many unfairly generalised their views, even assuming he was a drinker or drug user.

The irony wasn't lost on Rob. The person responsible for nearly ending his life with a lenient prison sentence was now leading a normal existence. This reality was harder for his mother, Val, to accept than it was for Rob himself.

Rob had been ready for his independence. He wanted to meet new friends and live away from his parents. Moving into his own self-contained flat brought much needed change into his life and the freedom he should be relishing at an early age. His parents had been incredibly supportive, but he wanted to relinquish the burden he had placed upon them for so long. "Val," had worked so hard to support him during his recovery. Their "mother and son" relationship had changed beyond recognition. She had become his long-term carer and he hated this. He had been bright, athletic and had a whole life of opportunity ahead of him which had changed in an instant on that fateful day.

Val had harboured anxieties about Rob moving into his own self supported home, a concern that had gradually eased over the past few months. The daily visits that were initially a constant had become less frequent, a shift that proved agreeable for everyone involved, including Rob.

7 Jitters

The kitchen echoed with the rhythmic thud of Matt's knife against the chopping board as he wrestled with an onion. The acrid scent filled the air, making his eyes smart and sting. From the distant hum of tires on gravel, he deduced that Nicole was back from work. Not exactly a culinary maestro, Matt found himself engaged in the rare act of cooking.

Nicole wearily trudged through the front door, the weight of the day clinging to her shoulders like a relentless burden. She shut her eyes momentarily, attempting to shed the accumulated stress from the long hours at work. Stepping into the comforting embrace of her home, a wave of relief washed over her.

With a tired sigh, she kicked off her shoes and collapsed onto the couch, letting its softness cradle her weary body. The silence enveloped her, a stark departure from the chaos of the office, a brief respite, a much-needed moment of solace.

Her eyes closed, she inhaled deeply, allowing the calmness of her surroundings to permeate her very being. Subtle scents of lavender and freshly brewed coffee wafted through the air, easing the tension that had etched itself into her muscles.

The day's challenges replayed in her mind, a symphony of complaints, unrealistic expectations, and navigating unforeseen setbacks. Yet, as she sat there, immersed in the tranquillity of her space, the realisation dawned, she had made it through another day.

Her shoulders gradually relaxed, the day's weight dissipating. In the quietude, Nicole indulged in a moment of self-reflection, acknowledging the resilience and determination it took to confront challenges head-on. Despite the demanding workload and the looming pressure, she had emerged victorious, finding strength in the sanctuary of her own home.

Matt entered the room with a smile and shouted "Bonsoir, Madam." She smiled back and he approached, embracing her with both arms, quickly following this by a loving kiss on her lips. Nicole was smartly dressed and carried a light scent of perfume. There was a real vulnerability to her, and he sensed goose pimples rise on her arms by a draught from the back garden.

Matt sat across from Nicole, his eyes betraying a mix of guilt and determination. He had something important to share, a decision that weighed heavily on his heart.

"Nikki," Matt began softly, taking a deep breath to steady himself. He kissed Nicole, looked into her eyes, and said "Je Vous aime." Quickly reverting to English, I need to tell you something.

Nicole's smile turned to a concerned look, "Why what's the matter?"

"I need to go back to England. My brother, Neil, he's unwell, and I can't stay away any longer as he needs my help."

Nicole looked at Matt, her eyes searching his face for any signs of hesitation or doubt. She knew all too well the depths of family bonds, the unbreakable ties that transcended time and distance. In that moment, she saw the pain etched in Matt's eyes, the internal struggle between his commitment to her and his duty to his family.

Matt continued; his voice tinged with emotion. "I never want to leave you, Nikki. You mean the world to me. But I can't bear the thought of my brother going through this alone. I hope you understand."

Tears welled up in Nicole's eyes as she reached across, gently taking Matt's hand in hers. She knew that love was not always a simple path, but a journey filled with challenges and sacrifices.

"Matt," she whispered, her voice filled with understanding. "I do understand, family is everything. You need to be there for your brother, and I will support you every step of the way even if I'm not there with you."

Matt's heart swelled with gratitude for Nicole's unwavering support. In that moment, he knew that their love was resilient, capable of withstanding the trials that life threw their way. They had built a foundation of trust and understanding, and together they would weather the storm.

As they sipped their coffee, Matt and Nicole began to discuss the planning of his journey. Nicole offered her assistance in making travel arrangements, ensuring that he could be by his brother's side as soon as possible. They vowed to stay connected, to bridge the physical distance with messages, calls, and video chats, keeping their love alive despite the miles between them.

"When are you thinking of going."

"This weekend seems as good as any, provided I can get tickets. I'm going to take the train to Paris then to London St Pancras, then straight across to Euston for another train up to Manchester. All being well I could leave early morning and be there late afternoon." Parting ways with Nicole carried a bittersweet weight, a poignant acknowledgment that their love was resilient, tethered by the profound understanding that, at times, duty beckoned in unforeseen ways.

Later that evening, Matt dialled his brother's number. "Hey Neil, it's Matt. Got a moment to chat?"

"Yeah, it's good. I've been looking forward to catching up, thanks for calling back. How've you been after all this time?" Neil inquired with enthusiasm. Although his voice held a lively tone, there was a hint of frailty and vulnerability, suggesting the passage of time had left its mark.

"No worries about yesterday; I was just a bit caught off guard and in the middle of something," Matt apologised.

"No problem, I'm sorry for hitting you up out of nowhere. Things have been rough with Sarah since the divorce," Neil's voice quivered.

Matt sensed a wealth of emotion being concealed and restrained.

Neil and Sarah appeared from the outside to have been that perfect couple. Happy, loving, wealthy, content and healthy. A couple who'd been the "benchmark" that other couples aspired to be.

A heavy silence hung in the air, burdening the conversation. Neil finally broke it, his words weighed down by the tragic situation surrounding Tom. "We're all still grappling with the shock of what happened. I feel lost, Matt, like I'm sinking. I can't face this. I'm deteriorating. The struggle is so intense that I can't even manage simple tasks anymore. Getting out of bed, putting on shoes and socks, it's all become an insurmountable challenge. Daytime has become a battleground, and staying awake is a fight I'm losing. And then there's Richie. He's entangled in something dark. His silence is deafening, and he just drifts in and out."

Matt, choosing his words carefully, paused before responding, "Just give me Richie's number, Neil. Tell me where I can find him." The weight of the words hung in the charged atmosphere, a declaration of determination in the face of overwhelming turmoil.

8 Back in town

Matt stood on the outskirts of the bustling railway station, his heart racing with a mixture of excitement and trepidation. The towering buildings loomed before him, casting long shadows that mirrored the uncertainties within his mind. After spending years away, he had finally mustered the courage to return to the place he once called home, Manchester.

As he gazed at the sprawling metropolis, memories flooded his thoughts, both fond and haunting. The city had always been a double-edged sword for Matt a place of dreams and aspirations, but also a breeding ground for anxieties, insecurities, and violence. It was a relentless whirlwind of noise, people, and expectations, where the rhythm of life beat faster, leaving little room for hesitation or respite.

Leaving all those years ago had been a conscious choice for Matt. The pace of urban life had become overwhelming, suffocating his spirit, and amplifying his anxieties. He had sought solace in quieter surroundings, where the symphony of nature replaced the cacophony of honking horns, loud voices and hurried footsteps.

Exiting Piccadilly station, he found himself stopping for a moment to stare at the "Victory in Blindness". A distinct statue depicting seven blinded soldiers from the First World War. Each man following the other with their hand on the shoulder of the man in front. The statue captured the essence of its meaning perfectly. Standing still he began reflecting about his own experiences of war and the historic futility of it all. The old cliché of there were never any true winners in war hung in his mind, just losers and those who suffered long term physical and mental injuries as a result. The blinded soldiers struck a chord and somehow symbolised something remarkably close and meaningful to Matt. Staring at the statues brilliant detail he doubted humanity would ever learn by it.

But now, circumstances had conspired to bring him back. Yet, as Matt stood at the threshold of his return, his mind was filled with doubts.

Would the situation swallow him whole once again? Would this fast-paced return drown out the tranquillity he had cultivated in his absence? The cacophony of the city streets mocked his apprehensions, daring him to step forward and embrace the chaos.

As he took his first steps into the urban maze, Matt's heart pounded in his chest. The familiar sights and sounds surrounded him, assaulting his senses. The symphony of car horns, the chatter of passers-by, and in the brilliance of daytime, the citys neon glow were both exhilarating and overwhelming.

His anxieties resurfaced like ghosts from the past. The fear of getting lost in the anonymity of the city, of being consumed by its relentless demands, threatened to paralyse him. Doubts gnawed at his confidence, whispering that he had made a mistake in returning, that he was destined to be forever caught in the city's merciless grip.

But in the chaos, there were glimmers of hope. Faces passed him by, their expressions a mix of determination, weariness, and resilience. The city was not just a beast to be conquered; it was a tapestry of human stories, each thread interwoven with triumphs and struggles.

Matt took a deep breath, steadying himself. He reminded himself that the city had also been a canvas for personal growth and connection. It had forged friendships, kindled passions, and provided opportunities for self-discovery. The challenges he faced here were not new to him.

9 Finding a Nest

Given his disabilities it often took Rob an hour or so to get moving in the mornings. The pins in his right knee and the compromised right hip limited his flexibility. As Rob stood up, his face contorted with pain, a constant reminder that he required medication to alleviate his nerve pain. The pain, persistent and unrelenting, lingered despite the medication, which, unfortunately, had the unpleasant side effect of inducing drowsiness.

Three weeks ago, he had struck up conversation with young girl named Mia while coming out of the community medical centre on the estate. He couldn't recall how she had even started the conversation, but she was the first person in a long while who had shown him the slightest bit of interest. The initial conversation had been difficult but relaxed and Rob described the pain he was suffering to Mia.

"I've shared with the doctor that the tablets prescribed seem to have minimal or no impact on alleviating my pain," he clarified.

Mia, ever the opportunist, trailed behind Rob as they exited the medical centre, eliciting curious glances from fellow patients. The question lingered in the air, why was she taking such a keen interest in Rob, who was visibly vulnerable?

Once outside and away from prying eyes, Mia called out, "Wait, stop, Rob! Ever thought about giving weed a shot to see if it helps with your pain?"

Rob's innocence and vulnerability prompted him to respond, "No, but why not?" He was open to trying anything that might alleviate his pain.

"But where would I get it to try?" he asked naively.

Mia smiled and calmly handed him a small snap-seal bag. "Here you go, give this a try."

Returning her smile, Rob's expression quickly shifted to a quizzical look. "What do I do with these dry green leaves?"

"Look, I can show you, but not here in the street," Mia replied with a sly grin.

"Well, um, just come over to my place; it's not too far."

"Do you live with anyone?"

"I've got my own flat; it's nice. You can come and check it out."

Mia couldn't help but smile; she had struck gold with Rob, naive, vulnerable, innocent, and living alone nearby on the estate. Jonesy had been pressuring her for weeks to find a spot to operate from. Rob might just be the opportunity they had been searching for, she mused.

Back in the flat Mia made no delay in asking Rob questions about, who he lived with and how often his parents came to visit. She was carefully weighing up Robs domestic situation and how she could exploit it.

Rob on the other hand, responded to these questions unaware that he was disclosing his own vulnerability. Right now, he was happy and grateful for Mias' company, despite being blissfully unaware of her evil intentions.

He perceived her as a newfound friend, akin to a toddler in the playground. The attention and interest she showed captivated him, and he welcomed it. In his perspective, Mia appeared genuinely kind, honest, and intent on aiding him in confronting the relentless pain he endured. Traditional medical interventions had proven futile, and he found himself at a point where experimenting with a swift "joint of weed" seemed like a plausible alternative. The battle against his chronic pain felt unending, leaving him frustrated with conventional treatments and drained from restless nights. Despite harbouring apprehension, hope mingled with trepidation fuelled his desire to explore this unconventional remedy.

At the kitchen table Mia rolled a joint, her hands trembling slightly. Rob sat in a chair and lit it, a little unsure what to expect. As he brought the slender paper to his lips, he inhaled deeply, letting the pungent smoke fill his lungs. Moments passed, and a subtle warmth of calmness began to envelop his body, as if a gentle blanket of relief were unfurling within him.

An ethereal calm washed over Rob, easing the tension that had held him captive for far too long. The pain, once an omnipresent companion, now took a backseat in his consciousness. Each breath he took seemed to carry away a fragment of his suffering, replacing it with a gentle euphoria that lifted his spirits.

As the minutes passed, Rob experienced a newfound sense of clarity. His mind, usually clouded by the unyielding torment of pain, was now free to explore uncharted territories of thought. The world around him seemed more vibrant, every colour heightened and every sound more melodic. He marvelled at the beauty he had overlooked in his struggle, grateful for this respite from his pain-induced haze. For the first time in years, a smile graced Rob's face, a smile untethered by anguish. As he sat there, enveloped in the embrace of peace and the gentle tendrils of smoke, he realised that cannabis had offered him more than just relief, it had granted him a glimpse of a life beyond his pain and suffering. With renewed hope Rob exhaled slowly, releasing the remnants of his pain into the atmosphere. The journey to managing his affliction was far from over, but in that moment, as the therapeutic properties of the herb wrapped around him, he found solace and a glimmer of peace as he slipped off to sleep.

Mia seized this opportunity to explore Robs flat. Her eyes scanned the rooms, searching for anything of value. Drawers were opened, cabinets rifled through, and closets examined with meticulous precision. She found various handwritten notes from an anxious mother, reminding him to do things. There were three ten-pound notes in a draw by the bed which she took without hesitation. Mia held the money in her trembling hands, conflicting emotions warred within her. Guilt gnawed at her conscience, but her drug dependency quickly irradiated this emotion.

It was clear Rob was vulnerable and Mia was going to take this opportunity going forwards to "Cookoo" his flat. She would 'flatter' and build Robs trust. A few compliments and keep him topped up with a bit of weed was all it might take. Mia would string Rob along as a potential girlfriend given his naivety. Her 'paymaster' Jonesy would be delighted with her and might even consider giving her a bit more 'free gear' off the back of it as her reward.

Mia continued this pattern of frequent visits to see Rob. From a distance, she keenly observed his vulnerability and emotional turmoil. With a natural penchant for manipulation, Mia found herself unable to resist taking advantage. Strategically positioning herself as a supportive figure in Rob's life, she engaged in casual conversations, displaying genuine concern for his well-being. Mia offered a sympathetic ear whenever he needed to vent, meticulously crafting an image of a caring and trustworthy friend, always prepared to lend a helping hand.

Rob began to confide in Mia, sharing intimate details about his personal life and the challenges he was grappling with. Mia listened attentively, feigning empathy, and understanding, while secretly weaving her deceitful plan. She gradually manipulated the conversations to uncover essential information about Rob's routine and life.

Mia knew she needed to gain unhindered access to Rob's flat to execute her ulterior motive. With careful precision, she exploited his vulnerability, showering him with false reassurances and promises of support. She created a facade of unwavering loyalty, assuring Rob that she would always be there for him. Taking advantage of Rob's trust, Mia convinced him that she could help alleviate his stress by organising his living space. She offered to clean, rearrange, and beautify his apartment, promising that it would create a more positive environment for him to heal and find peace. Rob, desperate for a sense of relief, gratefully accepted Mia's offer without realising her hidden agenda.

      She silently marvelled at the vulnerability of her new friend, knowing she had successfully deceived him. Mia's heart raced with excitement, thinking about the benefits this could bring.

10 Debts Grip

The weight of indebtedness settled upon Richie's young shoulders, pressing down on him like an insurmountable burden. It seeped into every corner of his life, tainting even the simplest moments with anxiety and dread. Sleep became elusive as nightmares of retribution played out in his mind, each one a vivid reminder of the dangers he had brought upon himself.

Every interaction with Jonesy was fraught with tension, a tightrope walk between obedience and defiance. Fear and resignation mingled within Richie's veins as he handed over drugs money, his self-worth slowly eroding with each transaction. He felt powerless, trapped in a vicious cycle he didn't know how to escape.

The shame of his choices became a constant companion, whispering harsh judgments and amplifying his feelings of worthlessness. Richie's once vibrant spirit had become dimmed by the weight of his secrets. He yearned for a way out, for a chance to break free from the clutches of his actions and the suffocating grip Jonesy now had over him.

As he sat in his solitary room, Richie's heart yearned for redemption. He knew deep down that the road to reclaiming his life would be arduous and strewn with obstacles. Yet, a flicker of hope persisted, reminding him that within despair, there was still a glimmer of resilience. With each breath, he steeled himself for the uphill battle that lay ahead, determined to find a way to break free from the shackles that held him captive.

****

The news of Tom's tragic demise didn't hit Matt as profoundly as one might expect. Death had become a familiar companion, a shadow lingering from the haunting memories of Iraq and Afghanistan. Two close friends lost to circumstances uncannily like Tom's fate had desensitised Matt to the emotions surrounding mortality. The perplexing question echoed in his mind, why were so many young men succumbing to the overwhelming struggles of life, resorting to the tragic choice of ending their own existence?

Drawing from his own battles, Matt understood the profound difficulty of clawing back from the abyss of despair. In the clutches of depression, it often felt like there were only two paths ahead. The first, a devastating plunge into the darkness of self-inflicted oblivion. The second, a daunting journey through the obscure tunnel of despair, a route known to few.

Fortunately, Matt had opted for the latter, and now he felt compelled to extend a helping hand to his brother after his touching private plea for assistance. The seed of a plan germinated in Matt's mind as he stood beneath the city's grey clouds. A sudden break in the overcast sky allowed rays of sunlight to cascade down, casting a warming glow despite the cold dampness in the air. It felt reminiscent of those mornings after gruelling nights on operations, the sun's embrace bringing solace to frozen bones.

Finding the car rental just off the train station concourse, Matt stowed his bags in the boot of a nondescript dark Ford Focus. Igniting the Sat Nav, he swiftly keyed in a postcode for his destination. Wythenshawe, not too distant from Manchester's centre, beckoned him. Matt harboured a deep yearning to reconnect with his old friend Jed, a reunion long overdue since their perilous patrols in the unforgiving terrain of Afghanistan. However, things would have to wait…

11 Lost

Richie found himself wandering around the town centre, feeling a strange mix of restlessness and boredom. With no plans or responsibilities weighing him down, he had the luxury of time on his hands.

Strolling down the bustling streets, he observed the vibrant energy that permeated the town centre. People hurriedly went about their business, shops displayed colourful wares, and the aroma of freshly cooked food wafted from the quaint cafes lining the street. With no specific destination in mind, he wandered from shop to shop, glancing at the array of merchandise but finding nothing that piqued his interest. He found himself drawn to the window displays, momentarily captivated by the crafted mannequins displaying the latest fashion trends. He daydreamed about a life filled with excitement and adventure, far removed from the mundane routine of his teenage existence.

Richie meandered into a bookshop, losing himself in the rows of bookshelves that held countless tales and knowledge waiting to be discovered. He picked up a book in the military section, flipping through the pages, but the words seemed to blur before his eyes. His mind wandered, lost in a sea of thoughts that ebbed and flowed, never settling on any one topic.

Leaving the bookshop, he continued his aimless exploration of the town centre. He watched street performers juggle, dance, and create magical moments that captivated the passers-by. He lingered near a group of buskers, listening to the rhythmic beats and melodies that filled the air, briefly finding solace in the harmony of sound. Time seemed to stretch endlessly, and his wanderings became a metaphor for his own search for meaning and purpose. He yearned for something to ignite a spark within him, to fill the void of purposeless that had settled upon his shoulders. But for now, he was content to wander, to let the hours slip away as he absorbed the sights, sounds, and sensations of the town centre.

Home life had become a little too unbearable to face since the death of Tom. Richie didn't want to burden his dad about how "pissed off and upset" he had become with his life. It always ended up with his dad preaching to him. He just couldn't bear to listen to it anymore. His mum had called him, but he had blamed her for all the chaos, arguments and family destruction that had taken place over the last couple of years. The call hadn't gone well, and Richie had told her not to call him again and put the phone down on her. Right now, he blamed his mum for a huge amount and wasn't in the mood for forgiveness.

As the sun began its descent, casting a warm golden glow upon the streets, Richie's aimless wanderings gradually ended. He found himself on a bench, watching as the town centre transformed under the embrace of twilight. A sense of tranquillity washed over him, and he realised that sometimes, it was okay to wander without a destination, to allow time to slip through his fingers and to simply be present in the moment. Richie slowly made his way back, carrying with him a sense of calm and a curiosity about where his life would lead him.

His phoned buzzed with a message from Jonesy, "Meet me at the Flat."

At the front of the flat, a prominent feature caught his eye, a sturdy set of metal security bars, firmly positioned in front of the entrance. These robust bars, like sentinels guarding the premises, conveyed a sense of protection and security that lay beyond them. Crafted from strong, durable metal, intricately woven in a pattern of intersecting lines and solid bars, forming an impenetrable barrier. They stood as a physical manifestation of the desire to safeguard the contents of the flat, deterring any unauthorised entry and dissuading potential intruders. These bars also offered a curious juxtaposition, an interplay of confinement and freedom. They kept the outside world at bay, creating a sense of seclusion and privacy within the confines of the flat. Behind the security bars, the occupants could find solace, enjoying the sanctuary of their own space, shielded from the unpredictability of the world beyond.

Despite their apparent functionality, the metal security bars could not completely suppress the human desire for connection. Behind them, the hum of life could be faintly heard, a muffled symphony of conversations, and the rhythmic pulse of illicit activities. It was a reminder that within those walls, lives were lived, memories were made, and schemes were nurtured.

Richie knocked and waited. After a short pause and much to his surprise Maxim answered the door with a warm smile, inviting him inside. As Richie stepped into the unfamiliar flat, he felt a mix of anticipation and curiosity. He had met Maxim during a chance encounter a good few times now, a friendly lad from Ukraine. Yet, here they were, brought together by a twist of fate and circumstances. On first impressions Maxim seemed like a decent guy although Richie couldn't be totally sure as conversations had been swift.

As Richie stepped through the doorway, a wave of mustiness assaulted his senses, immediately making it evident that cleanliness was not a top priority. The air felt heavy, laden with a mixture of stale odours and dust particles that danced in the faint light filtering through the grimy windows crying out to be opened to let in much-needed fresh air.

Richie reluctantly adjusted his eyes to the dim lighting, revealing a disarray of scattered belongings and neglected surfaces. The once vibrant colours of the walls had dulled over time, marred by smudges and streaks that hinted at years of neglect. Cobwebs clung defiantly to corners, their delicate threads swaying lazily in the stagnant air. It was a testament to the lack of attention given to even the most basic of cleaning routines. Neglected dishes, a stack of unwashed laundry, and forgotten remnants of meals littered the kitchen countertops, giving a glimpse into the apathy that had settled within the space.

As Richie surveyed the flat, his gaze was met with surfaces obscured by grime and smudges, leaving a film that seemed to have taken on a life of its own. Fingerprints and smears marked the once-clear windows, obscuring any view of the outside world. The bathroom, with its dull tiles and stained fixtures, exuded an air of neglect that made one hesitate to step inside. In every corner, shadows seemed to linger, hinting at a forgotten existence. It was as if the flat had absorbed the weight of its own neglect, each speck of dirt and every untended surface whispering tales of indifference and abandonment.

The uncleanliness of the place had surprised Richie. He thought Jonesy had been better than this, given how he portrayed himself to the outside world.

Mia greeted Richie with a false smile as he entered the lounge. "How you doing?"

"Yeah, I'm good thanks."

Mia's life had become a tangled web of struggles and shadows, an intricate dance with addiction that consumed her days and nights. Her once vibrant spirit had dimmed, eclipsed by the weight of her cravings and the constant battle within her own mind. Addiction had become her unwelcome companion, latching onto her with a tenacious grip. It whispered sweet promises of temporary relief, numbing the pain and loneliness that had settled deep within her soul. Yet, with each fleeting moment of respite, the shackles of addiction tightened, trapping her in a cycle of self-destruction.

Richie was suspicious of her addiction which often put her on the wrong side of Jonesy. Day by day Richie was getting a little more street wise although this "skanky flat" made him feel very much out of place.

Taking time to find an uncluttered seat Richie could sense Mia had been crying. There was a tense uneasy atmosphere in the room. Fidgeting in his seat he felt compelled to speak, "how you keeping Mia."

"Yeah good, but don't know where Jonesy's at."

Richie wasn't convinced by her response catching a glance from Maxim out the corner of his eye who discreetly shrugged his shoulder. "You sure?"

Mia paused and wiped her eye, "its……" Mia stopped mid-sentence on hearing something.

Determined to release his pent-up frustrations, Jonesy jammed his key into the lock with an aggressive force, his mind consumed by a torrent of anger and resentment. The door swung open abruptly, crashing against the wall and he stormed into the flat, his eyes blazing with an intensity that startled those inside. His frustrations had been mounting during the day and his patience had begun to wear thin. He had encountered one setback after another, and the weight of his mounting stress threatened to consume him.

Mia, caught off guard, jumped back, a look of confusion mixed with concern etched on her face. Maxim exchanged bewildered glances, their peace disrupted by Jonesy's abrupt and furious intrusion.

"Whoa, Jonesy! What's gotten into you?" Mia exclaimed, her voice laced with a hint of fear and concern. Maxim remained silent, his eyes now fixed on Jonesy, waiting for an explanation, yet ready to protect Mia if needed.

Jonesy's anger swirled within him, fuelling his words as he unleashed a torrent of frustration and blame, his voice filled with a bitter edge.

"What's up with you lot" he barked with a controlling, aggressive and authoritarian manner. He glared at Mia sensing he had interrupted a private conversation between them all.

"Nowt, we are great, you know, just catching up," Mia answered confidently. Her demeanour had changed in Jonesy's presence. Her vulnerability vanished with each word and Richie could see the hard outer shell of Mias' personality reappearing. It was obvious the sense of control Jonesy had over her. Richie and Maxim exchanged short glances, both noticing Mias' submissiveness to Jonesy's presence.

"You have a good time last night Mia?" Jonesy asked without giving her time to reply. "I heard it was a cracking party after I left," smirking at her. He looked at Maxim and Richie and cockily smiled at them too.

Slowly, the initial shock and anger of his entry began to ebb away, replaced by a glimmer of understanding. They recognised that Jonesy's outburst stemmed from a place of frustration and vulnerability, rather than a genuine desire to harm them.

After a prolonged silence, Mia spoke softly, her voice filled with a mix of compassion and caution. "Jonesy, we understand that you're going through a tough time, but taking it out on us isn't fair. Richie nodded in agreement, his gaze fixed on Jonesy with a mix of concern and forgiveness. "We're friends, mate," he added, his voice gentle yet firm.

Fully aware of his anger issues Jonesy changed the subject, "Anyway I've got a small job on for us all today." Reaching inside the waistline of his grey jogging bottoms he produced a large clear snap seal bag. It contained rocks of crack cocaine wrapped in cellophane. Jonesy threw the bag and a phone at Maxim. Maxim reacted and caught the snap seal bag but dropped the phone onto the carpet.

"Careful! Don't you go breaking that phone! I want you to take care of the business today, Maxim." Pointing at Mia and Richie, we are going to visit our new friend Rob "across the estate." There was another fleeting moment of silence as they contemplated what had just been said.

"Come on then, we need to get at it" Jonesy shouted angrily. He turned and walked to the front door shouting. "Oh yeah and Maxim, tidy this fucking flat up, it's a shit tip!"

The three youngsters looked at each, Maxim raised his shoulders and eyebrows in sync, suggesting they had little choice. Richie had seen a different side of Jonesy over the past few days and wondered what he was going to be asked to do next. Accepting gifts of "weed" from Jonesy hadn't been such a great idea it seemed. Richie felt a slight ratcheting up of pressure building in his mind. He owed a debt to Jonesy although it hadn't been 'called in yet.'

Walking from the flat Richie began to wonder what this 'pay back' was going to be. He had started to worry about what he was getting himself involved in and felt pressurised without being directly told he didn't have to do it. Quickly dismissing the expectations, he followed Jonesy and Mia out of the flat nodding a farewell to Maxim as he left.

Once outside in the street Richie asked, "where are we going?"

"You'll see when we get there," Jonsey remarked.

Mia. "You know what to do, we spoke about this yesterday. "Are you clear what needs doing?"

"Yeah, it's all fine, just don't go to heavy handed when you first go in, otherwise he might shit himself and have a meltdown," she responded.

The two set off on a purposeful stride across the expansive estate, their eyes gleaming with nefarious motives while Richie followed. With each confident step, Jonesy and Mia approached Rob's flat, their minds buzzing with excitement at the prospect of their deceitful takeover. Mia, the mastermind behind the plan, led the way, her sly grin revealing her warped eagerness to impress Jonesy.

"That's the flat there" Mia said, pointing to a ground floor maisonette. Jonesy took a seat nearby on a park bench. The other two quickly joined him. From this vantage point they gazed out across the urban park, eyes fixated on a ground floor flat nestled close to the park amidst the concrete jungle and surrounding urban landscape.

The flat, with its large windows and inviting facade, exuded an air of cosiness and tranquillity. Its brick exterior boasted a boring blend of 1960s dullness and an outdated concrete aesthetics, seamlessly blending into the surrounding area.

Richie had no idea what was happening, so he kept quiet and waited.

"We will sit tight here and wait for you Mia, just text me when you are ready" Jonesy instructed.

Mia stood up, pushed her hair back over her head like she was making herself more respectable and began walking across the park towards the maisonette.

12- Cuckooing

Rob had been agitated pacing around, unable to focus on anything constructive. The room around him was filled with mementos and trinkets that he had collected over the years. Each item held a special place in Rob's heart, a reminder of cherished memories and the joy they had brought him. His collection of model cars lined the shelves, perfectly arranged with meticulous care, while a stack of comic books stood nearby, waiting to be flipped through once again.

For the past hour he had been sat on the worn-out couch in his modest living room, his excitement palpable as he waited for Mia to arrive. Though time seemed to stretch endlessly, he clung to his anticipation with unwavering determination. Rob, with his warm-hearted nature and a perpetual smile etched across his face, had a newfound solace in the presence of Mia. Her visits brought a sense of comfort and belonging that Rob cherished deeply.

Anything that could break up the monotony of his day of being alone in the flat was good. The weather forecast was grim, and Rob hated going out in the rain. There had been no let-up in his social isolation recently which did little to help his downward mood. Rob craved for company. He had been expecting Mia and although she hadn't provided a time, to his mind she was late.

As the clock on the wall ticked away, Rob fidgeted with excitement, glancing at the door every few seconds. His mind was a whirlwind of anticipation and happiness, thoughts of her past visits replaying in his mind like a cherished movie.

Finally, a knock resounded through the apartment, sending Rob's heart into a frenzy of joy. With a wide grin, he practically leaped from the couch, rushing to the door with a spring in his step. As he swung the door open, Mia stood before him, her presence radiating warmth and familiarity.

"Mia!" Rob exclaimed, his voice brimming with unabashed joy. "You're here! I've been waiting for you."

Mia returned his infectious smile, glancing over her shoulder back across the park. "Hey, Rob! Sorry I'm a little late. How are you today?"

Rob's excitement spilled over into his words as he replied, "I'm great! Just been counting down the minutes until you arrived. Come on in!"

Mia stepped into the cosy apartment, her gaze taking in the familiar surroundings. She marvelled at the way Rob had meticulously arranged and kept his flat so tidy in comparison to where she had just come from.

As they settled into the familiar rhythm of their friendship, Rob's learning difficulties seemed to fade into the background. In Mia's presence, he felt accepted and valued for who he was, free from the constraints of his challenges. Despite Mias' intentions their conversations were filled with laughter and understanding, creating a space where Rob could truly be himself.

Mia on the other hand was just scheming right under his nose. She knew because of his learning difficulties he was too innocent and naive to see or understand what she was using him for.

After a short while Mia asked, "Rob is anyone due to visit you or are your parents planning to pop over anytime soon?"

Rob replied innocently, "oh no mums gone away with dad for a couple of weeks to Spain." It was the response Mia had wanted.

"Oh, that's nice but you shouldn't be so reliant on your parents. I'm always around, I can easily help you." Mia had taken a Rizla paper from its small cardboard folder and began rolling a joint with it.

"Yeah, that's nice, thanks" he said with a smile.

"Oh, I forgot to mention, my brother and his mate are popping over to meet me in a few minutes. I said they could come here, and I guessed you would be ok with that."

"That's fine, I didn't know you had a brother," Rob enquired inquisitively.

Mia finished rolling the joint and handed it to Rob. He lit the joint with renewed confidence, taking a long draw on it before slowly exhaling moments later. "Yeah, it'll be nice to meet," laughing and giggling as the toxins flowed through his body, he didn't finish his sentence.

Mia picked up her phone and sent a text, "Come on over, he is getting high."

Within minutes the doorbell rang. A mischievous smile played on her lips as she pondered the spontaneous plan that had formed in her mind. With a quick glance around to ensure Rob wasn't watching, she motioned for Jonesy and Richie to come inside. Their footsteps were cautious, as if treading on sacred ground, mindful that they were entering with illegal intentions in mind. Jonesy exchanged glances with Mia, curiosity and enthusiasm gleaming in their eyes.

Having not heard the doorbell Rob was a little startled when he first saw both men standing behind him in the Kitchen.

"Alright Rob?" Jonesy said in a confident manner.

"I'm fine thankyou, which ones your brother Mia?"

Mia placed an arm around Richie, "This is Richie, he is my younger brother."

Rob smiled back and nodded to Richie, "You don't look like each other."

Richie was taken aback by the random introduction Mia had provided and looked at her with suspicion etched on his face. Realising something was going on, he did his best to hide his shock from Rob and not give anything away. He had no idea why he was in Robs flat and wanted to know what was going on.

Richie felt a knot tighten in his stomach as he watched Jonesy and Mia eagerly discuss their plans. This sudden deviation from his comfort zone made Richie feel very uneasy. Jonesy and Mia were excited, their eyes gleaming with anticipation, but all Richie could feel was a sense of intimidation creeping over him.

Rob picked up the "part rolled joint" from the kitchen work top and casually asked Mia to light it which she did without hesitation. Why was she doing this, Richie thought?

Rob was enjoying the company of Mia and Richie found this strange and too bizarre for his liking. How did Mia know Rob? What was their connection or was he an old family friend of hers? The biggest question Richie pondered, was why Mia had introduced him as her brother? Right now, it was all too weird for Richie to comprehend. He didn't feel it was the right time or place to start asking questions.

Mia enquired, "Rob, would it be alright if I crashed with you over the next day or two? Rob now under the influence of the joint, appeared somewhat perplexed by the request but nonchalantly responded "yeah that should be fine, stay as long as you need."

Jonesy produced a large snap seal bag of gear from under his coat and shoved the contents into a kitchen draw. Mia moved towards Rob and stroked his hair seductively. "Rob we are going to leave our stuff here a couple of days before I move in. You don't mind looking after it for me, do you?"

Rob was smitten with the attention from Mia and was never going to object.

Jonesy was relentless in his pursuit of why he was here and placed more coke into another draw. Richie realised what was going on. Mia and Jonesy were muscling into this poor bloke's home and "cuckooing" it. Richie had heard about gangs doing this, but it was happening before his very eyes, and he wasn't comfortable with the situation he found himself in. His mind wandered to a different path, one that aligned more closely with his own values and aspirations. He yearned for stability and something in his life but had no idea what this was. The thought of venturing into this murky world, of taking risks that might lead to failure or disappointment, filled him with apprehension. He felt trapped, caught between his own dreams and the overpowering force of Jonesy and Mia's persuasive charm. Every event was making it harder and harder for him to walk away. Deep down, he had to find his own voice. He couldn't let himself be swayed by Jonesy's relentless drive to exploit others if it meant sacrificing his own happiness and principles. It was a difficult realisation to come to, as he had at one stage genuinely liked Jonesy and Mia valuing their friendship. Yet, he also knew that he had to honour his own path, even if it meant branching away from theirs.

Jonesy walked into the lounge and was sat on the couch flicking through channels on the television. Richie joined Jonesy leaving Rob and Mia in the Kitchen. Richie mustered up the courage to express his concerns and desires. He spoke up, his voice quivering slightly but filled with determination.

"I need to shoot off."

Jonesy's eyes narrowed, his face turning red with a sudden surge of anger. The once calm, confident aura that surrounded him seemed to dissipate, replaced by an unsettling intensity. His voice trembled with rage as he lashed out at Richie, his words biting like venomous snakes. "Shut the fuck up! You're staying put now until we all leave here together. You better start getting used to this house as I want you coming back here tomorrow to start serving up my gear"!

Mia entered and exchanged concerned glances with Richie, taken aback by the sudden outburst. They had seen Jonesy get frustrated before, but this was different. It was as if a switch had been flipped, unleashing a storm of fury that showed no signs of abating.

"What do you mean?" Ritche asked with a puzzled anxious expression, his innocence shining through in his response.

Jonesy leaped up energetically, moving close to Richie with a dominance reminiscent of an alpha animal establishing its position in the group. A hint of stale tobacco and an odour that suggested a lack of recent encounters with a toothbrush accompanied Jonesy's breath. "Hey, numbnuts," he said sternly, "you owe me for that weed and all the help I've given you. It's payback time, whether you're on board or not. If you don't follow my lead or try to fuck me over, you'll find out what happens to those who let me down."

The room was filled with an oppressive tension as Jonesy's anger escalated. His words became more aggressive, cutting through the air like shards of broken glass. Each sentence dripped with resentment and malice, causing Richie to retreat a step-in fear. It was a frightening sight, witnessing someone he had known to be affable, transform into an uncontrollable force. It became evident that Jonesy was not going to calm or back down. He seemed consumed by his anger, unable to find solace or reason amidst the torrential storm within him. The atmosphere in the room became suffocating, the weight of Jonesy's anger pressing down on them.

Jonesy brandished a Stanley knife, gently pressing it against Richie's left cheek without breaking the surface of his skin. Richie understood that Jonesy wasn't one to back down; he exuded danger and had the capability to support the implied violence. Any attempt by Richie to resist seemed futile, as overpowering Jonesy appeared unlikely. Even if Richie somehow gained an advantage in a physical altercation, it wouldn't necessarily bring an end to the impending violence. The next few moments rested solely on Richie's shoulders. Should he exit the scene? Confront Jonesy with a fight? Or yield and remain in the flat, awaiting the unfolding of whatever came next.

Richie dropped his shoulders, lowered his eyes, and took a small step back in a sign of submission. He spoke quietly and said, "OK I'll wait."

"Good boy," whispered Jonesy.

In that moment, Richie revealed his own vulnerabilities and weaknesses to Jonesy, who, being highly adept at recognising signs of submissive behaviour, swiftly picked up on them. Jonesy excelled at intimidation, having spent a lifetime using this skill on the streets. Richie, along with Mia and Maxim, had all found themselves ensnared in Jonesy's manipulative grasp. They were all young victims of his criminal exploitation, used solely for the purpose of generating money. The success of Jonseys endeavours relied heavily on instilling fear and employing intimidation tactics. He had been raised in a street environment where strength equated to toughness. Unlike Richie, who didn't have violent skills ingrained in him from an early age, Jonesy grew up in an environment where only the strongest thrived. Richie, hailing from a good middle-class family, possessed something Jonesy lacked: compassion for others. Violence and intimidation weren't inherent to most people, making them susceptible to intimidation. Jonesy recognised this and shrewdly exploited it to his advantage.

13 Uncomfortable Reunion

Neil's semi-detached residence on Whitbarrow Road represented a significant downgrade from the detached luxury executive home he had once owned. Nestled in a pleasant suburban street in Lymm, the move proved to be a considerable challenge for Neil. Downsizing after his separation from Sarah was particularly tough. Back then, Richie and Tom had been resolute in their decision to leave their mother's house and live with their father, a daunting adjustment for them as they were accustomed to the happy family home. Conversely, Sarah felt displeased about parting with her boys during their move. She resented it and held Neil responsible for orchestrating the situation, even though he hadn't manipulated the boys into moving in with him. Despite Neil's attempts to explain, Sarah remained unconvinced and unwilling to accept any other perspective.

Neil observed the car parking outside his house and waited anxiously behind the front door. Exhausted and disheartened, he couldn't summon the energy to dress appropriately, still clad in his old dressing gown and worn-out slippers. Falling into the habit of not dressing during the day, Neil felt drained and lacked motivation for the tasks that lay ahead. Convincing himself that there was no compelling reason to get up and dress became a regular part of his routine.

As Matt stood outside, his heart raced with the anticipation and uncertainty that hung in the air. It had been years since he last saw his older brother Neil. Gathering his courage, Matt took a deep breath and moved forward, prepared to rekindle the connection with the brother he had been estranged from for a significant amount of time.

When the front door opened, Matt was taken aback by Neil's dishevelled appearance. Time had etched deep lines on his face, and the once vibrant eyes now bore the shadow of illness. Memories of their joyful childhood, shared adventures, and echoing laughter flooded Matt's mind. However, the stark reality of Neil's condition became undeniable. The brain tumour had left its cruel mark, stealing fragments of his personality and memories. Neil, once a driven and proud individual, both in his work and appearance, now appeared as an old man approaching his final days due to the tragic impact of illness. Emaciated and markedly thinner since his diagnosis, his complexion was now "whiter than pale," and the skin on his lower forearms seemed thin and almost transparent. Struggling to stand upright without the support of the open-door frame, Neil's voice, too, had become frailer and more fragile since their phone conversation two days earlier. Contrary to the months estimated by doctors, Neil's appearance suggested he had only weeks, if not days left.

  Matt found himself utterly astonished and caught off guard by his brother's transformed appearance, which was barely recognisable. Fighting back the tears welling up inside, Matt grappled with the harsh reality of Neil's deteriorating condition.

  "Damn, Neil, why didn't you reach out to me earlier?" Neil chose to brush off Matt's comment. "Thanks for coming, Matt. I really appreciate you dropping everything for me. You can see I've been going through a rough time. How about you, Matt? How are things with you?" Neil was keenly aware that Matt had been struggling when they last saw each other all those years ago.

  "You know, I'm doing okay now and adjusting to my new life in France. It's a slower pace of life and certainly drier than here in the Northwest of England. It hasn't stopped raining since I arrived in the UK." Matt dropped his bag in the entranceway and feeling the skeletal bones of his brothers' shoulders, draped his arm around his brother's upper shoulder, providing support as they walked back into the lounge.

"Who's been helping you, Neil?"

"I have a carer, Mary, who just started coming in one a day a week, thanks to the perks of paying my taxes and national insurance all my working life. Honestly, Mary's care has been excellent and much welcomed. As for the boys, Richie has found it difficult." Neils voice began to quiver, his eyes fixed on the ceiling, lost in his thoughts. Moments of clarity were fleeting, but in this instance, something shifted within him. A wave of memories crashed against the shores of his mind, and suddenly, he remembered. He remembered the piercing pain that had recently ripped through his heart, the loss of his young teenage son, Tom. This emotional realisation hit Neil like a thunderbolt, leaving him breathless. Tears welled up in his eyes as he allowed himself to fully embrace the magnitude of his grief. He mourned not only for Tom but also for the years he had lost, the moments he could never reclaim. The guilt and regret washed over him, threatening to drown his already fragile spirit. His thoughts cascaded through the fragments of memories he had of his son. The laughter, the dreams they had once shared, the warmth of their bond, it all resurfaced in vivid detail. He recalled, Tom's bright smile, heard his infectious laughter, and felt his loving embrace. The realisation of what he had lost, what could never be recaptured, weighed heavily on his heart. He reflected on the brevity of life; the fragility of the connections we hold dear. He questioned himself, wondering if he had truly cherished each moment with Tom, if he had been the father he had strived to be. Regret gnawed at him, amplifying the ache in his chest and couldn't hold it together any longer. He dropped to his knees and began sobbing uncontrollably with his face down on the floor. Matt was hopeless at the sympathy thing and knelt beside his brother while placing his arm around him.

"Don't worry, Neil. I'm here for you, and I can help," he reassured in a sympathetic and caring tone.

"It's not me I'm worried about," Neil gasped through his sobs, the weight of his words heavy with despair. "I've let Tom down so terribly, and I can't wrap my head around why he did it. They say he was just larking around, didn't mean to do it. I just don't know. This is tearing me apart from the inside, along with this bloody awful tumour. I'm forgetting things, and I'm terrified for Richie. He's transformed so drastically, and I can't blame him. His anger burns against everyone, and I fear he's falling in with dangerous folks. You know, gang stuff? I'm sure he's in over his head. Thinks he knows it all, but he's not that streetwise. He won't listen to me, comes, and goes as he pleases. He hates me and his mother for putting him through all this! Will you talk to him, Matt? If anyone can set him straight, it's you. I know he respects your military background. There was a time he even talked about joining up to follow you. I'm hopeful he'll at least pause and listen to you."

"I can try, but I can't promise. You know I'm not one of these happy clappy social worker types. My patience is not the best when it comes to things like this and drugs."

"What do you mean Matt?"

"Let's just say I don't have a good record with drug dealers in the Manchester area". Neil looked at his brother with a questioning silence.

Tapping his brother on the shoulder and wanting to change the subject, "Come on Neill let's get you sat down, and I'll get a "wet on" for you." Neil smiled at his brother's military terminology for a cup of tea….

Matt grasped why the two boys had struggled so much with their parents' breakup. Like all the young individuals navigating the challenges of a family separation, they had received minimal support. Despite the school's attempts to assist, the boys rebuffed those efforts, avoiding discussing their fears and emotions.

The intense arguments and conflicts between Neil and Sarah had escalated to the point where the police were involved. Past incidents led to a referral to social services, unsettling the boys. Neil insisted there was no domestic violence, but Sarah had consistently tried to harm and tarnish him over the years, seeking favour from various agencies. Sarah had gone to great lengths to acquire what remained of Neil's possessions, including money from his failed business.

At one juncture, Tom and Richie were taken into a "Place of Safety" after Sarah, under the influence of alcohol, claimed Neil had attacked her in their presence. Her drinking had gradually worsened over time, making even the simplest discussions challenging for the entire family. Neil referred to Sarah as a functioning alcoholic, acknowledging her difficulty in drink, but he maintained he never resorted to violence. Sarah's drinking had steadily deteriorated, exacerbating an already strained situation. Neil found conversing with her, especially in the evenings, to be a nightmare. Despite her worsening drinking problem, Sarah's close friends remained unaware, as she managed to appear quite normal to the outside world the day after her bouts of heavy drinking.

Though they hadn't been troublesome boys, the family's break up had taken a heavy toll. Matt recognised the profound sadness in the situation and understood the urgency to assist Richie. Unfortunately, for Tom, it was too late, and everyone had to grapple with the enduring consequences. Richie, however, stood at a crossroads, and there was a chance to rescue him from the path he was currently navigating.

Neil and Matt sat on the couch drinking tea catching up on the lost years. Neil seemed interested in Matt's new life in France who kept his responses brief and avoided discussing his relationship with Nicole. The conversation inevitably veered towards the heart-wrenching topic of Tom's sudden death.

"Why did he do this? Was there other stuff going on at school?" Matt's inquiry dripped with empathy.

"Nothing, Matt. It was like he just reacted in the moment," Neil responded, his words laden with the unbearable weight of the situation. The coroner had officially deemed the death an accident, a classification that left everyone grappling with disbelief. Tom's impending funeral loomed like a sombre gathering, casting a foreboding shadow over them all.

"Neil, if I'm going to help Richie, I want to do it my way. It might not be pretty at times, and it might get confrontational, but I need you to support me when and where you can."

"Fine, Matt. We have to do what's necessary."

"What's Sarah going to say about this? You know she isn't my greatest fan and won't be thrilled about my arrival."

Neil, acknowledging Matt's enduring disdain for his ex-wife, didn't hold back. "Forget her, Matt. I don't care what she thinks; the woman is an utter nutcase. Richie loathes his mother for what she's done to us as a family. He won't even be in the same room as her. It's heart-wrenching, but I can understand why, and he won't talk to me about any of it." Neil's voice resonated with raw pain and frustration, adding a profound and powerful layer to his words.

As both men sat chatting in the living room, the calm ambiance was abruptly interrupted by the faint jingle of keys outside. The sound of metal scraping against metal resonated through the silent air, signalling Richie's return home. With a subtle click, the key found its rightful place in the keyhole, echoing a satisfying confirmation. A quiet creak followed as the door swung open, each footstep grew in volume, the familiar rhythm of Richie's gait reverberating through the hallway. The muffled thuds gradually grew closer, evoking a sense of anticipation. Finally, the muted shuffle of his shoes on the floor marked his presence.

"Whose car is on the drive?" he shouted just as he was entering the room before catching sight of Matt, "Oh it's you, alright." There was a short uncomfortable pause as Neil and Matt turned to face the startled Richie.

Richie's face became twisted with anger as he came face to face with his uncle. The tension in the room was palpable, the air thick with unresolved resentment. For as long as Richie could remember his mother had talked badly of Matt which had tainted his view of his uncle.

Matt had always been an observer, keenly attuned to the struggles and journeys of those around him. He recognised the familiar shadows that danced in Richie's eyes, the weight of poor choices and the allure of a destructive path. Deep down, Matt understood the pain and desperation that drove Richie into the arms of gangs and excitement, for he too had once battled his own demons.

With empathy in his heart, Matt decided to reach out to Richie, determined to offer a guiding light amidst the darkness that consumed him. He knew the road to redemption was treacherous, but he believed that everyone deserved a chance to change their course. He had to convince Richie that he had everything to live for and get away from the drug and gang culture in which he had become embroiled. Pull him back from the brink of self-destruction otherwise the outcomes would only mean two things, Jail or worse.

Matt's presence loomed over Richie, his casual demeanour and playful smile a stark contrast to Richie's clenched fists and furrowed brow. The strained silence between them seemed to stretch on indefinitely, each moment fraught with unspoken words and unhealed wounds. Richie couldn't quite put his finger on why he harboured such animosity towards his uncle. It was the way Matt always overshadowed him, effortlessly stealing the spotlight with his behaviour. Or it was the sense of superiority that exuded from Matt a former Commando, as if he had all the answers and Richie was merely an afterthought.

As the moment ticked by, Richie's anger swelled within him, threatening to erupt like a volcano. He struggled to find the words to articulate his frustrations, his voice caught in the suffocating grip of his emotions. But the fire burning in his eyes spoke volumes, conveying a simmering resentment that refused to be ignored.

Matt, sensing the storm brewing within Richie, tried to break the tension. He tried to strike up a conversation, aiming for a semblance of normalcy, but his words fell flat, the discomfort in the room intensifying with each passing moment. It was clear that this encounter was not going to be easily reconciled.

In the end, Richie's anger and animosity overshadowed any possibility of a peaceful resolution. Their encounter remained an unresolved clash of personalities, an exchange fraught with unspoken grievances. As Richie turned away, his heart heavy with unresolved emotions, he couldn't help but wonder if there would ever come a day when he and his uncle could find common ground, or if their strained relationship was destined to remain an irrevocable divide. Richie made his excuse and went upstairs.

Matt was struck by the size of Richie, considering he was just sixteen. Physically, he had grown since Matt last saw him, standing at an imposing six feet tall and showing signs of filling out, though there was still room for further physical development. Despite realising Richie lacked the physical ability to overpower him in a direct confrontation, Matt understood that this might be put to the test during any efforts to rehabilitate Richie. A confused and angered teenager, fuelled by testosterone, could still pose a formidable challenge. Richie, a troubled teenager, harboured a deep anger towards everyone in his world.

Matt turned to his brother and remarked, "He seems like a lost soul, doesn't he? I've encountered young lads like him back in the Marines. Lost, with little family support or positive role models. It's common for young men to seek excitement and that missing family bond elsewhere. That's why so many turn to the military. It appears Richie found his excitement and sense of belonging by joining a gang."

Trying to understand why young men chose a gang or the military was hard. These decisions could be vastly different or terribly similar. Each with its own set of consequences and outcomes. While both involved joining a close-knit community and taking on a distinct identity, the purposes and implications of these choices diverge significantly.

In the world of criminal gangs, the allure often lied in a sense of belonging and protection. Gangs often attracted those seeking a sense of family or camaraderie in environments where like Richie such support was lacking. However, this sense of belonging could come with a steep price to pay. By joining a gang, Richie had put himself at risk, both legally and physically, and could face long-lasting repercussions that could negatively impact on his life and those around them.

Contrastingly, the military offered a different path towards belonging and purpose. While it also involves a powerful sense of camaraderie and a tight-knit community, the military provides a structured environment with clear objectives and a hierarchy. Members receive extensive training, which instils discipline, leadership skills, and a sense of responsibility. Although military service can involve dangerous situations, it is governed by a commitment to upholding the values of service and sacrifice.

One notable difference between joining a gang and the military is the impact on personal growth and long-term opportunities. Joining a gang often perpetuates a cycle of violence and criminal behaviour, limiting chances for personal development and success.

In contrast, joining the military could provide individuals with a structured environment for personal growth and education. While both paths involve a commitment to a group, joining a gang and joining the military present starkly different outcomes. The decision between these two paths depends on an individual's values, aspirations, and the kind of life they envision for themselves. Matt just hoped Richie's values would get him through unscathed. Richie just needed guidance and someone like Matt to be prepared to give him time and commitment. Had Neil failed his boys, while he was too mixed up in his own marriage breakdown? Experts would say "No," but others like Matt with all his discipline and military background would say, "Yes."

14 Whispers in the Wind

At this time of year autumn had a special kind of beauty. The crisp morning breeze was carrying russet, amber and scarlet leaves in the air. Feeling the cold breeze on his face Matt watched the leaves swirl around. They reminded him of his days hanging under a parachute canopy. Fallen leaves, had collected at the gate in the shadow of the Church. Morning dew lay across the neatly cut grass. Chalky and lichen moss covered gravestones lined the pathway to the church entrance. Young people were milling around in small groups interspersed by remorseful looking adults. Some appeared to be teachers from Tom's school comforting many of the young girls who were tearfully upset. Confronting the harsh truth of a funeral and a young friend, someone they had once believed had a bright future ahead.

Matt had opted out of accompanying his family in the hearse procession, anticipating unbearable tension. He deemed it wiser to meet with Neil at the church instead. As Matt arrived and surveyed the scene, unfamiliar faces greeted him. On the far side of the church parking lot, a peculiar couple captured his attention. The woman, though feminine, seemed markedly younger than her male companion. Their demeanour piqued Matt's curiosity. The man, clad in inappropriate funeral attire, grey jogging bottoms and a dark puffer jacket stood out uncomfortably. Meanwhile, the woman, with her pallid complexion and dishevelled appearance, hardly looked the part for such a solemn occasion. Matt couldn't shake the feeling that they weren't there for the funeral at all.

Before long, the Herse arrived outside the church. Mourners began gravitating into the church ahead of the coffin that contained the young Tom. It became very apparent how unwell Neil looked when he was surrounded by healthier people.

Neil, once a sturdy figure with a commanding presence, had transformed into a frail and fragile-looking old man. His once strong and firm posture had now slouched, burdened by the weight of illness and years gone by. His body, once robust and energetic, had become a shadow of its former self. His limbs seemed delicate and fragile, as if a gentle breeze could sweep him away. The skin on his hands, weathered and thin, revealed the marks of a life filled with both triumph and tribulation. Neil's face, lined with countless creases, told stories of joys and sorrows, etching a roadmap of experience and wisdom. His hair, once a thick and vibrant mane, had now thinned and turned to wisps of silver, a testament to the passage of time.

As Neil moved, it was with a cautious and deliberate effort, as if every step towards the church was an arduous task. His movements lacked the vitality and strength of youth, replaced instead by a gentle and measured grace. Neil's voice, once commanding and resonant, had grown softer, his words carrying a fragile vulnerability. Though his body showed signs of weariness and age, the glimmer in Neil's eyes remained steadfast. Behind the spectacles perched on his fragile nose, his eyes held a flicker of the fire that had once burned so brightly within him. They were windows to a lifetime of memories, dreams, and the resilience that had carried him through the darkest of days. If only time could be wound back Matt thought.

Neil acknowledged his brother by raising his hand. Neil had never expected to be burying his own son as he struggled to walk behind the coffin on his son's final journey into Church.

Matt found funerals and going through the emotions of another sad event extremely hard. He been to enough over the years. All good young men in the prime of their lives taken way too early. Matt followed behind the family and felt like he was watching from a Bird's eye view, like he wasn't there. He avoided eye contact with Sarah. He wasn't even sure if she had noticed he was even there.

The atmosphere inside the church was heavy with sorrow, punctuated by the sounds of women and children in tears. Emotions ran high as touching tributes poured forth from Tom's friends and family. It was evident that Tom had been deeply cherished and admired, making his tragic fate even more heartbreaking. He had been let down by a family that failed to show him love, pushing him to the brink of despair.

As the congregation sat in disbelief, it was clear that nobody could have foreseen such a grim end to Tom's life. The profound impact of his loss reverberated throughout the room, leaving a lasting imprint on the young souls present, an experience they would carry with them for years to come.

Among the mourners, Neil stood out, his expression betraying a sense of utter defeat and desolation, as if the spark of life had been extinguished within him.

Matt felt a strong reluctance to be present in that place. His emotions churned within him, threatening to overwhelm him, and he struggled to maintain control. He had become adept at managing his feelings, honing this skill amidst the chaotic and violent scenes of combat that haunted his memories. As intrusive images flashed through his mind, he could sense the familiar signs of distress creeping in, the heat rising in his palms, the clamminess of his skin. The nervous tremors that often-followed moments of intense combat resurfaced, causing his hands to shake as he tightly clutched the order of service. It was a sensation he hadn't experienced in quite a time, a reminder of the battles he thought he had left behind.

Outside the church, by the graveside, a light drizzle began to fall, though it went unnoticed amidst the solemn proceedings. Matt remained on the periphery of the congregation, unable to bring himself closer to the heart of the ceremony. As the coffin was lowered into the freshly turned earth, he averted his gaze, unable to bear the sight. The overwhelming sorrow of the moment brought tears to his eyes, and he fought valiantly to maintain his composure. The service stirred up painful memories, reopening psychological wounds he had worked hard to heal during his time in France. As he grappled with his emotions, he questioned why he had subjected himself to this anguish once more. Why had he returned? Why not remain in France, where he could have avoided this emotional turmoil altogether?

Matt stared at his brother who was in turn looking at Richie. What must they be thinking right now Matt thought?

The Priest remained motionless and started to recite the final words, "Ashes to ashes, dust to dust."

Suddenly, Sarah's anguished cry pierced the air, her voice echoing with desperation. "No, no, no! Why, why, why?" she wailed, striking Neil's chest with clenched fists. Collapsing onto her knees, she seemed oblivious to the presence of others around her. Mourners nearby reacted quickly, rushing to her side to offer reassurance and help her to her feet.

Through her tears, Sarah directed blame at Neil, her sobs punctuating her accusations. As she was gently guided back towards the car park, her makeup ran in streaks down her tear-stained cheeks, blending with the rain.

Though physically shaken by the outburst, Neil managed to maintain his composure, remaining silent and impassive. He was hardly in a state to respond anyway. Meanwhile, Richie, incensed by his mother's behaviour, lashed out in frustration. "Just go! You're making a spectacle of yourself and embarrassing us all," he shouted.

Sarah, without a word, retreated into a nearby car, casting a lingering glance at her son before closing the door behind her.

The silence was deafening, leaving an anxious and sad atmosphere by the graveside. It was over and Tom was now at peace with the world. Richie looked at his father, embraced him for a moment without speaking then turned and walked off without saying another word.

Matt assumed Richie would offer his mother solace and support, but to his dismay, Richie ignored her completely. As Sarah looked towards Richie, her eyes filled with a glimmer of hope, only to be met with disappointment as he passed by her car without a second glance.

Richie approached the male and young female that Matt had noticed earlier, evidently familiar with them. They exchanged smiles and engaged in a brief, unheard conversation before a taxi arrived. Without a second thought, they all climbed into the taxi and departed, leaving Matt intrigued and determined to uncover their identities.

15 The Dark Trespass

    Richie, Mia, and Maxim entered the dimly lit flat, their senses tingling with a mix of anticipation and trepidation. As they stepped further inside, a faint scent of stale cigarette smoke lingered in the air. The silence hung heavy, broken only by the distant sounds of traffic outside. Their eyes adjusted to the low light, revealing a scene that sent a shiver down their spines. Two young women stood near the kitchen; their figures slightly obscured by the shadows. Dressed in revealing attire, their appearance suggested a world of hardship and vulnerability. The heavy makeup on their faces, coupled with the tired expressions, hinted at a life of struggle and desperation. The silence between them was deafening, as if an unspoken agreement had been made to maintain distance and anonymity. Richie, Mia, and Maxim exchanged uneasy glances, their eyes mirroring a mixture of curiosity, concern, and a deep-rooted sadness. The women's Eastern European features hinted at a distant homeland, carrying the weight of a thousand untold stories. It was evident that their presence in the flat was not accidental, and their aura spoke volumes about the unspoken world they inhabited. The women's eyes met briefly, their gazes carrying a silent plea for understanding. Yet, they remained resolute, offering no verbal response. It was as though the pain and suffering they had endured had muted their voices, leaving only the echoes of their past in the depths of their haunted eyes.

    Maxim, observant and analytical, surveyed the room, seeking clues to unravel their circumstances. He noticed scattered belongings, a tattered handbag, and worn-out shoes, lending a sense of humanity to these women who had been reduced to mere shadows in the darkness. The air was heavy with unspoken words, as Richie, Mia, and Maxim stood, a silent alliance forming between them.

Jonesy had been waiting at the flat and although aware Richie had been to his brother's funeral, made no reference to it.

"Right, youse two," pointing at Maxim and Richie. "You will go to Robs and keep pushing the gear from there. Don't forget to keep on top of Rob as he will still be twitchy. He needs to get used to us or were just goner have to gag him and lock him in a room if he becomes a problem. Jonesy threw a couple of bundles of cellophane wrapped snap seal bags at Maxim. "Let's push this stuff hard you two. Mia you're staying here with me as I've got business for you to sort out."

Mia's gaze lingered on Maxim, her eyes brimming with a mixture of worry and concern. They had been through so much together, their bond forged through countless trials and shared experiences. With just a glance, she conveyed a myriad of emotions, silently pleading for understanding. She knew Maxim's determination and fearlessness, his unwavering commitment. But this time, the weight of uncertainty lay heavy on her heart. The sight of the two young women standing in the kitchen had triggered a surge of apprehension within her, causing her mind to race with unanswered questions.

Maxim couldn't bring himself to speak for his fear of upsetting and antagonising Jonesy. As Mia locked eyes with him, her silent plea carried a depth of understanding that transcended words. She wanted him to see the cautionary glimmer in her gaze, to acknowledge the risks they were all exposed to.

Richie saw this nonverbal communication but kept quiet, feeling fearful it wasn't his place to speak up. Jonesy sensed the anxiety amongst the three and shouted, "Come on then you soft fuckers, let's get hustling, it's payback time!"

Maxim started to rock on the heels of his feet and plucked up the courage to speak, "Can't Mia come with us to keep Rob sweet."

"No, she fucking can't you little gobshite, she has business to attend too here. You just stick to what you're told to do, I'll stick to making the decisions, is that clear!" Maxim shoulders dropped while he took in a deep breath, turned, and began to leave the flat. Richie followed without saying a word.

As they left the apartment two Asian men arrived asking for Jonesy. They acknowledged each other with nods, and Richie pointed inside and shouted, "Hey Jonesy it's for you."

Getting out of ear shot of the flat, Maxim turned to Richie and said, "This is evil, we shouldn't be letting this happen to Mia."

Richie paused and wondered if Maxim was assessing his loyalty.

"What do you mean."

"Jonesy has me trapped because I owe him. Like you I am in debt to him and it's hard if not impossible to let go or escape, 'but you?' You could leave now, go back to your family, and run the risk of looking over your shoulder to simply avoid Jonesy. He doesn't even know where you live, does he? As for me I have nowhere to run and hide. It's the same for Mia. But you? Why are you doing this Richie?"

Richie stopped and looked at Maxim. His normally confident and jovial expression was replaced with a look of uncertainty and anxiety. As he stood facing Maxim, his eyes darted around, searching for answers that eluded him. His furrowed brows and the slight crease on his forehead revealed his unease. The worry etched upon his face spoke volumes about the thoughts swirling through his mind. Richie's fingers twitched nervously, a tell-tale sign of his anxiety, as he grappled with the unknown. The air of uncertainty and his previous decision making seemed to weigh heavily upon his broad shoulders, as if he carried the weight of the world in that fleeting moment. Richie was known for his quick wit and bold demeanour, but in that moment, his uncertainty was palpable. His lips, usually curved into a mischievous smile, were now pressed together in a tight line, betraying his internal struggle. The gleam in his eyes, usually brimming with mischief, was replaced by a glimmer of doubt and concern.

He stared at Maxim, seeking solace in the familiar comfort of his presence. Richie yearned for the unwavering support he knew Maxim could provide, hoping it could quell the tumult of doubts swirling within him. However, even in Maxim's steadfast gaze, he found no immediate respite, for Maxim seemed preoccupied with his own concerns.

"You know, that's a valid question, but honestly, I've got nothing else going on in my life right now. I'm just doing it because I initially thought Jonesy was a decent guy when I first met him," Richie admitted, his words tinged with uncertainty. "Oh, and he does know where I live." With that, Richie turned and walked away, leaving Maxim momentarily to contemplate the weight of his friend's words.

Jonesy picked up his mobile and flicked through the contact list before dialling. "What's happening my man," Jonesy said laughingly.

Billy was Jonesy's main enforcer. At six foot three inches in height, Billy was a huge bulk of a man and a loyal friend to Jonesy. His shaved head was complemented by his tattooed arms, sleeved from top to bottom. They had seen lots of action in the Gym, having spent years working the doors in Manchester's club scene he had gained a big reputation of a no-nonsense man who would be foolish cross in a physical confrontation. Billy had seen and dished out plenty of violence over the years and was well known to the local cops.

"Billy I've got a small job, fancy it?"

"Sounds good, want to give me the details."

"It's a simple one for a man of your talents, all you have do is pay two friends of mine a little visit at their new quaint home. Nothing to heavy, ruffle them up a bit and relieve them of their gear. They won't be expecting you and there is nothing for you to worry about as they are just two young kids. The gear is in the Kitchen, so you don't have to search far.

"Nice and simple then," Billy remarked. "I'll call youse later when it's done."

"Sweet Ill text over the address later." Jonesy hung up.

****

Richie knocked on the front door and waited. Rob answered with a naive smile which vanished when he saw Richie and Maxim standing on his doorstep.

"Where is Mia," he asked disapprovingly.

"Ah, she is unwell and can't make it now. She asked if we could pop by to see how you are doing and spend a bit of time keeping you company. Before he even had time to answer Maxim and Richie were inside the flat. Rob had a perplexed expression etched upon his face. His brows furrowed as he observed the presence of the unfamiliar strangers standing in his sanctuary. Confusion danced in his eyes, mixing with a hint of agitation.

With a childlike innocence, Rob approached Richie, his voice quivering as he questioned their presence. "Um, excuse me. Can I ask... why are you in my flat?" His words carried a mix of vulnerability and frustration, as he struggled to comprehend the intrusion that had disrupted his familiar routine. The expressions of Maxim and Richie, mirroring a mix of surprise and empathy. They understood that Rob's learning difficulties rendered this encounter even more disorienting for him, amplifying his need for answers and reassurance.

In response to Rob's earnest inquiry, Richie stepped forward, his voice gentle and soothing. "Hey, we're really sorry if we've startled you. We're here to help and support you."

Rob's agitation began to wane slightly as he absorbed his words. A flicker of understanding crossed his face, although his questions still lingered. He wanted to grasp the why and the how, to make sense of this unexpected intrusion into his safe space. Trying to find the right words, Rob continued his inquiries, his voice tinged with a mix of curiosity and frustration. "But... I want to see Mia. And why have you come into my flat?" His eyes searched Riches facial expression, hoping for clarity amidst the confusion that clouded his thoughts. Recognising the need to provide Rob with honest answers while balancing the sensitivity of the situation. Richie explained their purpose, describing how Mia had asked them to come round, help him out and keep him company for a while. Rob's brow unfurled, his countenance slowly transforming from agitation to a sense of acceptance. Though he might not fully grasp the intricacies of the situation, he understood it, that these two strangers had arrived with good intentions, aiming to help rather than harm him. As Rob absorbed their explanation, his trust in the strangers began to take root. Their calm demeanour and genuine concern resonated with him, easing his initial agitation. In that moment, he chose to believe that they had entered his flat for a reason, a purpose that would bring him the understanding he sought. With newfound reassurance, Rob nodded slowly, his gaze shifting between the strangers. Though his learning difficulties might make it challenging to process the intricacies of the situation, he was ready to accept the mysteries that had brought these strangers to his doorstep unexpectedly.

  Maxim, driven by a sense of duty, began to search through the drawers of the kitchen. His hands moved methodically, his eyes scanning for any signs of illicit substances hidden within. As he sifted through the contents, his phone buzzed incessantly, its notifications demanding his attention. Maxim couldn't help but feel a pang of frustration as the messages poured in, prospective punters reaching out, seeking a connection to acquire drugs. With each ping, Maxim's resolve hardened. His focus shifted from the immediate task at hand to the urgent need to find the gear Jonesy had left. A sense of urgency and excitement pulsed through Maxim's veins. The messages on his phone served as a stark reminder of the imminent dangers faced by those ensnared in the clutches of addiction. Each plea for drugs represented another life hanging in the balance, another soul teetering on the edge of self-destruction. It also signified to a dealer like Maxim there was important money to be made. The juxtaposition of these simultaneous realities weighed heavily on him, highlighting the interconnectedness of lives caught in the web of substance abuse and exploitation. In the meantime, they started getting round Rob, encouraging him to go in the lounge, relax have a brew and smoke a spliff.

When the first door knock came, Rob jumped to his feet with an intention of answering it.

"Sit down," Maxim shouted, "Richie is expecting friends, so you don't need to get up." Rob shocked and a little scared by Maxim's reaction sat back down with a look of worry etched on his face.

The initial knock on the door marked the beginning of a significant shift for the rest of the evening. Initially tense with each subsequent ring, Rob gradually grew accustomed to the interruptions as the night progressed, eventually easing into a more relaxed state. He found solace in the moments when Maxim treated them to pizza and beer. Despite his confusion over the growing number of visitors at his doorstep, he opted to brush it aside.

As the evening settled in, following their successful first day of dealing, everything had unfolded seamlessly. With a substantial amount of cash to show for their efforts, Ritche and Maxim shared laughter, revelling in the simplicity and efficiency of their money-making venture. Why bother with laborious, low-paying jobs when this offered such a straightforward and lucrative alternative? Despite the inherent risks, the ease and minimal effort required, coupled with the slim chances of getting caught by the authorities, made it an appealing proposition.

Just as they were beginning to unwind, Maxim's phone interrupted the moment. Ritche observed Maxim's demeanour shift as he conversed with Jonesy. "No worries, it's been a solid night. Cheers, mate. I'll stick around here and drop off some more tomorrow." The call concluded as swiftly as it had begun.

With no alternative accommodation available, Maxim seemed resigned to spending the night at Rob's place. Meanwhile, Ritche harboured a subtle unease about staying overnight in Rob's home. As Rob slept soundly in his chair, Maxim began to doze off beside him there was a knock at the door. Ritche rose from his seat and approached the door, the sound echoing through the quiet room. In the drowsiness of the moment, Maxim stirred awake, momentarily disoriented. "Wait, did we get an order?" he called out, his voice tinged with confusion. But before Maxim could fully grasp the situation, Ritche had already unlatched the front door, unaware that no one had placed an order.

With a sudden click of the latch, the door violently swung back on its hinges, striking Ritche squarely in the face with a brutal force. The impact sent him staggering backwards, crashing to the floor in the hallway. Before he could even gather his bearings, the menacing silhouettes of three masked men clad in balaclavas stormed into the apartment.

"Give us the damn gear and money!" one of them bellowed, delivering swift, merciless kicks to Ritche's head as he lay defenceless on the ground. The blows left him seeing stars, rendering him unable to react or even utter a word. Blood filled his mouth, and his vision began to blur as the assailants swiftly bypassed him and barged into the lounge.

Maxim struggled to regain his footing when a powerful grip seized him by the throat, wrenching him off balance. Before he could react, a massive fist crashed into his face, sending a jolt of pain shooting through him. Simultaneously, another assailant swung a glass vase, shattering it against the back of Maxim's head with brutal force. The impact split his skin, blood spraying from the wound as the vase shattered into shards. "Where's the fucking gear and money!" one of the intruders repeated in a loud and intimidating manner.

Maxim had no time to respond as the two males were already searching his pockets, taking all the cash and remaining drug wraps. The third male had forced Rob face down onto the lounge carpet standing on the back of his neck. Rob was petrified and had pissed himself through his jogging bottoms. "You fucking dirty bastard screamed the third male!"

The chaos continued as the intruders ransacked the kitchen, their hurried footsteps echoing through the tense silence. Suddenly, one of them barked, "Alright, let's move!" With swift efficiency, the trio dashed out of the house, their presence fleeting as they vanished into the night. In less than sixty seconds, it was all over. It took Ritche and Maxim seconds to gather themselves, their senses reeling from the abrupt violence. With urgency, Ritche grabbed a kitchen cloth and pressed it against the back of Maxim's head, staunching the flow of blood. Meanwhile, Rob remained motionless on the carpet, paralysed by fear.

"What the hell do we do now, Maxim?" Ritche's voice trembled with uncertainty.

"I don't know, but I'm getting out of here," Maxim declared, snatching his jacket, and bolting out of the flat without a second thought.

Left standing in the aftermath, Ritche felt a surge of panic. Rob's continued sobbing echoed in the room, a stark reminder of the trauma they had just endured. Ritche could feel the swelling around his right eye, a painful reminder of the chaos that had unfolded. With the commotion undoubtedly attracting attention, Ritche knew he had no choice but to flee. There was no way he could explain his presence to the police. With a heavy heart, he turned and ran, leaving behind the shattered remnants of their once peaceful evening.

16 Shattered Blue line

PCs Dave Russell and Steve Lomax responded promptly to a high-priority call regarding a suspected aggravated burglary with an ongoing disturbance. The only information provided to the two officers was from an anxious neighbour who wished to remain anonymous, expressing concern that a vulnerable individual was being targeted by burglars.

Dave, a fresh-faced officer eager to apply his high-speed, blue-light driver training, was joined by Steve, the seasoned veteran of the team, whose years of service surpassed his colleagues combined. Steve had long outgrown the thrill of racing around with blue lights and sirens blaring, having witnessed numerous younger officers succumb to the pitfalls of overzealousness. He understood that Dave's enthusiasm would eventually wane, much like his own and that of many others who had endured the relentless pressures and stresses of police work. The attrition of officers on shift and the unyielding public expectations amidst dwindling resources weighed heavily on Steve.

Upon arrival at the scene, Steve calmly informed the control room of their presence, allowing them to ease off other patrols still enroute. As they approached the address, the sight of the wide-open front door and illuminated lights signalled trouble. Smudged footprints on the exterior hinted at forced entry.

With caution, Dave entered the hallway, announcing their presence, "Police, is anyone home? Please identify yourselves." Silence greeted their call. As they traversed the hallway, signs of a disturbance became evident, a shattered vase littered the floor near the entrance. Despite the eerie quiet, the distant murmur of a television broadcasting Northwest football results emanated from the lounge. Steve and Dave moved forward together, their senses heightened, as the faint sounds of someone crying reached their ears.

Exchanging glances to confirm they both heard the same sounds, Dave and Steve proceeded cautiously into the lounge. There, they found a distraught man lying face down on the carpet, his sobs echoing through the room. Assessing the scene, they noticed blood and broken glass elsewhere, adding to the mystery of the situation.

Uncertain of the circumstances they were dealing with, the officers grappled with questions: Was the man a perpetrator or a victim? Whose blood, was it? Were there others present? Assessing such situations was second nature to frontline police officers, and they knew they had to act swiftly. While officers took time to develop this skill, Dave appeared to excel at it.

Dave gently initiated communication with the shaken man, trying to piece together the events leading up to their arrival, while Steve conducted a thorough search of the flat, relieved to find no one else inside. Updating the control room via radio, Steve informed them that the situation involved an aggravated burglary with the offenders now gone.

As the chaos settled, Dave managed to coax Rob into a nearby chair, his emotional state resembling that of a distressed child. Despite the turmoil, it was just another day's work for the seasoned officers.

Approaching Rob with compassion, Steve knelt, offering comfort and support. However, despite their efforts, Rob struggled to articulate what had transpired, repeatedly mentioning "Mia's brother" being present during the break-in. Aware of the challenges posed by Rob's condition in ascertaining a detailed account of what had happened , Steve knew that forensic evidence would be essential in piecing together the events. Despite the obstacles, the officers remained committed to their duty, navigating the complexities with diligence and empathy. It became clear that Rob's learning difficulties hindered his ability to provide coherent information complicating any subsequent investigation.

Before departing, Dave made sure to check the front door, ensuring it could be securely locked. To his surprise, he found it intact, suggesting the intruders had unlatched it rather than forcibly breaking in. Despite the chaos, it seemed nothing valuable had been taken, leaving the officers perplexed about the motive behind the intrusion. Once they ensured Rob would be okay for the night, the officers left the scene. As they settled back into their vehicle, Steve couldn't help but voice his frustration. "Just another tough job for us to document," he grumbled. " But I have a hunch there might be 'cuckooing' involved here." With a resigned shrug, he glanced out of the police car window. "Yet another unsolved crime to add to our database," he sighed, the burden of unresolved cases weighing on him.

****

Matt jolted awake in the dead of night; his senses heightened by the unsettling sound of movement echoing from downstairs. His heart raced, adrenaline surging through his veins as he strained to discern the source of the disturbance. Glancing at the illumination dials on his faithful military watch he saw it had just gone past three in the morning. As he sat up in bed, the darkness engulfed him, accentuating the eerie silence that hung heavy in the air. Matt's mind raced with a flurry of possibilities, his imagination conjuring up the worst-case scenarios. Fear tinged with determination coursed through his veins, propelling him into action. With cautious steps, Matt slid his feet into his trainers, silently cursing the creaky floorboards that threatened to betray his presence. He tiptoed through the darkened hallway, his breath held in anticipation. Every creak, every rustle, magnified the tension that filled the house. Reaching the top of the stairs, Matt peered down into the shadows below. The faint glow of a streetlight filtered through the curtains, casting eerie shadows on the staircase. The sound of movement persisted, growing more distinct with each passing second. His instincts took over, pushing him forward despite the knot of apprehension tightening in his gut. Matt descended the stairs with measured steps, his senses on high alert. The air grew thick with anticipation as he neared the origin of the sound. As he reached the ground floor, his eyes scanned the dimly lit surroundings. The flickering light from a malfunctioning hallway lamp cast an eerie glow, playing tricks on his mind. Matt's ears strained for any sign of the intruder's presence, his mind racing with the possibilities. A sudden creak from the kitchen drew his attention. His breath caught in his throat as he edged closer, his heart pounding against his ribcage. He braced himself, ready for whatever awaited him beyond the threshold. With a mix of fear and determination, Matt pushed open the door, revealing the scene before him. His eyes widened in surprise as he beheld the source of the disturbance.

There stood Richie in the kitchen, his back turned to the door as he poured himself a drink. Matt feeling a wave of relief wash over him, quietly entered the room detecting the lingering scent of Cannabis in the air. It was evident Richie had been indulging in it before returning home. "How's it going Richie."

As Richie turned to face his uncle, Matt couldn't help but notice the evidence of a recent physical altercation etched on Richie's face. Richie's eye was swollen, a fiery shade of red, clearly indicating pain. It wasn't the first time Matt had witnessed such a bruise, a familiar sight from his days in the Marines, where late-night escapades often resulted in similar injuries.

"What's been going on, Pal?" Matt asked sympathetically, already anticipating Richie's response.

"Nothing much, you know just had a small disagreement with someone."

"Oh right, seems like a big disagreement to end up with an eye like that. You might want to be careful. There are some bad people out there willing to hurt you?"

"What yah talking about," tutting angrily with a poor gangster type accent he had now somehow inherited.

Matt's heart ached with concern as he sat down with his nephew, his voice laden with earnestness as he tried to convey the gravity of the situation. He knew the dangers that lurked within the dark underbelly of gang culture, and he desperately wanted to steer Richie away from its treacherous path.

"Richie, I've seen firsthand the devastation that comes with being mixed up in this gang culture," Matt pleaded, his eyes filled with a mix of love and concern. "It's not the life you want, trust me. You have so much potential, so many opportunities ahead of you."

But Richie, stubborn and defiant, met Matt's pleading gaze with a resolute stare of his own. The lure of the streets and the sense of belonging he found within the gang held a seductive grip on his young mind. He had grown accustomed to the adrenaline, the camaraderie, and the false sense of power that came with it.

"You can't fool me, Richie. You're just a middle-class kid getting mixed up to your neck in shit. I know it and you know it. Seems to me you're getting involved with people who are way out from your comfort zone. You need to be careful. Get out why you still have the chance, would be my advice. Do something constructive with your life. Don't throw your life away with these wasters! I can see how it's changed you in the brief time that I've been here. How do you think your behaviour is helping your dad? Who were your two friends I saw you rushing away with yesterday?"

"Just some friends, why?"

Look Richie I've been around the block and I'm not stupid, get away from all this before it gets too late for you.

The drugs game is a lonely place, and you will only loose in the end.

"Dunno what you're talking about, I aint involved in no drugs and never have been so get off my case." His denial of what he was doing was obvious to Matt and his heart sank at Richie's response. His voice trembling with a mix of frustration and desperation, "Richie, they might seem like they've got your back, but this is a dangerous path you're on. Those bonds you think are strong could crumble in an instant. They're exploiting your potential, your future." The weight of Matt's words hung in the air, a silent plea for Richie to see reason. He knew that breaking through the wall Richie had built around himself would be a monumental task. It was a battle between the love of family and the allure of a world that promised power, money, and acceptance.

Richie's gaze hardened; his voice tinged with defiance as he pushed back against Matt's concerns. "You don't understand what it's like out there, Uncle Matt. Im doing what I want to do and don't need no preacher telling me otherwise."

Richie stood up to go to avoid any further discussion as he knew his uncle wasn't stupid. Richie ignorantly walked past Matt avoiding further eye contact before heading for the kitchen door. Matt's voice softening as he reached out to his nephew. "Richie, I know it's tough, but there are other paths, safer paths that can lead you to a better future. I don't want to see you fall victim to this cycle of violence and despair and you're capable of so much more."

But Richie, enveloped in the intoxicating allure of the gang culture, shook his head, refusing to yield to Matt's pleas. The walls he had built around himself seemed impenetrable, his conviction unyielding. In that moment, Matt felt a sense of helplessness, with the knowledge that he couldn't force Richie to change his path. All he could do was continue to be there for him, hoping that Richie would find his way back to a life that promised hope, not despair.

"Night then," Matt sighed and walked into the lounge in quiet thought. Quietly flicking on the TV, he lowered the sound, sat in a chair, and decided to wait for a while. Waiting was something Matt had become particularly good at….

****

After a couple of hours, Matt meticulously ensured that all the TVs and lights were switched off before making his way upstairs. As he passed Richie's bedroom on the small landing, he noticed that the door was slightly ajar. Peering inside, he could hear the steady rhythm of Richie's deep breaths, a sign that he was sound asleep. Despite whatever turmoil Richie had been embroiled in, it had negligible effect on his ability to find rest. Drawing on his expertise in navigating the darkness during his military days, Matt cautiously entered Richie's room. Moving with silent precision, he took note of the placement of Richie's mobile phone on the bedside cabinet. With deft fingers, he retrieved the device before silently slipping out of the room.

Back in his own room, Matt wasted no time in figuring out the PIN number to unlock Richie's mobile phone. He began by examining the screen under the room lights, searching for telltale waxy fingerprint marks. Four numbers stood out, showing obvious signs of frequent use, indicating to Matt the combination for unlocking the device. With a straightforward deduction, Matt pieced together the PIN code, realising that Richie, like others, had opted for his date of birth. With practiced ease, Matt discreetly installed a covert tracking software app onto the phone. After a brief syncing process with his own device, Matt was satisfied with the results. Carefully placing the phone back in its original position next to Richie, who remained oblivious to the covert operation unfolding around him, Matt quietly resumed his vigil, confident in his newfound ability to monitor his nephew's movements.

With the software successfully installed, Matt gained the ability to pinpoint the exact location of Richie's phone. Knowing that teenagers, including Richie, were typically inseparable from their mobile devices, Matt felt assured that Richie wouldn't even realise the covert software had been installed, even if he were to search for it. With this tool at his disposal, Matt could keep a close eye on Richie's movements. However, aware of the challenges that lay ahead in the coming days, Matt recognised the importance of getting a few hours of sleep. He understood that he might not have opportunities for a rest in the coming days.

17 Texting in touch

Maxim had spent the night on a friend's cold and uncomfy sofa. Despite the kind offer of help he had been asked to leave when the friend had to set off for work at 6am. Since then, Maxim had been wandering around town getting cold and contemplating what he would do next as he had missed calls from Jonesy and Richie. He dialled into his voicemail and listened to the recordings. The first being from Jonesy. "Maxim, call me, where are you, what's going on!

The next message was from Richie, "I'll meet you in the cafe at 10am".

Mia had been woken early by a call from Jonesy telling her to get round to Robs house. He hadn't given her a reason but ordered her to check the drug stash in Rob's kitchen. She had planned to go straight to the front door but noticed an unfamiliar red Land Rover parked outside. There was a smartly dressed professional looking woman, in her mid-fifties glancing at the front door talking to Rob. Deciding to avoid any interaction with Rob, Mia pulled up the hood of her jacket and briskly walked past the address, keeping within earshot. As she passed, she overheard a conversation between Rob and a woman, his mother.

"I told you it wasn't safe, Rob. You should move back home with me and your dad," she urged.

"Don't be stupid, Mum. It's going to be fine," Rob retorted confidently.

"Alright, but make sure you call me once the police have been round. Don't let anyone in that you don't know," she instructed firmly yet with a hint of nurturing concern.

The word "police" lingered in Mia's mind as she walked out of earshot. Once around the corner, she quickly dialled Maxim's number. The phone rang, but before it was answered, she received a message: "Meet me & Richie at Elvira's Café at 10 am."

Mia and Maxim began an exchange of text messages,
"Wtf is going on, Police going to Robs!!!!!?"
"It went shitty last nyt will speak L8er."
"Where's Richie!?"
"Fuck knows!"
"OK see u 2 @ 10".

Mia called Richie, but it went unanswered, so she followed up with a message, "Call me! u, OK?"

Feeling uncertain about where to go, Mia was adamant about avoiding Jonesy's flat at all costs until she knew what was happening. She dreaded facing his wrath over whatever had transpired the previous night. "Screw it," she muttered to herself, deciding to head to the café and wait until she heard from Maxim and Richie. As she walked, her phone buzzed with a text message, but to her dismay, it was from Jonesy: "Call me."

"Can't speak I'm with people, 5 O at Robs, so didn't go near, will call u l8er."

"If you C or hear from Maxim or Richie, tell them to call me NOW!"

Mia was under no illusion that something had gone wrong last night, and Maxim and Richie were not in Jonesy's good books.

****

As Matt finished assisting Neil into the lounge, they both heard Richie descending the stairs. They turned to catch a fleeting glimpse of him throwing on his jacket and rushing out of the house without a word. Neil, preoccupied with his own discomfort, barely had time to register his son's bruised eye before the front door slammed shut. Neil glanced at Matt with a mix of disbelief and concern, too unwell to delve into the situation further. "What's gotten into him?" he asked, his voice laced with worry.

"I'm not sure, Neil, but I'll find out," Matt reassured him. "I'm about to try and figure out what's going on. Will you be okay here today? It might take me a while."

"Yeah, I'll be fine, Matt," Neil replied gratefully. "I really appreciate your help and for coming home to do this for me. My carer will be around later to assist with lunch, so don't worry about me. Just focus on getting Richie sorted."

18 Elvira's Café

'Elvira's' was a back street no frills café on the edge of the town. The scent of freshly brewed coffee mingled with the aroma of hearty, home-cooked fried breakfast, enveloping the cosy space. Inside, a tapestry of characters unfolded, each adding their unique thread to the vibrant fabric of the café. At a corner table, a group of elderly friends gathered, their laughter echoing through the air. Their wrinkled faces told tales of a lifetime, their shared memories intertwining with the present as they swapped stories over steaming cups of tea. They were a testament to the enduring bonds forged over years of friendship and shared experiences. Near the window, a young artist hunched over a sketchbook, lost in a world of swirling lines and vivid colours. With each stroke of the pencil, her imagination came alive, creating art that would capture the essence of the neighbourhood's spirit. The café provided the perfect sanctuary, a space where creativity could flourish amid the clatter of dishes and the hum of conversations. In another corner, a tired construction worker sat alone, his calloused hands clutching a mug of strong coffee. His worn-out boots and dusty overalls spoke of years of arduous work, his tired eyes reflecting the toll of physical labour. The café provided a haven of respite, a place to refuel both his body and spirit before heading back to the demanding tasks that awaited him. At the counter, a harried mother juggled a crying baby on one hip while desperately searching for her misplaced phone in her bag. The café served as a sanctuary for her too, a temporary escape from the chaos of motherhood. Amidst the clatter of dishes and the chatter of customers, she found solace in a hot cup of coffee and the understanding smiles of fellow parents who shared in the daily struggles of raising a family.

Gill who ran the place was from a tough working-class family in Manchester. A little overweight and in her mid-fifties, her upbringing allowed. A warm-hearted soul with a perpetual apron tied around her waist, navigated the bustling space with grace and familiarity. Her genuine smile and kind words made each customer feel like family, as she effortlessly managed the symphony of pots clanging, orders being shouted, and the comforting hum of conversation. Many of her customers were good local people carrying with them their daily life struggles. Her bubbly personality made it hard, if not impossible to not to like her infectious non-judgemental personality and she could draw a smile out of anyone, however hard a time they were having in life. In this humble backstreet café, the towns working-class community found more than just a place to satiate their hunger and thirst. It was a hub of connection, where neighbours became friends and strangers became familiar faces. Amidst the backdrop of clinking cutlery and the symphony of diverse accents, the café embodied the spirit of the neighbourhood, a testament to the resilience, warmth, and camaraderie of its people. And so, in this unassuming space, the tapestry of characters continued to weave their stories, each cup of coffee a catalyst for connections, conversations, and shared experiences.

Richie entered and saw Mia sitting at a table by the window alone and deep in her thoughts. She was halfway through her breakfast of 'beans on toast' when Richie slid onto the chair joining her. The concerned expression on Mia's face said everything to him as he stared at her.

"What happened Richie, I heard the Police are going to Robs flat. I walked past earlier, and he was stood there sad, looking at the door with a woman who I guessed was his mum."

Before he had time to answer, Gill appeared at the side of the table, "what can I get you my sweet." Gill was far to street wise and picked up on their demeanour, noticing Richie's badly swollen eye trying to make light of the situation, "Oh dear looks like you've been in the wars my sweet, what happened to you."

"Ah nothing, just banged my face at work, stupid I know but I'll be Ok, thanks for asking, I'll have a full English and a coffee please."

Gill sensed he wasn't telling her the full truth and glanced at Mia, raised her eyebrows, and exaggerated the dotting of her pen on the paper note pad she was holding. "Coming right up my sweet" before turning and walking back towards her kitchen. Richie began to relate the previous night's events while Mia listened patiently. Part way through reciting his account Maxim arrived. He looked dreadful, as if he hadn't been to bed all night. He was shivering from the cold and quickly sat down next to them both. He was close to tears and very agitated, "oh my god what will we tell Jonesy about this. I can't go back and see him after all his gear and money has been stolen. I must leave; he will hurt me. I came here to have a better life, it's just worse than I could ever expect. "I'm scared, I have no money and I can't get help!"

Mia interrupted and whispered assertively, "Just fucking calm down a minute Maxim and keep your voice down."

Gill arrived back at the table looking highly suspicious of the three, "Ok my friend, don't tell me you're the sparring partner to this one," she enquired jokingly while pointing at Richie with her pen. "What can I get you?"

Maxim missed the sense humour in Gills tone, "I'll just have scrambled eggs, two toast and coffee."

"Ok my sweet it's on its way," turning and heading back towards the kitchen.

"Do you know who they were?" Mia asked.

"Of course, we fucking don't," Richie replied angrily who was beginning to realise he was way in over his head.

"Ok calm down big man, that aggression got you nowhere last night so don't take it out on me," Mia responded abruptly. This is what Jonesy, and his guys do to people like you and me. He can control us now because we all have a drugs debt to him. I wouldn't be surprised if he arranged this himself, to get you turned over like this. That way he can hold you both to ransom. He aint going to let you off lightly or let you walk away that easily. He needs the likes of you two, to run his gear and do the dirty work for him. To do that he needs a hold on you both and this event last night was the answer. You're vulnerable and have no obvious escape from it. He knows you're not going to run and tell the cops. Well, at least it was just cash and leftovers from the gear you had left to sell," Mia remarked, trying to maintain a sense of perspective. "You two didn't have to resort to this or choose this way of life," she said, her voice tinged with disappointment as she glanced at Richie, shaking her head momentarily.

"Especially you, why on earth did you chose this route when you could have easily done something else with your life. I didn't have a choice going into the care system as a young vulnerable girl. Every day I still wish I could wake up and discover my life is a horrible dream, but it isn't. Unlike you I didn't have that choice as I was a young innocent victim of the care system. A system Jonesy knows how to play and operate until it gets its poisonous grip on you. If I can offer any advice, you both need to get away from this as soon as you can."

Sipping at his hot cup of coffee Richie looked downbeat by what he had heard, "Its worse than that, they took the big block of coke from the kitchen."

Mia blew out a long sigh and said, "shit, you'll never going to be able to pay back that debt, or certainly not in the time Jonesy gives you. Your goanna have to make some massive "payback" before he is happy the debt is cleared."

Richie and Maxim looked at each other. Worry written all over their faces, no one spoke while they contemplated their situation.

****

Matt sat in his car, engine purring softly as he observed the lively café scene across the road. Glancing at his mobile phone, he confirmed that Richie, or at least his mobile phone was inside Elvira's café, thanks to the tracking app's seamless operation. Positioning his car discreetly between two work vans, Matt maintained a discreet surveillance post, his gaze fixed on the café from across the street. As rain drizzled lightly down, droplets formed on the windscreen, providing a convenient cover in the overcast weather. The wet conditions obscured visibility from casual passersby, affording Matt a measure of stealth as he kept watch. His gaze remained fixed through the café window, drawn to a corner table where Mia, Richie, and Maxim were seated. From afar, he could discern Richie engaged in lively conversation with a man and a woman whom he recognised from the funeral. The woman seemed to have Richie enthralled, gesturing emphatically as her expressive hands underscored her words. As Matt sat in his car, he watched their interactions with a mix of yearning and admiration, feeling as though he were witnessing characters from an intricately woven spy narrative. Each person complemented the others perfectly, effortlessly sharing their thoughts and opinions. However, a bittersweet reality anchored Matt to his car seat, preventing him from joining them. Though he longed to be part of their world, he had his reasons for remaining a silent observer, concealed within the confines of his vehicle. Utilizing the app's microphone feature, he strained to catch snippets of the conversation unfolding inside the café. Despite the background noise, he could feel his anger simmering as he listened to their vulnerability, realising how easily one man had exploited them. Determined to uncover the truth behind Jonesy's hold over them Matt knew he had to delve deeper into their world.

Mia set down her cutlery after finishing her breakfast and pushed her plate forward slightly. "I don't think we have any choice. You need to speak to Jonesy. Avoiding him won't help anyone," she said firmly.

Richie pondered for a moment before responding, "Maybe we should call him and have him meet us here. It's safer, and he's less likely to flip out in public."

"Sounds like a plan," Mia agreed.

Richie pulled out his phone and began searching for Jonesy's number, grumbling about how slow and unreliable his device had become. Unbeknownst to him, the covert monitoring software was sapping his phone's memory.

Finally finding the number, Maxim had wasted no time in dialling. "Where the hell have you been?" came Jonesy's irritated voice through the phone.

Trying to keep his voice low and discreet Maxim replied, "We got badly turned over last night and it all came on top. I'm with Richie and Mia at Alveria's café, can you come and meet us."

"Wait there and don't go fucking anywhere, I'll be ten minutes."

Maxim placed the mobile down on the table and looked at the others, "He's on his way."

Matt noticed two male building workers approaching the van parked in front of his car. Their nonchalant glances briefly swept past him, their priority clearly fixated on reaching their van and escaping the relentless rain. Amidst the bustling flow of pedestrians and cars on the street, Matt found solace in blending seamlessly into the urban backdrop, reassured by the bustling activity that he wasn't drawing undue attention to himself. Shortly after, a sleek dark Mercedes GLC cruised by and smoothly parked in an empty spot ahead of Matt's car. Two casually dressed young Black men, in their late twenties, emerged from the vehicle. After scanning the street, they leisurely made their way across the road toward the café. Matt's intuition strongly hinted that one of these men was Jonesy. Although the driver seemed strikingly familiar, Matt struggled to recall where he might have encountered him before.

As Matt listened to Mia's voice coming through his phone, "They've just pulled up outside."

While Matt wasn't particularly daunted by the physical stature of the two men, confident in his ability to prevail in a hand-to-hand confrontation if it came to that, he understood all too well that encounters with individuals like Jonesy seldom devolved into mere fisticuffs, as they frequently wielded weapons. Clad in oversized hoodies with their hoods drawn low to obscure their features, they projected an air of defiance and rebellion with every step. Their strides were deliberate, their demeanour oozing aggression. Tattoos peeked out from beneath their sleeves, each marking a chapter of a life lived on the fringes of society. With a forceful push, the heavy glass front door swung open, admitting two young gang members into the quaint cafe. Their negative energy preceded them like an ominous cloud, causing a momentary hush to fall over the room as if the very air held its breath in anticipation of their arrival. The cafe patrons stole nervous glances, their discomfort palpable in the air. The once vibrant atmosphere now seemed tinged with unease. Baristas paused mid-pour, their hands trembling ever so slightly, while servers tried to maintain their composure as they balanced trays filled with steaming cups of coffee.

Gill, sensing an impending disturbance, swiftly intercepted them. "What can I get you two gentlemen?" she inquired with unwavering confidence, asserting her authority as if the café were her domain. With her presence, she made it clear that there would be no room for mischief while she was in charge. Their eyes narrowed as they scanned the room, searching for something or someone. Their gazes darted from face to face, challenging anyone who dared to meet their eyes. With a disdainful smirk, Jonesy leaned forward, the faint scent of cigarettes wafting from his clothes. He spoke in a low, gruff voice, laced with an undercurrent of danger. His words dripped with arrogance, demanding attention from anyone within earshot. The other gang member, arms crossed over his chest, radiated an intimidating presence. His piercing gaze swept the room, his eyes locking onto individuals for a moment longer, as if daring them to challenge his authority. The subtle flexing of his muscles beneath his hoodie suggested a readiness for confrontation.

"Two coffees will do, thanks," Jonesy replied with a dry smile, gesturing towards Mia, Richie, and Maxim, who all appeared visibly anxious at their arrival. Their presence cast a shadow over the once welcoming space, with tension crackling through the air like an electric current.

"His boxing coach, perhaps?" Gill interjected, attempting to inject a hint of levity into the situation. Without waiting for a response from either man, she swiftly added, "Take a seat, I'll bring the drinks right over." It was Gill's subtle way of acknowledging that she had unmistakably recognised them, while also asserting her authority in the Café.

Without preamble, Jonesy addressed the group, "So, you're the amateurs who let my stuff slip through your fingers! When am I getting all my gear and cash back?"

Richie and Maxim exchanged a glance, silently communicating before Richie, his voice tinged with uncertainty, responded, "I... I don't know. I'm not sure what to say."

Jonesy's voice sliced through the air, dripping with scepticism. "You don't know?" he questioned; his tone laced with disbelief. "Here's what's going to happen: Mia will lay low for a few days until things calm down, then she'll pay our friend Rob a visit. Meanwhile, you two will get back in there before the weekend and start pushing gear nonstop, 24/7. Once you've coughed up enough of my cash, then we'll talk about what comes next... Do I make myself clear?"

Maxim nodded in acknowledgment, while Richie remained silent, his mind reeling in shock. The harsh reality of his predicament hit him like a freight train, crystalising his awareness of being in way over his head. Memories of the events of the past few days whirled in his mind, each one a painful reminder of how he had ended up entangled in this mess. As he glanced at Mia and then Maxim, Richie felt a sinking sensation in the pit of his stomach, realising he had no clear escape from this wretched, debt-laden situation. Jonesy, sensing Richie's turmoil, spoke in a hushed tone, careful not to attract unwanted attention from other patrons. "Listen, posh boy," he began sternly, "you better grasp what I'm saying. You've stepped into my world now. This isn't a game you can dip in and out of. You're swimming with the massive fish now. It was easy taking from me, wasn't it? But now, it's payback time. Understand?"

As Jonesy spoke, Matt observed the conversation unfolding from his vantage point near the café window. With each word, it became increasingly evident that Richie was cornered, left with no option but to comply with Jonesy's demands. As Matt pondered his next move, the gravity of Richie's situation sank in, he was embroiled in the drug trade far more deeply than Matt had ever realised. Determined to intervene and extricate Richie from this perilous predicament, Matt resolved to devise a plan to "bail him out" and ensure his safety, far away from the clutches of these dangerous men. Having reached his limit, Matt slid across the centre console and stepped out of the front passenger door of his rental car, onto the pavement. Casting a quick glance toward the café, he noted that none of the group seemed to be monitoring the street outside. Seizing the opportunity, Matt swiftly made his way to the blind side of the Mercedes, crouching down near the rear bumper to discreetly affix a small tracking device underneath. In a matter of seconds, the task was complete, unnoticed by any onlookers. With a smooth motion, Matt straightened his jacket as he rose to his feet, then calmly walked away down the street, intent on putting distance between himself and the scene before Jonesy returned. Matt was already focused on the next phase of his mission.

19 The Burden of Love

Neil, the pallor of his skin drained of its usual vitality, lay slumbering in an armchair, his body slouched and frail. The contours of his face were etched with exhaustion, shadows accentuating the sunken hollows beneath his eyes. A thin blanket barely covered his fragile form, as if seeking solace in its meagre embrace. His breaths came shallow and laboured, accompanied by the occasional cough that rattled through his weakened chest. The lines of pain and weariness etched themselves upon his forehead, evidence of the silent battle being waged within his body. Each inhalation required a herculean effort, as if his lungs were burdened with the weight of the world. Matt, sat nearby, his gaze fixed on the flickering images emanating from the television screen. His eyes wandered occasionally, gravitating toward Neil's motionless figure, filled with a mixture of concern and aching sadness. Matt's face bore the marks of sleepless nights spent tending to his brother's needs, etching a narrative of unwavering support and unconditional love. The sounds from the television, though playing in the background, seemed distant and muffled, unable to penetrate the depths of Matt's thoughts. His attention was firmly anchored to the sight of Neil's frailty, a constant reminder of the fragility of life and the weight of responsibility placed upon his shoulders. A sliver of sunlight filtered through the window, casting a soft glow upon Neil's face, illuminating his gaunt features with a melancholic radiance. Matt watched as Neil's chest rose and fell in an irregular rhythm, a painful symphony that mirrored the uncertainty of their shared journey.

In the stillness of the room, Matt's heart echoed with the weight of unspoken words and unshed tears. His love for Neil, a bond forged through shared memories and unbreakable loyalty, enveloped him like a protective shield.

He yearned for Neil's recovery, for the restoration of his brother's health and vitality, even as the weight of reality bore down upon him. As Matt remained perched on the edge of the chair, his weary eyes never strayed far from Neil's slumbering form. He knew that within the confines of that chair, he was more than a spectator. He was a guardian, a mountain of unwavering support and a source of comfort in the face of uncertainty. And as he silently watched over his brother. Matt's love radiated from every fibre of his being, a testament to the strength of the sibling bond that bound them together, even in the darkest of moments. He had noticed Neil was often devoid of conversation simply because he was so tired. Hardly surprising Matt thought given he had been feeling so unwell from his recent treatment. Matt had prepared and eaten a small evening meal earlier, but Neill had just pushed bits of food around his plate choosing to leave it on the tray next to his chair.

   As Neil stirred from his sleep Matt suggested that he would help his brother back upstairs into bed. That way Neil could get comfy, be less disturbed and fall asleep when he wanted. With a determined resolve etched across his face, Matt approached the armchair where his seriously ill brother, lay. The weight of responsibility pressed upon his shoulders, but he pushed aside his own fatigue, drawing upon a hidden well of strength. Gently, he reached out, his hands trembling ever so slightly as they found their place beneath Neil's fragile frame. In that moment, Matt's love transcended into physical strength, as if his bond with his brother had granted him an extraordinary power. He lifted Neil's weakened body with utmost care, mindful of every breath and movement, ensuring that no harm would befall him. Neil's head lolled against Matt's chest, his once vibrant hair now a mere whisper of its former glory. Matt cradled him tenderly, his heartbeat synchronising with the rhythm of Neil's shallow breaths. The weight of his brother in his arms was both a reminder of the gravity of the situation and a testament to their unbreakable connection. Step by careful step, Matt navigated through the room, guided solely by his love for Neil. The air seemed hushed, as if the universe held its breath, acknowledging the gravity of the moment. The weight of Neil's frailty became a shared burden, fuelling Matt's determination to provide solace and comfort. With each footfall, the distance between the armchair and the bed grew shorter, as Matt's resolve pushed aside any doubt or hesitation. He gently eased Neil onto the soft expanse of the bed, his movements slow and deliberate, as if overseeing the most delicate of treasures. His pyjamas hiding his almost skeletal and frail physic. It was a sombre feeling pulling the duvet over his brother knowing he didn't have much longer in this world.

Once Neil was settled, Matt lingered by his side, his hand reaching out to brush against his brother's fevered brow. He whispered words of comfort, his voice a soothing balm amidst the chaos of illness. Matt's eyes glistened with unshed tears, a mixture of fear and hope intermingling in the depths of his gaze. As he stood by Neil's bedside Matt knew his brother was "closing in" on death. Their eyes locked on one another, and he could see a tear in his brother's eye without uttering a word. Caught up in their thoughts and memories that they had once shared together. Great childhood happiness of playing as young brothers. Missed moments, lost opportunities, scrapes and scraps, regrets, and sometimes immense sadness. Life was tough at times, and this was another one of those moments. The clock of life was ticking, and it would eventually stop for everyone. There was total silence in the room as both brothers stared at each other caught in the moment of stillness. Neil slowly produced his hand from under the duvet. Matt clasped it tight with his and felt it was icy cold to touch.

"Thank you, Matt, this means a lot," Neil gently whispered. It was a precious moment between the two brothers. Without speaking they knew what was coming. The Doctors had advised that they could do little more than palliative care and both men knew it was just a matter of time. All Matt wanted to do was ensure Neil last moments remained comfortable and he felt cared for and loved in his own home.

"Get some rest Neil." With a final lingering look, Matt turned away from the bed, carrying the weight of responsibility as if it were a mantle upon his shoulders. The room seemed to exhale, the silence now filled with a sense of purpose and determination. Matt's footsteps echoed through the room as he left, his heart filled with a fierce resolve to stand by his brother's side, no matter what happens.

Matt turned off the light, paused to take a deep breath and walked out.

Downstairs he picked up his mobile and sent Richie a message.

"You need to come home asap, your dad is very unwell!"

Matt saw there was also a message from Nicole. "Hello darling, I hope everything is going Ok back there in the UK. All good here Love and Miss You xxx."

Matt replied, "Love and miss you darling. Will call in a couple of days."

Matt couldn't bring himself to call or speak to Nicole. The thought of it was too upsetting for him to dwell upon Seeking to divert his thoughts, Matt busied himself by clearing the plates from the lounge and loading the dishwasher. Leaning against the kitchen units, he activated the monitoring app for Richie's mobile while he brewed a cup of tea. Finding nothing noteworthy on the tracking app, Matt returned to the lounge with his freshly brewed drink. Settling into his seat, he retrieved his dash camera from his bag and captured the still images of Jonesy. With a clear image of Jonesy attached, Matt composed a text message and sent it. "Hi Jed, it's been a while. Simply curious, have you ever encountered this individual? I'm currently on a job in the

Northwest and was wondering if he's crossed paths in your line of work."

Within seconds Matt had a reply.

"Can you speak privately; you need to be careful Matt"!

Matt was not surprised by Jed's response, "yes, I'm free now.

Matt's mobile quickly rang.

"Hi Jed thanks for calling."

"Matt are you alone to speak."

"Yes, no problem."

"Ok, what I'm going to say is confidential and just for you only. I will get sacked if my Law firm finds out I've spoken to you. That guy in the image goes by the name of Jonesy, but his real name is Kyle Jones. We have done big defence cases with him and his family over the years. All drugs and violence stuff and he has miraculously managed to keep out of jail all these years, which rightly or wrongly is down to excellent work from us! It comes down to alleged witness intimidation and people being too scared to speak up when needed too. He is connected to a large family in South Manchester and years ago his brother Darnell along with a couple of others were gunned down in a pub Car park. It was a big case and hit the national news."

Matt felt the pit of his stomach tighten and took a long pause while he gathered his thoughts ensuring he gave nothing away by his reactions. Jed's comments had been a shocking reminder of that eventful night all those years ago.

"Are you still there Matt?" Jed asked to break the silence.

"Yeah, Im still here."

Jed continued, "It created years of "tit for tat" gang related shootings in South Manchester with rival gangs trying to muscle in on the vacant turf that was freed up by those killings. They never did catch anyone for it although there were rumours circulating about who had done it. There was even a crazy suggestion that a Homeless tramp had done it, but nothing ever came of it. After the Darnel murder, Jonesy took it upon himself to get involved in the drugs game in a big way. I haven't personally seen or heard from Jonesy in a long time. Rumours suggest he had made his money and had left Manchester because he was getting paranoid about being shot. I don't believe that for a moment , which is why you need to be careful. Can I ask why you are asking about him?"

"No, you can't Jed, let's just say it's to do with security but you have been extremely helpful to me. Please be assured from an "old oppo" that I won't pass on any of this info to anyone, you have my absolute word and guarantee over that."

Thanks Matt, "just be careful, oh and how long are you up this way?" Jed asked thoughtfully.

"Don't know really, family stuff going on, but I'll be back on my way to France very soon. Stay connected and thanks for being a great friend." Matt hung up and sat in his chair sipping at his brew thinking hard about what he had just heard from Jed. Matt looked at his mobile and saw Richie was heading in the general direction of his home. The tracker on Jonesy's car indicated the vehicle was stationary on an estate in Manchester.

The creak of the front door signalled Richie's return, but this time, there was a noticeable shift in his demeanour. Gone was his usual swagger, replaced by a heavy air of concern that weighed down his every step. Matt couldn't ignore the worry etched on Richie's face; it was as if the weight of the world rested squarely on his shoulders.

"How was your day?" Matt inquired, trying to gauge Richie's state of mind.

"Pretty shit, if I'm honest," Richie replied, his voice tinged with a hint of defeat.

"Well, we all have rough days," Matt offered, his tone gentle but firm. "But remember, there's always a way through stuff. It might take time and courage, but solutions are always there. Are you worried about your dad?"

Richie cleared his throat, his vulnerability breaking through his tough exterior. "Yeah, I am," he admitted, his voice faltering slightly.

Matt sensed the heaviness in the room, the unspoken tension hanging thick between them. Richie shifted uncomfortably in his seat, the weight of impending conversation pressing down on him.

"Look, Richie," Matt began, his words heavy with sorrow. "Your dad... he's not doing well. And as hard as it is to say, I don't think he's going to make it. We're talking days, maybe less. There's nothing more we can do for him except be there, make him comfortable. I'm here for you, Richie, but we need to start thinking about what comes next. Where will you live? What will you do for work? Are you going back to school?"

As the weight of reality sank in, Richie's gaze dropped, the gravity of the situation settling heavily upon him. Matt's unwavering strength wavered for a moment, his own uncertainty peeking through the cracks. Matt could see his questions were just filling Richie's head with problems and issues with which he just couldn't cope. Richie couldn't digest the enormity of it all and was unable to think with any clarity. At the same time, he was the victim of criminal exploitation, what was called "County lines." It was obvious Richie was finding it impossible to deal with it all and wasn't open to help.

"Look Richie, I can help, but you have to ask me for help?"

Richie cast a brief glance at Matt, a small, appreciative smile playing on his lips. "Thanks, but I'll just take it one day at a time for now. Did you know I once wanted to join up and earn my Green Beret like you, but Mum and Dad talked me out of it after what happened to you," he confessed, his voice tinged with a mixture of regret and longing.

Matt's brows furrowed in surprise at Richie's revelation. "Is Dad upstairs?" Richie inquired, concern lacing his words.

"Yeah, he's asleep, but I'm sure he'd appreciate a brief visit," MAtt confirmed. Richie rose from his seat, nodding gratefully to Matt before heading upstairs to his father's bedside.

20 Intrusion in the Shadows

With determination etched across his face, Matt sat before his computer screen, fingers poised over the keyboard, ready to delve into the vast depths of the internet. It was time to uncover the enigmatic life of Jonesy, a person whose secrets held the key to a puzzle Matt was desperate to solve. His eyes narrowed, focused on the glowing pixels that held a wealth of information. Matt knew that the digital realm was a vast expanse, a virtual landscape where traces of one's existence were scattered like fragmented breadcrumbs. He was prepared to sift through the vast sea of data, undeterred by the challenge that lay before him. Taking a deep breath, Matt began his quest, fingers dancing across the keys in a symphony of clicks and taps. Search engines whirred to life; algorithmic gatekeepers poised to assist him in his pursuit. Keywords and phrases flowed from his fingertips, each query a thread to be tugged upon, unravelling the tapestry of Jonesy's life. Websites, social media platforms, and online communities became Matt's playground. He honed his amateur investigative skills, navigating the digital landscape with a mix of intuition and logic. Like a modern-day detective, he followed the digital footprints left behind piecing together a portrait of the elusive Jonesy. In the depths of online forums and social media profiles, Matt discovered fragments of Jonesy's past. Photographs and anecdotes hinted at a life shrouded in mystery yet touched by profound experiences. Each new revelation fuelled Matt's curiosity, driving him deeper into the digital rabbit hole.

Minutes turned into hours, and hours into an eternity as Matt traversed the vast expanse of cyberspace. His eyes grew weary, but his determination remained unyielding. He knew that within the web of the internet, answers lay waiting to be discovered. Finally, after tireless searching, Matt struck digital gold. He unearthed a trove of information, a mosaic of Jonesy's life pieced together from disparate sources. The picture that emerged painted a complex individual, someone who had traversed unique paths, hidden beneath layers of anonymity. As Matt absorbed the revelations before him, a sense of triumph surged through his veins. He had peeled back the veil of secrecy, exposing the truths that eluded. Yet, amidst the victory, a humbling realisation dawned upon him, the internet was both a fickle friend and a formidable adversary, a realm of possibilities and obscurities. Closing the browser tab, Matt leaned back in his chair, contemplating the wealth of knowledge he had acquired. Jonesy certainly was living above his means for someone who didn't appear to be in any gainful employment. The enigma of Jonesy had been cracked, but the journey had only just begun. Armed with newfound insight, Matt knew he held the key to unravelling the web of intrigue that surrounded Jonesy's life, one thread at a time.

****

In the hushed stillness of the early morning, Matt's car glided smoothly through the shadowed streets of the Manchester estate. His palms clung to the steering wheel, a faint tremor betraying the weight of his anticipation. The moon's soft glow cast elongated silhouettes across the quiet roads, while a gentle mist clung to the air, veiling the world in a shroud of secrecy. Guided solely by the glow of streetlamps, Matt positioned his vehicle with practiced finesse, navigating the network of roads and cul-de-sacs. Each turn was executed with precision, calculated to evade prying eyes, and minimize any chance encounters. His heartbeat, quickened by a potent mix of nerves and excitement, reverberated in his ears, a steady reminder of the importance of remaining unnoticed. Matt knew he couldn't afford even a whisper of suspicion. He had a purpose, a mission that demanded discretion and anonymity. As the car glided to a halt near his destination, Matt exhaled a breath he hadn't realised he was holding. The estate slumbered; its occupants blissfully unaware of the clandestine presence that now stood at its gates. Discreetly parking a couple of streets away from where he wanted to be, he surveyed the area, scanning the surroundings for any signs of life. The last thing Matt wanted to do was compromise the only vehicle he had access to. Individuals like Jonesy were always scanning their surroundings, looking out for enemies, threats, and cops. Gently easing the car door open, Matt emerged into the cold, dew-kissed embrace of the morning. His footsteps were light, barely disturbing the fragile peace that enveloped the neighbourhood. He was focused and in mission mode, like a phantom in the darkness. He moved with grace, hugging the shadows, his senses heightened to every creak and rustle, anticipating cameras were everywhere on the estate. Matt was here to do "his little recce" and was aware every movement could be traced and tracked by a keen detective should it ever come to it. The night was silent and scattered lights flickered in the windows of homes. Like stars punctuating the darkness, these signals of warmth and comfort cast a soft glow onto the world outside. Each illuminated dwelling whispered stories of its occupants, their lives unfolding behind closed doors. As the world slumbered, these lights stood as silent sentinels, a testament to the quiet moments and untold dreams that danced within the walls of these homes, offering glimpses into the intimate tapestry of human existence. The energy wastage would get environmentalist trembling in their wellies, but he didn't expect to see them here on a tough estate as the privileged often preferred to operate in the safer places to get their messaging across.

    Matt didn't have time to dwell or assume anything. The working week in this part of town didn't mean much too many of the residents. In the realm of ambition and productivity, generations of the families had chosen to sponge off the Government. A subset of individuals content to linger on the fringes of society, their gaze fixated on the prospect of being supported by the state. With a reluctance to engage in diligent employment, they eagerly embraced a life of idleness, seeking refuge in the safety net woven by others. Driven by a sense of entitlement, they manoeuvred through the intricate loopholes of the system, ever ready to exploit its provisions. Though opportunities abound, their inertia blinded them to the potential for personal growth and self-sufficiency when it was easier to blame others or turn to crime for fast easy cash. "The takers of society" as Matt called them had no intention or motivation to get out and work for their money or pay their way. Matt hated the left side of Society and Government, who always looked for excuses to pander to the shirkers. "It's not fair" was a phrase he grown tired of hearing.

    Modern and bright L.E.D street lighting had made this part of the estate feel safer for law abiding residents. The downside to better lighting made it much harder for him to move around unnoticed. The abundance of home security systems, door cameras and other lighting made it almost impossible to move without leaving some kind of signature as to his presence. The key to beating this was thinking ahead and staying switched on. Making his identity impossible to recognise as he moved. That way if the 'shit hit the fan' it would make it much harder for any investigator to trace or worse identify him. Cover from parked vehicles, staying close to garden hedges and moving close to the building lines assisted in keeping an extremely low profile. Pausing in the shadows and plotting his every move, Matt made timely progress to his target address. His non-descript clothing, dark cap and neck warmer pulled up over his face kept a large part of him hidden and unrecognisable. If someone were to keep a lookout, spotting him wouldn't be a challenge. Therefore, his main concern was to move stealthily, avoiding any chance of detection. Matt had observed a number, thirty-seven, on a door in the background of one of Jonesy's pictures during his investigation. Knowing Jonesy's car's location from the tracker, Matt pinpointed number thirty-seven as his initial destination for reconnaissance which stood as a typical semi-detached house, emblematic of a 1970s council housing estate. Access to the sides of most properties in the estate proved simple. Driveways or modest front gardens adorned many of the homes.

With utmost caution, Matt approached, slipping into a rear garden from a neighbouring street. Every muscle in his body tensed with the anticipation of the risks ahead. The moon cast feeble light, offering mere glimpses of his path, and veiling the surroundings in a dim, otherworldly glow. The night air hung heavy with silence, disrupted only by the gentle rustling of leaves under his careful tread. But amidst the tranquillity, a distant bark echoed through the estate. Matt's heart skipped a beat as his ears strained to locate the source of the sound. Panic surged through his veins, threatening to betray his presence. Dogs had been a constant pain during his deployments in Iraq and Afghanistan especially at night. These dogs had come close to compromising patrols when they were snooping around close to enemy positions. The fury pests would be everywhere and find you when you least expected it. Most would just stand barking, attracting others to join the pack. Thankfully, most UK homeowners kept their dogs inside after dark.

Matt blended seamlessly with the night, his figure merging with the darkness, a ghostly apparition navigating the terrain of secrecy. His eyes flickered with determination, unwavering in their focus. Silent as a whisper, he reached his destination, his pulse now a steady drumbeat of purpose. With practiced ease, he positioned himself carefully in the rear hedge line so he could see inside the property. A thrill tingled through him as he looked inside, from the darkness outside. The interior appeared stage like and the world around him remained oblivious to his presence. He embraced the challenge of remaining unseen. Two figures sat hunched over a coffee table, their eyes fixated on the piles of cash before them. The table's surface was strewn with stacks of banknotes, their denominations varying, forming a small mountain of illicit wealth. The room reeked of tension and secrecy, as the aroma of cigarette smoke mingled with the faint scent of forbidden transactions.

Silence hung heavy in the air as the two men methodically counted the stacks, their fingers gliding over the paper with practiced precision. Their eyes darted back and forth, meticulously ensuring that no note went unaccounted for. The weight of their responsibility resonated in the furrowed brows that marked their faces, a stark contrast to the cool indifference that danced in their eyes. Every flick of a note, every muted whisper of crisp currency, amplified the gravity of their enterprise. Their movements were measured, deliberate, a choreographed ballet of criminal intent. Time seemed to stand still as the room enveloped them, shielding their activities from prying eyes. Though surrounded by the fruits of their illicit labour, a palpable tension emanated from their gazes. In that shared moment, a silent agreement passed between them, acknowledging the risks they faced. They knew that their actions existed out of sight of everyday life, and that their empire of cash could crumble with a single misstep. Yet, despite the danger that loomed, a veneer of confidence clung to them. Their lives were intertwined with the allure of quick fortunes and the seduction of the forbidden. They were modern-day outlaws, skirting the fringes of legality, driven by a thirst for power and the spoils it bestowed. Their eyes briefly met, sharing an unspoken understanding of the life they had chosen. They were two players in a high-stakes game, fully aware that the stakes were not only measured in pounds but in the potential consequences that lurked just beyond their secret sanctuary.

In that room, the hum of hushed conversations and the shuffle of cash counted reverberated through their beings, a reminder of the choices they had made. And as the money piled higher, their destinies intertwined further, forever bound by the allure of a life lived on the edge of the law.

After a moment of remaining motionless Matt was content, he wouldn't be noticed and slowly produced a small pair of binoculars from his pocket. Matt knew he was invisible to the two males inside the house but couldn't relax. Despite his experience he never relaxed doing close target surveillance work. To "see and be unseen" took nerve and confidence in your abilities. His sense of vulnerability remained high, but he had been in more dangerous situations. Albeit on this occasion he wasn't carrying a full loaded assault rifle, for his personal protection should the need arise. With binoculars pressed against his eyes, Matt peered through the lenses, his gaze focused on a figures standing inside. As the magnified view sharpened, a surge of recognition coursed through his veins. There, amidst the activity, was Jonesy, unmistakable in his distinctive demeanour and appearance. Matt's heart quickened, excitement mingling with a tinge of apprehension. He watched intently, observing Jonesy's every movement, committing each detail to memory. Binoculars became a conduit, bridging the physical gap between them, allowing Matt to study his target from a safe distance. In that fleeting moment, a surge of determination surged within Matt, fuelling his resolve to uncover the truth that lay hidden beneath Jonesy's enigmatic facade. Jonesy looked relaxed and confident. Why wouldn't he? He was ripping people off, plying his trade almost unhindered by the Police, and making 'stacks' of cash doing it. Matt wondered how long it would take to make this amount of money himself from his honest day job as a local tradesman.

Suddenly in the stillness of the night, the gates to the side of the house creaked open, their metallic hinges protesting the intrusion of movement startling Matt. The sound hung in the air, a dissonant melody of trespass and stealth. Shadows of men danced along the edges of the gate, their dark tendrils stretching like phantom fingers into the depths of the property. Eyes widened in anticipation as Matt, hidden in the cover of darkness, observed the scene unfold. Each motion was deliberate, each step calculated to minimise any chance of detection. The gate swung open just wide enough for the intruders to slip through, its ancient metal frame whispering secrets of clandestine intent and a shiver of unease ran down Matt's spine. The tension in the air grew palpable, as if the very surroundings held their breath, sensing the presence of unwelcome visitors. Matt's senses sharpened as he kept his gaze fixed on the gate and those inside the house. Each subtle movement, every hushed rustle of foliage, felt magnified, as if the world had conspired to amplify the arrival of the intruders. He couldn't afford to make a single mistake, knowing that the line between discovery and anonymity hung precariously in the balance. Matt saw the silhouettes of three males moving silently into the garden behind the house where the interior lights made them more visible. He thought they were associates of Jonesy but quickly realised these three males were here with bad intentions. Matt caught sight of a flicker from a large Machete held by one of the males, another was holding what looked like a baseball bat. He heard one quietly speak and although he couldn't hear exactly what was said it didn't sound like English. Matt could just make out a couple of their faces. He didn't dare move for fear of being seen. In the cover of darkness, the three figures moved with calculated precision towards the rear of the house. Their steps were swift, yet silent, betraying a familiarity with their nefarious intent. Shadows clung to their forms, obscuring their identities, as they closed in on their target. With methodical ease, they approached the patio doors, their bodies tense with anticipation. The night held its breath, as if aware of the impending chaos that would soon be unleashed. They knew the risks involved, but their determination to seize control outweighed any fears that threatened to surface. Their gloved hands gripped the tools of their trade tightly, each instrument a conduit for their aggression and malice. Their minds homed in on the moment at hand, the pulsating thrill of the hunt. They were predators stalking their prey, driven by a motive known only to them. With a swift, synchronised motion, the intruders smashed through the patio with a scaffolding pipe. A resounding crash shattered the silence, the sound echoing through the area like a harbinger of chaos. Inside, the two unsuspecting 'cash counters' were taken aback, their senses jolted from complacency to alarm. Panic filled the air, mingling with the scent of illicit activities. The intruders moved swiftly; their intentions clear as they closed in on their targets.

A battle of wills ensued, the clash of desperation and determination reverberating through the walls. Chaos erupted within the confines of the house with glass shattering everywhere. The intruders wielded a calculated ferocity, their actions driven by a mix of vengeance and opportunity. Jonesy's associate jumped to his feet but was struck across the arm by a machete, opening a massive gash, exposing bone, and rendering the arm useless as it slumped downwards to his side. He staggered back with blood spraying from his wound screaming in agony. The room had become a battleground, a clash of opposing forces vying for dominance. The nights silence shattered by aggressive shouts of defiance mingling with grunts of pain. Amid the mayhem, Jonesy had turned and sprinted out of sight into the front of the house choosing the option of "flight" rather than "fight. His blood soaked; cash counting friend wasn't so lucky as the scaffolding tube struck him across the back of the head with such force it floored him instantly. Anyone would be lucky to survive such blunt force impact to the back of the head. Had Matt just witnessed a murder? The three attackers didn't pursue the escaping Jonesy focusing their attention by grabbing the cash on the table and stuffing it into their pockets. This was what they had come for.

The man wielding the scaffolding tube stepped into the lounge and removed his balaclava to reveal his identity. It was Maxim and he was "taxing" back and proving what a toxic world Richie was getting wrapped into. Maxim had now raised the stakes, and the escalation of violence was heading upwards. Where this left Richie in this gang culture of "tit for tat violence," Matt could only wonder. As chaos reigned within the confines of the house, Matt's heart pounded in his chest, a mix of fear and adrenaline coursing through his veins. The cacophony of shouts and crashing sounds served as a stark reminder that time was running out. At this moment, his focus shifted to more pressing matters: ensuring his escape before the inevitable arrival of the police.

With eyes darting around, scanning for an exit route, Matt's mind raced, calculating the best course of action. Every second counted, each passing moment bringing the police closer to the scene of the turmoil he had unwittingly found himself in. He made a swift exit from the garden in the confusion. Matt had to ensure he didn't draw attention to himself as he moved back towards his car. Taking a deep breath to steady his nerves, Matt slipped into the shadows. Every step he took, every turn he made, brought him closer to freedom, but the stakes remained perilously high. The sound of approaching sirens pierced the night air, their wailing chorus growing louder, urging Matt to quicken his pace. Panic surged through him, urging him to abandon all caution and sprint towards the nearest road. But he knew that a hasty, reckless escape could be his downfall, leading the police directly to him. Breathing heavily, Matt knew he couldn't afford to linger. He knew that the danger was far from over, that his actions would have consequences that reverberated long after his departure. But for now, his focus was singular, to navigate the streets, to elude capture, and to disappear into anonymity, leaving behind a scene of chaos that would forever remain etched in his memory.

Having skillfully evaded detection, he reached his car with silent relief. As he slipped behind the wheel, a wry smile tugged at the corners of his lips "Shit I'm getting too old for this crap," he muttered to himself shaking his head in disbelief. There was still work to be one.

21 Reluctant Redemption

Neil successfully made it downstairs in time for breakfast, casually asking about the previous night without realising the tumultuous events that had transpired for Matt. Matt, still reeling from the unexpected violent burglary he witnessed, hadn't anticipated such a question. "Yeah, I slept okay, but I didn't hear Richie come home. Did you?" Neil shook his head in response.

Taking a seat at the kitchen table, Matt's focus shifted to the bowl of cornflakes before him. He spooned a mouthful into his mouth, relishing the familiar crunch and comforting taste. Eating his breakfast, the soft hum of the television drifted into his awareness, drawing his attention. The news readers urgent voice captured his curiosity, prompting him to turn his gaze toward the screen, momentarily forgetting his spoon in hand.

"Police are investigating a murder in Manchester, where a man in his late twenties was found with fatal head injuries following a disturbance at the address in Wythenshawe. Police are appealing for witnesses and anyone with information." The news bulletin unfolded, revealing details of a chilling murder that had taken place just hours ago. Matt's spoon hovered mid-air, suspended by the gravity of the news. His eyes widened, fixated on the images and the words that spilled from the screen, painting a picture of a crime scene and a life cut short. A mixture of shock and fascination washed over him, the cereal forgotten as his attention became consumed by the unfolding news. The vibrant colours of the cornflakes dulled in comparison to the vividness of the crime story that unfolded before him. The taste of the cornflakes lost its appeal as the weight of the news sank in. Matt's mind whirled with questions and speculations; the ordinary breakfast scene transformed into a nexus of intrigue. He contemplated the motives behind the murder, the lives affected, and the ripple effects that would inevitably follow. As he continued to watch, the spoon clattered against the bowl, abandoned in favour of this unexpected revelation. The cereal grew soggy, forgotten as his thoughts raced, propelled by the scene he had witnessed. In that moment, breakfast became an afterthought, an inconsequential backdrop to the unfolding drama that demanded his attention. The television news held him captive, transporting him into a world where the ordinary had given way to the extraordinary.

****

Jonesy stormed into the flat, his face contorted with seething anger. Behind him stood three unfamiliar men, their expressions tense and formidable, casting an aura of intimidation that Richie and Mia found unsettling. "Where the hell is Maxim?" Jonesy's voice boomed, filling the room with palpable tension.

"We have no idea," Richie responded, still appearing unsure why Jonesy was so angry and annoyed. "We were both here last night getting ready to do what you asked us. We haven't seen Maxim since yesterday," he continued.

"He is getting banged up now," Jonesy shouted through gritted teeth.

Amid their conversation, Jonesy's eyes darted around the room, as if gauging the level of security that enveloped them. A sudden intensity flickered in his gaze, and with a swift motion, he reached into his coat pocket, producing a sleek, black automatic handgun. The sight of the weapon sent a jolt of surprise through Richie, his startled expression mirroring the gravity of the situation.

"Take this," Jonesy urged, his voice low and urgent. He extended the firearm towards Richie, his eyes conveying a mixture of trust and apprehension. The weight of the gun rested heavy in the room, its presence altering the dynamics of their encounter.

Richie hesitated, his hands instinctively recoiling from the lethal object before him. He had never imagined himself in possession of such power, nor did he fully comprehend the implications of accepting it. Yet, a sense of duty tinged with fear compelled him to reach out and accept the firearm, the cold metal pressing into his trembling palms.

As his fingers closed around the grip, Richie couldn't help but feel the weight of responsibility settle upon him. The gun symbolised a dangerous threshold crossed, a pivotal moment that would forever alter the course of their lives. He looked at Jonesy, their eyes locking in a silent exchange of shared understanding."

Jonesy cautioned, "Take this strap and keep it safe, if you see Maxim, you are gonna 'pop a cap' in him, so he doesn't get up. No one comes and does that to me. He is now nasty and I aint having this. You need to get my "pees back," understand?" his voice a whisper in the tense atmosphere. "We can't afford any mistakes."

Richie nodded; the gravity of the situation etched upon his features. He felt the weight of the gun pressing against his side, a constant reminder of the stakes he faced. A mixture of fear and determination coursed through his veins, as he vowed to protect their secret, knowing that the consequences of failure would be dire. In that fleeting moment, Jonesy's trust had been placed in Richie's hands, a bond forged by necessity and the shared burden of their actions. Their destinies were now inextricably intertwined, tied together by the dangerous dance they had chosen to embark upon.

With a steadying breath, Richie tucked the gun into his waistband, concealing it beneath his clothing. He glanced at Mia, who looked away knowing she couldn't do a thing. Mia's gaze shifted uneasily towards Jonesy, a flicker of concern passing through her eyes. Her disapproving frown deepened, and she nervously bit her lower lip, her body instinctively recoiling from having seen the weapon. The room grew heavy with an unspoken tension, and Mia's discomfort became palpable. She had never been comfortable in the presence of firearms, their very existence a reminder of the potential for violence and harm. As her eyes met Richie's, she silently implored him to refuse the offer, to reject the dangerous path that lay before him. But her voice remained locked within her, stifled by the weight of the situation. Mia understood the gravity of their circumstances, the risks they were undertaking. Yet, she couldn't help but feel a surge of disappointment, a sharp pang of disapproval at the choices being made. The gun symbolised a dangerous escalation, a departure from the path of caution and into the realm of recklessness.

  The gravity of Jonesy's request weighed heavily on Richie, causing a wave of overwhelming nausea to wash over him. The mere thought of being tasked with ending the life of a friend felt suffocating, as if he had been casually asked to run a mundane errand. The juxtaposition between the mundane nature of the request and its profound, tragic implications left him reeling in disbelief. Richie found himself in a bewildering situation, unsure of Maxim's whereabouts from the previous night and completely in the dark about the events that had unfolded. Despite his lack of involvement, he felt inexorably drawn into the turmoil. The thought of being entangled in whatever had transpired filled him with a sense of dread. Attempting to distance himself from Jonesy only seemed to exacerbate the situation, as the spectre of violence loomed ever closer, leaving Richie feeling powerless to break free.

  Sensing Richie's anxiety Jonesy approached him, "Look. this aint no game no more. You're in this, you owe me, and I want you to find Maxim and sort him." Richie could feel his chest tightening from the stress and anxiety being placed on him by these crazy demands. Without waiting for a response, Jonesy strode out of the flat, his three henchmen trailing behind him. A heavy silence settled in the room as Mia and Richie processed the weighty exchange they had just experienced. "What's your next move now?" Mia inquired, her tone laced with urgency and concern.

Richie buried his face in his hands, tears streaming down his cheeks as he crumbled under the weight of his emotions. "What am I supposed to do?" he choked out between sobs. "I'm completely messed up with all of this. Why is all of this happening to me? My dad is dying, and now I'm drowning in all this chaos. If I go to the cops, they'll throw me in jail."

Agitated by the unfolding events, Mia's voice rose sharply as she exclaimed, "Listen, Richie, going to the cops isn't an option. You need to track down Maxim, figure out what the hell he's done, and retrieve those 'pees' pronto. It's the only chance we've got to avoid becoming the next targets in this chaotic mess." Richie continued to weep as the realisation hit home that he was way out of his depth and Mia could see this.

"Listen, Jonesy has no loyalty anyway. They're all cut from the same cloth, just looking out for themselves. They'll betray anyone, especially if you're not part of their inner circle. And let's not kid ourselves, they have a deep-seated disdain for women, treating us like garbage," Mia remarked, her words tinged with suppressed anger evident in her tense posture. Pulling out her phone, Mia scrolled through local news reports, her brows furrowing as she quickly pieced together the situation. "Looks like someone's been killed, and my bet is on Maxim being involved. That's why Jonesy's so furious," she added before glancing back up.

Richie, his face streaked with tears, withdrew his hands to reveal a handgun resting on the table before him. It was a Beretta 9000, compact yet deadly, its weight heavy with significance. Memories of shooting firearms with his father at the gun club flooded Richie's mind as he examined the weapon. He removed the magazine, confirming it was fully loaded with live rounds. With practiced caution, he cocked the gun, checked the chamber, and then secured the safety catch. Placing the loaded magazine back into the handle, he carefully wiped the gun, hoping to erase any trace of his fingerprints. He tucked the weapon securely into his jeans, relieved to have made it safe for the time being, knowing it wouldn't accidentally discharge without proper preparation.

    Mia was taken aback by Richie's familiarity with the handgun. She had never encountered a loaded firearm before, and its presence made her deeply uncomfortable. "Please, Richie, don't do anything reckless," she pleaded, her voice trembling with fear. "This situation is spiralling out of control, and I want no part in it." Standing up, she fixed Richie with a solemn gaze. "Think carefully about your next move, Richie," she implored before turning to leave. The weight of the revelation that Richie had been tasked with killing their friend was too much for her to bear. She couldn't bring herself to face it.

22 The Curry Mile

The Curry Mile formed a vibrant part of Wilmslow Road, cutting through the heart of Rusholme in South Manchester. Renowned for its plethora of luminous neon signs adorning Pakistani, Bangladeshi, and Indian eateries, this stretch of the city drew in throngs of visitors nightly. Yet beneath its bustling exterior lay a shadowy underbelly of illicit activities, unbeknownst to passing pedestrians. Nestled within this lively enclave stood Spice Land, an unassuming Indian restaurant that blended seamlessly with its neighbours. Despite its outward appearance, Spice Land was operated by Bangladeshi staff, a fact hidden from casual observers. These employees, deeply grateful for their positions, demonstrated unwavering loyalty and discretion. Employment at Spice Land was a privilege reserved for those in the mainly Asian community with the right connections and endorsements, secured through familial ties and word-of-mouth referrals. Iqbal and Mohammed, two brothers with a shared penchant for adventure and risk, had embarked on a clandestine endeavour that operated surreptitiously above their bustling restaurant. As owners of a popular eatery, their business thrived with satisfied customers filling the tables below, oblivious to the secretive dealings occurring just above their heads.

The two English-born Pakistani brothers had been raised in Rusholme; their entire lives steeped in the vibrant tapestry of the neighbourhood. As third-generation Pakistani men, they grappled with the complexities of identity and belonging, torn between their British upbringing and the pull of their Pakistani heritage, deeply intertwined with strict Muslim values. Adaptable and shrewd, both brothers had learned to navigate the delicate balance between cultural identities, particularly when it came to their entrepreneurial pursuits. Their family had spent over three decades building the business from humble beginnings as a corner shop to a flourishing enterprise in the restaurant industry. Following the passing of their father, the business experienced a surge in growth. Presently, the brothers boasted ownership of three thriving restaurants, along with a portfolio of rental properties, primarily utilised as Homes of Multiple Occupancy (HMO) in the area. These properties served a dual purpose, providing accommodation for their staff, many of whom were undocumented immigrants working off the books to avoid taxation and potential government scrutiny. Despite the precarious nature of their situation, the staff remained grateful for the shelter and employment provided by the brothers' enterprises. Externally, the brothers' business empire projected an image of success and garnered respect within the local community. Their presence at the mosque, often accompanied by generous donations, further solidified their standing. However, beneath this facade lay a hidden truth: their legitimate business served as a mere cover for their extensive drug operation, where the real profits were reaped. While whispers circulated among elders at the mosque regarding the brothers' involvement in illicit activities, such suspicions were ignored. The prospect of probing deeper into the matter posed risks, as law-abiding citizens feared repercussions such as intimidation or ostracisation for speaking out. Thus, a prevailing culture of silence prevailed within the community, where turning a blind eye was deemed preferable to stirring up trouble. Restaurants served as the ideal vehicle for the brothers to launder substantial sums of cash. Whether through manipulating financial records or conducting transactions entirely in cash, they could easily obscure the movement of funds. With no effective oversight mechanisms in place, authorities struggled to track the flow of money. Even if they were to sell hundreds of curries each night, the sheer volume of transactions made it impossible for authorities to accurately monitor or verify income. As a result, the laundering of drug proceeds remained a straightforward and unchecked endeavour, facilitated by the limited resources of an understaffed and underfunded His Majesty's Revenue and Customs. Hidden from view behind their restaurant, access to the rear was discreet and unassuming, tucked away from the lively activity of Wilmslow Road. Concealed within an inconspicuous door, a narrow staircase beckoned the brothers into a realm far removed from the aromatic aromas and clinking of plates downstairs. As they ascended the steps, their thoughts shifted from the realm of food and hospitality to one of clandestine deals and covert operations. This covert enclave became their clandestine sanctuary, a concealed space where their illicit business flourished in secrecy.

As the clock ticked and the sun dipped below the horizon, the restaurant downstairs would buzz with activity, staff bustling about, taking orders, and serving delectable dishes. The brothers, however, operated in a world detached from the aromatic delights wafting up from the kitchen. They delved into the realm of whispered conversations, navigating a complex web of connections that extended far beyond the boundaries of their establishment. Their staff, loyal and dedicated, diligently performed their duties below, unaware of the clandestine activities transpiring above them. The brothers had taken great care to maintain a strict separation between the legitimate business they presented to the world and the enigmatic dealings conducted in secrecy. It was an invisible wall, guarding their dual existence, and they were the only ones who possessed the key to unlock its mysteries. Through their calculated manoeuvres and astute decision-making, Iqbal and Mohammed had carved out a niche in the intricate underworld of illicit business. In their secluded sanctuary upstairs, the brothers discovered an ideal hub for coordinating their operations. Here, the distinction between lawful and unlawful activities became increasingly blurred, and the allure of forbidden ventures grew stronger. However, despite the tangible anxiety and apprehension gripping the police force, especially considering the complex issues surrounding racism and political correctness in contemporary society, the Police neglected to thoroughly investigate or confront this clandestine underworld. Their reluctance to confront uncomfortable realities only served to allow the brothers silent realm to flourish unchecked. The brothers knew the risks, and the consequences of being discovered could shatter not only their hidden empire but also their carefully built reputation. And so, they continued their dual existence, balancing the fine line between the legitimacy of their establishment and the exhilarating thrills of their illicit empire, all while the oblivious world continued below, savouring the flavours they had to offer.

Maxim's heart pounded in his chest as he approached the dimly lit office, his footsteps echoing in the silence. The weight of unease settled upon his shoulders, threatening to overwhelm him. This was no ordinary gathering; he had been summoned to sit at a table with Iqbal and Mohammed.

As Maxim stepped into the room, he was immediately struck by the beauty of the oak table positioned at its centre, exuding an air of elegance. The aroma of Indian cuisine lingered in the air, adding an unexpected layer of sensory richness. Gradually, his eyes adjusted to the dim lighting, revealing the imposing figures of Iqbal and Mohammed seated side by side. Their stern countenances and icy stares sent a chill down Maxim's spine, amplifying his already palpable nervousness. With a dry throat, he swallowed hard, feeling the clamminess of his palms as he reluctantly took the empty seat, they offered him. The atmosphere crackled with an unspoken tension, the air heavy with the scent of danger. Maxim struggled to maintain his composure, aware that he stood in the presence of power and ruthlessness. Every movement, every word, was carefully measured, acutely aware that a single misstep could have dire consequences.

Iqbal, his face etched with deep lines of experience, regarded Maxim with a piercing gaze. A formidable presence, he exuded an aura of authority that commanded respect and demanded obedience. Beside him, Mohammed, the enforcer, emanated an unsettling aura of silent menace, his eyes scanning Maxim with an intensity that sent shivers down his spine. Mohammed was over six foot in height and thick set, where Iqbal could be mistaken for an accountant who was much smaller, slimmer, and geekier in appearance. Together, they formed an unbeatable team, orchestrating intricate deals that remained concealed from prying eyes. Their clients, ranging from high-profile individuals to shadowy figures of the underground, trusted their discretion and expertise. The room was crowded with half a dozen imposing Asian men, their presence casting an intimidating shadow over the space. Among them were two figures Maxim recognised from his encounter at Jonesy's place, known only by the names Bilal and Raja. Loyal and trusted confidants of the brothers, they added an extra layer of intimidation to the already tense atmosphere.

Maxim's mind raced, his thoughts a whirlwind of uncertainty. How had he found himself entangled in this web of criminality? His palms grew clammy, his nerves threatening to betray him. The weight of their collective gaze felt suffocating, as if they could see through his every facade and uncover his innermost secrets. He pulled a heavy chair from beneath the table. The brothers wanted to talk business and understand the events of the previous night. Media reports were already circulating around the city, and they knew the dead victim had been a cousin of the Darnell family. Their words hung in the air, each syllable laden with implications. Maxim felt a knot forming in his stomach as the realisation sank in, he was being drawn deeper into their world, ensnared in their dangerous games. The choices before him seemed impossible.

As he sat there, a pawn in their twisted game, Maxim's mind raced, searching for a glimmer of hope, an escape from this suffocating existence. His hands trembled, his voice caught in his throat, as he struggled to find the words to respond. In this fateful meeting, he would succumb to their demands, knowing the consequences would be dire. The table before him became a battleground of silent tension, an arena where destinies hung in the balance. Maxim's eyes flickered between Iqbal and Mohammed, his heart torn between fear and uncertainty. In this pivotal moment, he knew that his choice would shape the course of his life forever, forever altering his fate and those around him.

A small brown sealed envelope lay conspicuously on the table. Iqbal's hand hovered over it briefly before casually sliding it across to Maxim. "This is yours for last night's work," he stated matter-of-factly, his tone revealing little emotion. It's a job well done on your part. Just be vigilant for any signs of trouble or the cops, and keep your lips sealed. If you happen to get arrested, don't utter a word."

Iqbal's gaze sharpened as he continued, "And what about that mobile?"

Without waiting for a response, Iqbal slid a business card across the table toward Maxim. "Call this number for our lawyer," he instructed curtly.

Maxim's hands shook as he reached for the business card, his fingers tracing the embossed letters with trepidation. The weight of its significance settled heavily upon him, the implications of needing legal counsel sinking deep into his bones. The burner phone he clutched tightly in his other hand suddenly felt heavier, its presence a stark reminder of the dark path upon which he had unwittingly embarked. He stared at the device, its screen a glaring testament to his descent into the underworld of addiction and desperation. The list of missed calls from unknown numbers seemed to mock him, each one a haunting reminder of the chaos and turmoil that now consumed his life.

The phone had fallen into his possession, a secret burden he couldn't easily discard. His initial curiosity had given way to a profound sense of unease, a burden of guilt that he carried upon his shoulders. Each missed call carried with it a story, a life hanging in the balance, seeking temporary solace in the very darkness that threatened to consume them. He knew the streets whispered tales of this phone, a lifeline for those ensnared by addiction. It was a number known only to the desperate, the destitute, and the broken. The urgency of their calls, the desperation in their voices, weighed heavily on Maxim's conscience. In the stillness of the room, he contemplated the phone's fate, his mind wrestling with the moral dilemma it posed. "Yeah, it's here," sliding it across the table in exchange for the envelope.

"Great stuff, you're working for us now, forget Jonesy. You trust us now and stay with us. We will help to protect you," Iqbal replied with a smirk on his face. Iqbal looked at the mobile and scanned through the contact list. "Good" he replied and slide the mobile back across the table to Maxim. "I want you to go back dealing in the same area in Manchester. Just do what you're doing in the same area. If you get any problems just let us know and I'll send the boys across. We will get gear to you and exchange the cash and you can take your 10%."

Maxim didn't feel he was able to negotiate, "Ok fine."

Mohammed's voice cut through the tension, his tone carrying a weight of authority. "Listen up. We're trusting you here, but don't even think about double-crossing us. You know what happens to those who try."

"Got it," Maxim replied evenly, though inside, turmoil churned. His life had spiralled into chaos, and there seemed to be no way out. Returning to Ukraine wasn't an option; he couldn't bear the thought of facing the questions and scrutiny of social services again. Selling drugs had become his only means of survival, his daily struggle for existence. But with

Jonesy seeking vengeance and his missing cash, the stakes were higher than ever.

Iqbal rose from his seat and moved closer to Maxim. "That's all for now. You're free to go," he announced calmly with a smile, handing Maxim another mobile phone. "This is yours. Keep it safe. Someone will be in touch in a few days." With a subtle gesture, Iqbal directed Bilal to accompany Maxim out of the room. Mohammed remained silent, but his nod conveyed acknowledgment. Maxim returned the gesture with a slight nod of his own before turning to leave. As he walked out the door, he could feel the weight of all eyes in the room following his every step.

Iqbal glanced at Mohammed, his expression serious. "We should watch him closely for now. He's young, but we can easily maintain control over him. Our main concern is whether he'll survive long enough to prove useful to us."

Mohammed's smile was tight, betraying his underlying scepticism. "Time will tell. He appears sharp and savvy, especially for a Ukrainian," he remarked with a hint of disdain. It was evident that Mohammed harboured little patience or regard for individuals from Eastern Europe.

Outside Maxim stood in the alleyway behind the restaurant, his heart pounding with anticipation. The weight of the brown envelope in his hands sent a surge of nervous excitement through his veins. He knew the contents held the power to change his circumstances, to offer him a lifeline amid uncertainty. With trembling hands, Maxim carefully tore open the envelope, revealing a stack of cash neatly tucked within. His eyes widened as he counted the fifty-pound notes, his fingers tracing over each note. Six grand lay before him, a small fortune that held the promise of new beginnings and a chance to escape the shadows that had haunted him. The sight of the cash both exhilarated and intimidated him. It was a double-edged sword, a tangible reminder of the risks he had taken and the dangers that still lurked in the shadows. Maxim had become entangled in a web of uncertainty, where each step forward carried the weight of consequences yet to be fully realised. He glanced around, ensuring he was alone in the alley, before stashing the cash inside his jacket pocket. The weight of the money pressed against his chest, a constant reminder of the choices he had made and the risks he had undertaken. It was a symbol of both opportunity and danger, a fragile balance that he had to navigate. As he stepped out of the shadows and back onto the bustling streets, Maxim's mind raced with possibilities.

Emerging swiftly onto Wilmslow Road, he couldn't shake the sense of vulnerability amidst the hustle and bustle of ordinary life. Knowing Jonesy's extensive connections in this part of South Manchester only heightened his unease. Subconsciously, he pulled his hood up, hoping it might offer some semblance of anonymity, a feeble attempt to avoid being recognised. Boarding a passing city-bound number 43 bus, Maxim found a seat and pulled out his mobile. A glance at his screen revealed missed calls and texts from Richie and Mia. Curiosity gnawed at him as he wondered what they knew about the events of the previous night. As he scrolled through his messages, his heart sank when he came across a text from an unknown number. Its contents turned his stomach, and he slumped back in his seat with a heavy sigh, trying to push away the sickening feeling it provoked. With a feeble attempt to ignore the message, he hastily stuffed his phone back into his pocket.

It simply read, "**PAY BACK, we're coming for you.**"

23 Shadows of Surveillance

With a mixture of trepidation and determination, Matt went into Richie's empty bedroom, his movements masked by the silence of the house. He knew time was of the essence and worked swiftly. Taking out a small covert camera from his pocket, Matt's fingers danced over its sleek surface, ensuring its settings were adjusted for optimal performance. He located the perfect vantage point, a spot that would capture activities without arousing suspicion. His hands moved with practiced precision as he secured the camera, expertly concealing it in the room's decor. The device blended seamlessly, hidden amongst the trinkets and personal belongings that adorned the surroundings. Matt stepped back, his gaze lingering on the covert camera, a potent symbol of the secrets it would soon unveil. A mix of guilt and necessity gnawed at Matt's conscience. He knew that his actions crossed boundaries, intruding upon Richie's privacy. Yet, the weight of the circumstances forced his hand. He needed to uncover the truth, to unravel the mysteries that surrounded them, and this covert camera was one of the means of doing so. As he made his way out of Richie's room, a lingering unease settled within Matt. The line between friend and foe had blurred and couldn't help but wonder about the repercussions of his actions, the potential fracture it might cause in their fragile relationship. But with each step he took, Matt steeled his resolve, reminding himself of the greater purpose at hand. It was a necessary gamble, a risk he had to take to protect what mattered most.

Matt's mobile vibrated, signalling Richie's movement as he was heading back home. With the aid of the app, Matt had unrestricted access to Richie's messages, revealing a clear urgency in Richie's attempts to reach Maxim. Matt couldn't shake off the uncertainty about Richie's involvement in the recent murder; each message potentially held grave implications. If the police caught wind of Richie's implication, they would seize and analyse his mobile, leading to dire consequences for Matt. He urgently needed to wipe the software to minimize his risk of entanglement. The recent homicide had escalated tensions, and the police would be intensifying their scrutiny on Jonesy and his associates.

****

As darkness enveloped the scene, Matt's gaze sharpened as he spotted Jonesy's unmistakable black Mercedes, parked unattended near a cluster of apartment blocks. A blend of curiosity and caution surged through him, compelling him to delve deeper. Bringing his car to a halt, his heart raced with anticipation. The sight of the empty vehicle stirred a whirlwind of questions in his mind, sparking a glimmer of hope that this might be an opportunity to glean vital information. Sensing the urgency of the moment, Matt knew he had to seize this unexpected discovery, all while remaining acutely aware of the looming risks. His foremost objective? Uncovering Jonesy's whereabouts. Finding a prudent parking spot, he decided to 'sit it out' and watch for a while. Matts gaze fixed on the sprawling estate that stretched out before him. The night enveloped the landscape, casting an eerie glow on the worn-out buildings and cracked pavements. A dim and melancholic atmosphere hung in the air, accentuated by the low, glowing orange streetlights that dotted the area. As he surveyed the scene, Matt's eyes traced the flickering lights that struggled to pierce through the darkness. They danced like distant embers, offering feeble illumination to the dilapidated surroundings. Their soft glow lent an otherworldly quality to the environment, as if time itself had slowed down in this forgotten corner of the city. The car park stood as an island of emptiness amid the bustling estate. Rows of vehicles were scattered haphazardly, their once vibrant colours fading under the weight of neglect.

The worn-out tarmac beneath seemed to whisper stories of hard lives and broken dreams, a testament to the struggles that had unfolded within this unforgiving neighbourhood. Despite the desolation, Matt found himself drawn to this place. He had always been captivated by the raw and unfiltered realities of life, searching for meaning and beauty amidst the most challenging circumstances. He had seen it before in so many foreign deployments. It was here, among the decaying buildings and flickering lights, that he discovered a profound sense of humanity. In the distance, he noticed figures moving through the shadows, their silhouettes distorted by the dim illumination. The residents of the estate went about their lives, their faces etched with resilience and determination. Despite the hardships they faced, a glimmer of hope still shone in their eyes, refusing to be extinguished by the darkness that enveloped them. As Matt continued to observe, he couldn't help but feel a surge of empathy for the inhabitants of this neglected neighbourhood. Their struggles were a stark reminder of the vast disparities that existed within society, but also a testament to the indomitable spirit that resided within each person. A marked police car arrived; its vivid high visibility markings cast a glow across the darkened street. The vehicle came to a halt near a worn-out, two-story flat, it's peeling paint and cracked windows telling a tale of neglect. Unbeknownst to the officers, Matt observed their arrival from a distance, his curiosity piqued by the unfolding scene. With a collective sense of purpose, three officers stepped out of the car, their boots hitting the pavement with a determined stride. Their uniforms and authoritative demeanour marked them as guardians of the law, ready to face any challenge that lay before them. Matt watched intently as the officers closed the doors of the police car, their reflections shimmering momentarily against the vehicle's windows. They exchanged words, their voices hushed in the stillness of the night, before embarking on their path towards the two-story flat. As they approached the entrance, their shadows elongated by the dim glow of the nearby streetlights, Matt's curiosity deepened. What had prompted this visit? What events had unfolded within the confines of one modest dwelling in the block to warrant the attention of the law? The officers climbed the concrete stairs, their steps muffled by the weight of anticipation. Matt noted the cautious glances they cast, their eyes scanning the surroundings, ever alert to potential dangers. Each officer bore the weight of their responsibility on their shoulders, embodying the delicate balance between justice and compassion. The officers reached the door of a flat their gloved hands gripped the doorknob, their unspoken determination radiating in the air. After a short pause, the door opened, and a figure of woman appeared. Matt took out his binoculars and saw Mia. The officers had a short conversation with her and with a swift motion, they entered the realm of the unknown, disappearing inside out of sight.

Matt's mind raced with questions as he continued to watch, hidden in the shadows. What awaited the officers inside? Would their presence bring relief, or would it unleash a storm of chaos and consequences? He couldn't help but wonder about the lives affected by their arrival, the fragile threads of fate intertwining in this one crucial moment. Time seemed to slow as Matt remained transfixed, caught between the desire to unravel the mysteries of the first floor flat and the respect for the officers' duty. As Matt's gaze remained fixed on the closed door, his imagination took flight, weaving narratives of hope, despair, and redemption. In this fleeting instant, he realised that even in the shadows, every action held the power to shape lives and alter destinies. After a tense interval, the officers reappeared at the door of the flat, their demeanour betraying no hint of suspicion or concern. With an air of nonchalance, they made their way back to their waiting vehicle and drove off into the night, oblivious to the fact that Matt had been meticulously tracking their every move, his senses attuned to every subtle gesture and nuance.

Matt opted for a strategy of observation and patience. He reasoned that if the police had sufficient cause to remove anyone from the property, there would have be a commotion. Jonesy, true to form, was unlikely to cooperate willingly; his allegiance lay firmly with the laws of the urban jungle, where the Police was regarded as the adversary.

To stave off the boredom, Matt reached over and flicked on the radio, finding solace in the music as he allowed himself ample time for contemplation. As the last notes of a song faded away, the local news headlines pierced through the airwaves. "Police have identified the victim of last night's fatal attack in Manchester as twenty-five-year-old Jerome Darnell, a father of two from Manchester." Matt recognised the surname and the coincidence from years gone by didn't pass him by without a moment of inner reflection. Another tragic young life wasted in the violent murky world of the gangs and drugs. Matt reflected to those last moments in the pub car park all those years ago. Nothing had changed since his acts of "Honourable Retribution," all those years ago. A violent night which had in the end made minor difference to society. No one would ever know what had happened that night except of course, Matt who intended to keep it that way.

Matt observed movement as the front door creaked open, casting a shadow onto the balcony as it widened. Mia emerged cautiously, her gaze darting around as if she were searching for someone. Finding no one along the concrete corridor, her attention shifted to the car park below. Once satisfied, she gestured with her right hand, signalling to someone inside. A white male promptly exited, followed closely by Jonesy and another Black male. They moved with an air of urgency, briskly making their way down the open corridor. The four descended toward the waiting Mercedes, their movements suggesting an underlying tension. Within moments the group had occupied the vehicle, the engine started and pulled off at speed. Matt remained seated, opting to stay put rather than follow the Mercedes. He checked his mobile to track its movements, confirming that it was indeed leaving and headed toward central Manchester.

With the coast clear, Matt seized the opportunity to proceed with the next phase of his mission. Exiting the car, he advanced toward the flat with a calculated and strategic demeanour, meticulously scanning his surroundings. As he ascended to the first floor, Matt's senses sharpened, alert to the presence of a young couple who crossed paths with him in the internal stairwell. Fortunately, they were too engrossed in each other's company to spare him a second glance. As he reached the front door of the flat, a sense of uncertainty lingered in Matt's mind regarding whether anyone else remained inside. Though the shroud of darkness suggested vacancy, he couldn't shake off a nagging doubt. He stood in front of Jonesy's flat, his heart pounding with anticipation. He knew he shouldn't be trespassing and felt vulnerable on the long and open corridor which overlooked the car park. Despite his lingering unease, Matt recognised the necessity of retrieving items from inside the flat. After ensuring there were no prying eyes, he took a deep breath and rapped firmly on the door. Ready with an imitation council worker's badge, he'd prepared to bluff his way through any potential encounters, claiming to be conducting routine checks. However, met with silence, he retrieved a door picking kit from his jacket pocket, grateful for the convenience of online shopping on eBay. Glancing up and down the corridor to ensure no one was nearby, Matt pushed hard against the door with his Elbow to evaluate the resistance of the locking system. The door flexed at the top and bottom indicating it was held by a Yale type lock. Inserting the plastic slide and suitable pick, Matt clicked open the lock seconds. He pushed the door open just enough to slip inside, ensuring that he left no visible signs of forced entry. Once inside, he closed the door gently behind him, his senses on high alert. The flat was eerily still, with only faint rays of light peeking through partially closed internal doors. He was hit by a warm stale smell which took his breath away. Instinctively Matt pulled up his neck warmer to cover his nose and mouth. Matt hesitated for a moment, contemplating the ethics of his actions. But he reminded himself that he had a genuine concern, and he was determined to conduct his mission. He put on latex gloves while his eyes adjusted to the darkness. As he moved through the flat, Matt took note of the subtle signs of absence. He wasn't going to touch or do anything unnecessary that could leave a trace to his presence. There was untouched mail on the hallway table and rubbish all over the floor. Matt knew what he was looking for in the living room and picked up a couple of mugs and empty cans, placing them into a plastic bag he took out from his coat pocket. Undeterred, Matt moved on to the kitchen, opening cabinets and drawers one by one. His hands brushed against cold cutlery and ceramic plates, his mind racing with the possibilities of what he might find. He collected used cigarette ends and sealed them into another bag. It was Jonesy's DNA that he was after, and these items would hopefully contain it in abundance. And then, he spotted it, a small notebook tucked beneath a stack of papers on a desk. Its worn cover and dog-eared pages hinted at its importance. With trembling hands, Matt opened the notebook, his eyes scanning the hastily written words.

Page after page, he discovered fragments of Jonesy's thoughts and transactions. Who owned him money, rows of cash figures and various mobiles with names next to them. But amidst the mundane entries, a single page stood out, a list of names, accompanied by cryptic notes. Matt's heart raced as he recognised familiar names, including Mia, Maxim, and Richie. It was a connection he had anticipated but was still surprised over. Realising the significance of his discovery, Matt quickly ripped the page from the book, ensuring that he had removed all evidence of the name list. As Matt made his way toward the front door, his mind raced with questions. What did the list mean? Why were their names included? And most importantly, where was Jonesy heading? The weight of the unknown pressed heavily on his shoulders, fuelling his determination to save Richie.

Matt glanced at his mobile, startled to see the Mercedes was heading back and only minutes away from his location. Something had gone wrong, Jonesy must have changed his plans or forgotten something.

Exiting the flat, Matt carefully locked the door behind him, erasing any trace of his presence. With a newfound sense of purpose, he retraced his footsteps back down the stairwell into the car park just as the Mercedes took up the same vacant space it had left. It was a remarkably close call for Matt as he jumped in his car, unnoticed by the occupants of the Mercedes. He had obtained all the items he had sought and for now his night was over.

24 Terrifying Encounters

Mia strolled towards the meeting spot, her steps quickening with each familiar face she spotted near the fountain at the heart of the City centre in the darkness. As she drew closer, her smile widened, mirroring the joy reflected in the expressions of her half dozen friends. Warm hugs and enthusiastic greetings were exchanged as she reunited, each embrace a testament to the strength of their bond through the care system and children's homes. It had been too long since they had all gathered like this, and the air was charged with excitement, promising hours of cherished camaraderie ahead. For Mia, meeting up with her only friends provided a much-needed escape from the weight of her current circumstances. Eager to embark on some carefree time, the group unanimously agreed to kick off their outing by exploring the precinct's latest arcade. Amidst peals of laughter and lively banter, they navigated through the vibrant maze of flashing lights and captivating arcade sounds. The atmosphere crackled with excitement as they engaged in friendly competition, challenging each other to an array of thrilling games. In an instant, the jovial ambiance shattered as a clamour erupted near the arcade's entrance. Mia, and her companions whipped their heads around to witness a menacing group clad in intimidating attire, barging into the arcade. It was a notorious rival gang, renowned for their aggressive demeanour and territorial conflicts. Fear tightened its grip on Mia and her friends. The once vibrant arcade transformed into a tense battlefield in a matter of seconds. The rival gang members were looking for trouble, shouting profanities and pushing innocent bystanders out of their way. Two of Mias group quickly took shelter behind a row of arcade machines, hoping to avoid detection. Mia exchanged a glance with the others, her instincts urging her to find safety as well. With a silent nod, she darted toward an exit at the back of the arcade, hoping to escape the clutches of this dangerous situation.

Adrenaline coursed through their veins as Mia and two of her friend Sam and Jodie sprinted through the dark corridors, the sound of chaos echoing in their ears. The distant cries of frightened people mingled with the heavy thuds of boots against the concrete floor, spurring them to run faster. They burst out of the arcade into the open air, their lungs gasping for breath. The familiar sights outside offered little solace as they realised the rival gang was in pursuit. Determined to keep themselves and their friend's safe, they made a split-second decision to run toward the nearby car park, hoping to lose their pursuers in the maze of cars. With every step, Mia and Jodie pushed themselves to their physical limits. Sam dropping off their pace turned in another direction and quickly disappeared from sight in the confusion. Panic fuelled their escape, blurring the surroundings into a whirlwind of motion. They zigzagged between parked vehicles, narrowly evading capture.

Among the gang's ranks was a hardened member feared for his ferocious demeanour and his steadfast companion, a massive, aggressive XL Bully dog. Another of their group, Jake, had fallen behind, his breath ragged as he desperately tried to keep up. The fear in his eyes was tangible, mirroring the terror that gripped each member of their group. Perceiving a chance to establish dominance and install fear, the dog, used as a symbol of power, was unceremoniously unleashed from its leash, setting the ferocious beast loose to wreak havoc. In an instant, chaos erupted. The unleashed dog lunged forward, its powerful muscles propelling its massive frame towards their friend Jake, who was now running for his life. The dog had been trained with aggression; its instincts honed to strike fear into the hearts of anyone unfortunate enough to cross its path. Jake's fear only motivated his desperate escape, his adrenaline pumping as he sprinted with all his might. But the enraged bully, stoked up by its handler's command and years of ruthless conditioning, closed the gap between them. Its thunderous barks reverberated through the street, filling them with a chilling chorus of aggression.

The moment of impact was both swift and brutal. The crazed dog sank its razor-sharp teeth into Jake's leg, tearing through flesh and muscle with a savage intensity. Jake's agonised scream pierced the air, intermingling with the chaos unfolding around them. The gang members, revelling in their power, watched with sick delight as the dogs' jaws clamped down, refusing to relinquish its grip. Mia's heart sank as she witnessed the horrifying attack. Fear and anger intertwined within her. In that critical moment, she knew she had to just keep running as the vicious dog's relentless assault continued, each laceration deepening the wounds on Jake's leg. The thundering footsteps and deranged laughter of the gang began to fade, offering a sliver of hope to Mia and Jodie. They slowed down, catching their breath behind a row of parked cars, their hearts pounding in their chests. Sweat streamed down their faces as they tried to comprehend the intensity of what had just happened. Regaining their composure, they cautiously emerged from their hiding spot, scanning the area for any sign of danger. The shopping precinct had returned to its usual state of normalcy, oblivious to the turmoil that had unfolded. Taking a moment to steady themselves, Mia and Sam sought out their friends, eager to ensure their safety. They raced through the street, their hearts pounding in their chests as they desperately searched for their friends. The encounter with the rival gang had left them shaken, but their worry for their friends overpowered any fear they felt. Each turn they took seemed to stretch the minutes into eternity, their footsteps echoing in the silence. As they rounded a corner, their eyes widened in horror at the sight before them. There, lying motionless on the cold pavement, was Jake. His body bore the marks of a brutal assault, his face swollen and bruised, blood staining his clothes. Jakes leg injuries by far the worse and Mia's hands flew to her mouth, stifling a gasp of disbelief that he had been stabbed so badly. Jodie stood frozen, her eyes welling up with tears as she struggled to comprehend the extent of the violence inflicted upon their friend. It was a chilling sight, a grim reminder of the dark underbelly that existed even in a City centre.

Shaking off their initial shock, Mia and Jodie rushed to Jakes side, their hearts heavy with a mix of anguish and determination. They knelt, gently cradling their injured friend, desperate to offer a semblance of comfort during the chaos. "Mia, we need to get help," Jodie whispered, her voice choked with emotion. Mia nodded, her eyes welling up with tears as she carefully assessed Jakes injuries. It was clear that Jake needed immediate medical attention but didn't wish to implicate themselves in the incident by calling the emergency services from their own mobiles.

Supporting one another, Mia and Jodie rose to their feet, determined to find help as quickly as possible. With Jakes safety at stake, they knew they couldn't afford to waste any time. Through the deserted streets, they hurried, their urgent footsteps resounding in the night. They pounded on doors, desperately seeking assistance from any willing soul who could lend a hand. Each rejection stung, but they refused to give up. Finally, a kind-hearted resident opened their door, concern etched across their face as they took in the distress of Mia and Jodie. Without hesitation, they dialled the emergency services, ensuring that help was on its way.

Relief flooded Mia and Sam as the wail of approaching sirens pierced the tense air. They remained outside, their anxious gaze never straying from their injured friend, silently urging time to hasten its pace. With the arrival of paramedics, a glimmer of hope pierced through the veil of worry that had enveloped them.

25 Farewell

Richie's footsteps felt heavy as he approached the door of his home. The weight of the world seemed to press down upon his shoulders, an unspoken heaviness that foretold the sombre scene awaiting him inside. The once familiar threshold now held an air of sorrow, signalling the inevitable farewell to his beloved father. With a trembling hand, Richie reached for the door handle, the creaking sound echoing through the hushed hallway. As he stepped inside, the atmosphere held its breath, as if time itself paused in reverence for the bittersweet moment that was about to unfold. He made his way towards his father's room, each step a mix of trepidation and longing. The hallway seemed to stretch impossibly, a corridor of memories intertwining with the anticipation of an imminent loss. The scent of antiseptic filled the air, mingling with the heavy silence that hung like a veil. Pushing the door open, Richie's heart sank at the sight before him. There, lying in a bed that had become his father's sanctuary, was a frail figure consumed by the ravages of illness. The lines etched upon his father's face told stories of a life fully lived, but also of the battles fought in the shadows.

Richie approached the bedside, his voice choked with emotion as he whispered, "dad... it's me, Richie, I'm here."

His father's eyes fluttered open, the flicker of recognition briefly illuminating his weakened features. It was a moment of connection, a fleeting bridge that transcended the confines of time and mortality. Richie's heart ached, knowing that this would be their final exchange, their last chance to say all the words left unspoken. Taking a seat by his father's side, Richie clasped his hand gently, a lifeline grounding them both amidst the uncertainty. Memories flooded his mind, the sound of his father's laughter, the wisdom imparted with every word, the unconditional love that had shaped his very being. He wanted to hold onto those moments, to etch them into his soul, but he also had to find the strength to let go. Richie hadn't been brought up to show emotions. His father had never been the 'cuddling type.' Although he felt the urge to do something, he couldn't even bring himself to hug his father. How do you show loving emotions when you have never been shown or encouraged before he wondered. In the hushed room, Richie poured out his heart, sharing stories, expressing gratitude, and seeking forgiveness for the shortcomings that had inevitably woven through their relationship. It was a dance of vulnerability, a final act of love and closure that brought tears streaming down both their faces. As the night light filtered through the curtains, casting a soft glow upon their intertwined hands, Richie felt a sense of peace enveloping the room. His father's laboured breaths whispered of the inevitable, drawing them closer to the edge of farewell. Time slipped away, minutes turning into hours, as Richie sat vigil by his father's side. In the quiet moments, he marvelled at the strength and resilience that his father had exhibited throughout his life, even in the face of impending mortality. It was a legacy that would forever be etched upon Richie's soul, a guiding light to carry forward. Richie had relentless thoughts whirling through his head. He was finding it hard to focus on anything let alone the enormity of his father's condition. Hours earlier he had been asked to execute a friend, now he was sitting next to his father watching him die. To make it even more unreal, Richie had a handgun shoved down his jeans and couldn't see a way out of his predicament.

  Twelve months ago, he had a father who was fit and healthy. A younger brother who appeared happy and getting on with his life. Now he had a father days away from death, a younger brother buried less than a week ago, an instruction to assassinate his friend and a crazy war veteran uncle he hadn't seen in years watching over him. An overwhelming sense of anxiety had consumed him, leaving him feeling adrift in a sea of uncertainty and anger. He ran his hands through his tousled hair, a nervous habit that offered little solace in this moment of overwhelming confusion.

The weight of the world secmed to bear down on Richie's shoulders, pressing him further into a state of unease. Every decision he faced appeared to be shrouded in a haze of doubt and mistakes. Each step forward veiled in a cloud of uncertainty. The path that once seemed clear had now become obscured, and he found himself questioning his every move. Amid this internal chaos, Richie felt an acute sense of being lost. He longed for a compass to guide him through his own mind, to provide him with the clarity and direction he so desperately sought. But the compass eluded him, leaving him feeling disoriented and alone in his struggle. As he gazed at his father, the world outside seemed distant and unfamiliar, mirroring the disarray within his own soul. The once-familiar sights and sounds that brought comfort now appeared alien, adding to his sense of isolation. He yearned for a sense of purpose, a glimmer of hope to break through the clouds of despair that hung heavy upon him. In this moment of profound vulnerability, Richie understood that he needed to confront his anxiety head-on. He realised that he couldn't allow himself to be paralysed by fear and doubt. It was time to take small steps forward, even if they felt uncertain and shaky. He needed to find the strength within himself to navigate this disorienting maze. To discover the path that would lead him to a way out and a sense of peace and fulfilment. He took a deep breath, drawing upon the reservoirs of resilience that lay hidden within. Though anxiety still gnawed at his core, he resolved to face it with courage and determination. It would be a long journey, with no guarantees of success, but he was ready to fight for his own sense of purpose and find his way back from the depths of his confusion.

Adjusting pillows, Richie kissed his father's forehead with a long pause before quietly turning to avoid waking his father and left. Richie had tears in his eyes as he headed for his bedroom. Desperate to remove the gun shoved down the front of his jeans he naively thought it would be safe in his bedroom.

There was one message on his phone. "You heard owt from that little foreign shit!"

Richie threw his mobile on the bed and pulled the Berretta handgun from his jeans. He held it out to his front and began examining it closely. Twisting it around in his vice like grip he felt an immense sense of power in his young, confused mind. As he stared at the guns detailing, he caught a glance of himself in the mirror. He didn't recognise his reflection. What had he become? How on earth had he got into this crazy situation? Standing alone with a loaded handgun in his hand, with instructions to kill another human. Richie turned, opened the wardrobe, and stuffed the gun behind his clothes.

****

Richie awoke with his heart racing as he heard his father's laboured breaths echoing through the house. Panic gripped him like a vice, squeezing his chest and clouding his thoughts. He sprinted down the hallway, his feet pounding against the cold floor, desperate to reach his father's side. As he burst into his father's room, a wave of fear crashed over him. His father lay in bed, his face pale and his body wracked with coughs. The struggle for breath was evident in the way his chest heaved, each inhale a battle against an invisible enemy. Richie's hands trembled as he reached out, his voice choked with emotion as he called out to his father, desperately trying to rouse him. Time seemed to stand still as Richie watched his father's eyelids flutter, then close. The room was filled with a deafening silence, broken only by the sound of his own racing heartbeat. The panic that had been simmering within him erupted into a full-blown storm, consuming him entirely. He felt an overwhelming sense of helplessness, his mind racing with worst-case scenarios.

"DAD DAD DAD," he shouted.

Richie began to sob at the sight of his dying father, "dad! Dad! what's up, are you Ok?"

Neil's eyes began rolling and he fell in and out of consciousness, finally passing out.

"Dad are you Ok! Can you hear me?" Richie shouted.

"Matt! Matt!" Richie's voice reverberated through the house, filled with urgency and desperation. Every syllable carried the weight of a life hanging in the balance. Matt sprinted through the house, the sound of his own pounding footsteps echoing in his ears. With each stride, his hope intensified, knowing that he needed his strength and knowledge to confront this terrifying situation.

As Matt burst into the room and screamed, "Call an ambulance."

Tears covered Richie's face, his voice quivering with a mix of fear and determination as he dialled for an Ambulance. "Matt, we need to do something. dad's not breathing. We must help him!"

Matt grabbed his brother and pushed his head back to help clear his airway. He could see Neil was in poor shape and searched for his pulse, but there was none. Matt had seen this "look of death" countless times on the battlefield. Matt focused, and with a trembling hand, he reached out and grabbed Richie's shoulder, pleading for him to remain calm. The weight of responsibility settled upon Matt's shoulders, and the urgency in his voice ignited a fire, shattering the grip of uncertainty. Matt dragged his brother off the bed and laid him on the floor without ceremony. Taking a deep breath, Matt nodded, his expression determined. Together, they would fight for Neil's life.

Side by side, Richie and Matt knelt beside Neil's motionless body. Matt guided Richie through the steps of CPR, their hands working in sync, desperately trying to breathe life back into Neil. The room was filled with a symphony of chaos, Richie's desperate cries, Matt's focused instructions, and the rhythmic compressions that were their lifeline of hope. Time became a blur as they poured every ounce of their strength into the resuscitation efforts. Sweat trickled down their foreheads, their muscles straining with each compression. Doubt and exhaustion threatened to creep in, but they pushed them aside, love for Neil fuelling their determination.

Despite the valiant efforts it was clear Neil had passed away by the time the Ambulance crew arrived. The paramedics had done their best, but it was little consolation.

It was a catastrophic blow for Richie and the paramedics sensed this. He was heartbroken sobbing on his knees holding his father's hand.

Matt had another "fly on the wall moments" like he was having a weird dream and longed to wake up from it.

The atmosphere in the house hung heavy with grief as Richie and Matt stood side by side, their hearts weighed down by the sudden loss of Neil. The arrival of the police had brought a sombre stillness to the home. Officers moved quietly, their expressions marked with a mix of professionalism and empathy.

The room buzzed with hushed conversations, a chorus of whispered condolences that seemed to float in the air. As the minutes turned into hours, the crowd of emergency workers began to disperse. Slowly, the house emptied, leaving Richie and Matt standing in the remnants of their shattered world. Silence settled upon them, broken only by the creaking of floorboards and the distant hum of passing cars. The weight of Neils absence pressed heavily upon their shoulders, a constant reminder of the void left behind. They stood amid memories, surrounded by the echoes of a life forever altered.

Richie turned to Matt; his eyes filled with unspoken questions. But now, as they stood on the precipice of a future without their father and brother, they couldn't help but feel lost, adrift in a sea of unanswered emotions. Words eluded them, as if the enormity of their grief had rendered language insufficient. They shared a silent understanding, knowing that no words could ease the ache in their hearts or erase the lingering questions that haunted their thoughts. In this moment, their bond as nephew and uncle became a lifeline, a source of strength amidst the overwhelming uncertainty. Memories of Neil life flooded their minds. Laughter shared around a dinner table, the sound of Neils voice telling jokes, the warmth of his presence during challenging times, fragments of a life intertwined with theirs. They clung to these memories, seeking solace and reassurance within their depths.

Richie and Matt sat in the lounge; their eyes fixed on a photograph that captured a moment frozen in time. They allowed themselves to feel the weight of their sorrow, to acknowledge the vastness of their loss. In the quietude of that shared space, they found solace in the company of each other.

Eventually Matt spoke, "It's going to be so hard over the next few days and weeks Richie. You can and will get through this, but you're going to have to think carefully. I can stay here for a couple weeks to help you, but it might be best if you go back and live with your Mum," Matt murmured softly.

"I aint doing that, no way am I moving back in with her, especially after the way she treated dad. I'm not even telling her my dad has died. She didn't even care when he was alive so why should she care now."

Matt looked at Richie and saw a distraught young man whose life had been turned upside down. Matt had often seen these emotionless signs of shocked behaviour. Coping with death and the sudden brutality of it often took years to overcome. The human mind could be scrambled by traumatic events in seconds but often took years of sensitive support to ever recover fully. Matt knew the brain could be a troublesome beast to manage after traumatic events. Most found their own unique ways of dealing with it but knew that with the correct support and right guidance Richie could find his way out of this trauma maze and adolescent confusion. The most critical issue Matt had to do deal with was how to help Richie break his association with Jonesy's gang.

The house started to feel chilly as the adrenaline rush had begun to leave both men. Matt walked over to the fireplace, knelt, removed the brass plate, pressed the ignitor switch while turning the small black gas valve. After a couple of loud clicks, the fire burst into life as blue and red flames licked their way over the imitation coals. A wave of warmth passed over Matt like the morning sunshine when he had been a young Marine on operations. He turned and looked at Richie, unsure how to approach the subject.

"Who are these bad guys you're getting mixed up with Richie," your Dad and I had been worried about what you've been getting caught up in, and what you are doing with these people?"

Richie reacted exactly how Matt expected. Shouting back and going on the attack. "What are you talking about? I'm doing nothing and to be honest it's got nothing to do with you."

"So why are you overreacting in this way? If you haven't got anything to hide what's with the overreaction and attitude to my simple questions?"

"I'm sick of people like you and others jumping in with comments about what I'm doing. I'm knocking around with friends and doing nothing wrong so just get off my case and leave me alone."

"Ok so what are you going to do about work or are you going back to studying. Without a good plan what do you think is going to happen?" enquired Matt.

"Look, you might be my uncle, but my dad's just died, and I don't need to tell you shit. So, mind your own business and leave me to it. In fact, once dads' stuff is sorted you can go back to wherever you came from. I'll look after myself thanks. I don't need you or my Mum to do that!"

Eager to avoid and hide from the next round of questions, Richie stormed off upstairs.

Matt sat back in his chair, sighed to himself, and looked back into the heart of the fire.

26 Battle Scared Resilience

Matt's senses jolted to life as the blaring alarm of his weathered Casio G shock watch shattered the tranquil stillness of the early morning. Grogginess weighed heavily upon him as he rubbed his eyes, struggling to shake off the remnants of sleep that clung stubbornly to his mind. A haze of confusion clouded his thoughts as he groped for the reason behind setting the alarm in the first place. Then, like a bolt from the blue, the events of the previous night crashed over him with the force of a tidal wave. Matt's heart plummeted as the realisation of daily life dawned upon him: he had forgotten to put the rubbish bins out. Annoyance surged through his veins, propelling him out of bed with an urgency bordering on panic. As he hurried towards the window, the distant rumble of the council bin men grew louder, filling him with a sense of dread. He pulled back the curtains, his eyes widening as he watched the large garbage lorry make its way down the street. The bins of his neighbours were being emptied one by one, while his own sat untouched. A mixture of frustration and disappointment washed over Matt. He had always prided himself on being responsible and organised, but this slip-up had caught him off guard. He knew the consequences of forgetfulness, but the bins were the least of his priorities right now.

Matt stood before the bathroom mirror, his aging upper body exposed and vulnerable. The reflection staring back at him revealed a landscape marked by the passage of time. His once-toned physique now carried the wear and tear of life's battles, visible in the scars and wrinkles etched across his skin. As he reached for his razor, his fingers traced the lines of a particularly prominent scar, a memento from a combat injury long ago. It served as a reminder of the fragility of life and the resilience required to overcome adversity. Matt's gaze lingered on the scar, appreciating the story it told, both the pain endured, and the strength gained. Even after all these years he would stand naked from the waist up to wash himself a lesson imprinted on him from his Commando training. The basics of a 'shit,' 'shower' and 'shave' were taught to every recruit irrespective of background or upbringing. In the realm of Royal Marine Commando training, diligence became an ingrained virtue, woven into the fabric of every recruit's being. From the moment Matt stepped foot on the hallowed grounds of the Commando training centre, he was indoctrinated in the importance of meticulousness. Every task, no matter how seemingly mundane, demanded a razor-sharp focus. The simple act of polishing boots evolved into an art form, as recruits painstakingly buffed every inch, ensuring not a speck of dirt or scuff mark remained. Each uniform worn was immaculate, with creases sharp enough to cut through the air.

In the field on operations, diligence could be a matter of life or death. A slight oversight, a momentary lapse in concentration, could have dire consequences. From the precise arrangement of equipment on a combat vest to the careful inspection of weapons, no aspect of personal gear was left to chance. Every clip, fastening, and strap had to be checked and double-checked, for lives depended on it. Navigation exercises became a symphony of awareness. Matt learned to read the terrain, analysing the subtlest contours and features. He honed his ability to spot minute landmarks and navigate by the stars, his senses sharpened to a heightened state of perception. In the field, a misplaced footstep or a misread map grid could lead to disastrous consequences, and so he learned to tread with utmost caution. In combat scenarios, confidence became a weapon. Commandos, like Matt meticulously planned their movements, studying the enemy's habits and vulnerabilities. They analysed every outcome, preparing for various contingencies. The success of his missions hinged on exploiting the smallest weaknesses, capitalising on the slightest opening. Even in the face of exhaustion, the relentless pursuit of detail never wavered. Commandos pushed their physical and mental limits, training their minds to remain sharp and focused even under the most gruelling conditions.

Matt learned to spot the smallest changes in his surroundings, attuned to the whispers of the wind, the rustle of foliage, and the distant crack of a branch. It was through this unwavering attention to detail that he gained an edge, an advantage that set him apart from civilian life that failed to understand any of this. For those like Matt who embraced this ethos, mindfulness ceased to be a mere requirement, it became a way of life. It permeated every facet of Matt's existence, transcending the confines of training and embedding itself within his core principles. It reflected Matt's dedication, his commitment to excellence, and his unwavering pursuit of mastery. And so, in the crucible of Royal Marine Commando training, Matt's diligence emerged as a sacred principle, a guiding light that transformed raw recruits into highly skilled warriors. It was this relentless devotion to the finest nuances, the smallest particulars that sculpted individuals capable of operating at the highest echelons of elite military environment.

Matts eyes shifted to his sagging skin, a testament to the relentless march of time. The muscles that had once defined his chest now seemed less prominent, their vitality fading. The sight sparked a twinge of melancholy within him, a bittersweet reminder of the passage of youth and the inevitability of aging. His mind raced with a whirlwind of emotions. He contemplated the choices made and the paths not taken. Regret and nostalgia mingled with acceptance and gratitude. Each wrinkle and line bore witness to the experiences that had shaped him, the laughter shared with colleagues, the challenges overcome, and the lessons learned. Yet, amidst the introspection, a newfound appreciation began to blossom. Matt recognised the beauty in the imperfections, the stories told by the battle scars and weathered skin. Each mark carried a chapter of his journey, a testament to a life lived with purpose and determination.

As he picked up his razor, Matt met his own gaze in the mirror, a flicker of resilience gleaming in his eyes. He acknowledged the changes that time had brought, but he refused to let them define him. The strength that resided within him extended far beyond the surface, transcending the physical manifestations of age. With each gentle stroke of the razor, Matt carefully shaped his facial hair, reclaiming a sense of control. He allowed himself to embrace the evolving image reflected at him, a visual reminder of his ongoing transformation. There was beauty in the raw authenticity, in the acceptance of his flawed and aging self. In this vulnerable moment, Matt made a silent promise to himself, a commitment to cherish the journey, to celebrate the battles fought and won, and to find joy in the simple act of living. As he finished shaving, he looked at himself once more, a newfound self-assurance radiating from his eyes. Clad in his vulnerability, Matt stepped away from the mirror, feeling a sense of liberation.

Matt peered into Richie's room only to find it empty, prompting a disappointed shake of his head. "Does this lad ever sleep?" he mused to himself.

Downstairs, Richie was already dressed and engrossed in a bowl of cereal in the kitchen. A brief, awkward silence hung between them as Matt entered the room, attempting to lighten the mood with a quip about missing the bin men due to a lie-in.

"Oh, right," Richie responded with little enthusiasm, barely lifting his gaze from his cereal.

"Thirsty?" Matt offered, filling the kettle with tap water.

"Nah, I'm good, thanks. I'm heading out in a bit," Richie replied, absentmindedly scratching his head as he scanned the contents of the fridge for alternative breakfast options.

"Shouldn't we be discussing your dad's funeral arrangements?" Matt suggested, voicing his concerns.

Richie ambled over to the dishwasher, depositing his bowl inside with a clang. "Like I said, I've got it covered. I don't need you breathing down my neck," he retorted sharply before storming out of the house, leaving Matt to ponder his next move.

As Matt mulled over the situation, it became apparent that Richie was harbouring unresolved anger, and cooperation would be hard to come by. It was shaping up to be a challenging day ahead. He picked up his phone and dialled Nicole. The international dialling tone took time to engage before it began to ring.

The distance between them suddenly felt insurmountable as he longed to hold her close, seeking solace in her comforting presence. The ache of his brother's loss weighed heavily on his shoulders, and he knew he needed to share the painful news with her. Matt's heart raced with a mix of anticipation and apprehension. He could already hear the echoes of Nicole's voice in his mind, her warm and soothing tones that had always brought him comfort. After agonising seconds, she picked up, her voice filled with excitement and longing.

"Matt, mon cher, it's so good to hear your voice," Nicole greeted, her voice tinged with eagerness.

"Ca va Bien, et toi."

Nicole's calm, soothing voice washed over Matt, evoking a wave of longing and nostalgia. "I'm well, thank you, and I'm glad you're doing okay. I've really missed you. Any idea when you'll be coming back home to me?"

A brief pause followed, during which Nicole sensed a shift in Matt's demeanour. "What's wrong?" she inquired gently; her concern evident in her tone.

"Neil passed away last night, and it's left Richie in a real mess," Matt revealed sombrely.

Nicole's voice quivered with emotion as she responded, her love and empathy pouring through the phone. "Oh, Matt, I am so sorry... I can't even begin to imagine what you must be going through right now. My heart breaks for you, mon amour."

"I'm going to stay another week or so to make sure Richie gets the support he needs and to sort things out," Matt explained, his voice tinged with resolve.

"Oui, yes, yes, of course it is. Do you want me to come over and help?"

"No, its fine, you need to work and help out there,"

Nicole's voice softened, filled with compassion, and understanding. "Matt, my love, I am here for you, no matter the distance. Take all the time you need. Your family needs you now, and I will be waiting for you, ready to wrap you in my arms when you return. Lean on me from afar, and we will get through this together." In that moment, Matt felt the immense power of their connection, a lifeline that transcended the physical miles. With Nicole's unwavering support and understanding, he knew he could navigate the difficult days ahead, finding strength in her love. With a mix of anxiety and curiosity, he held the phone to his ear, engaged in an intense conversation with Nicole. Their conversation ebbed and flowed, carrying the weight of their emotions across the distance that separated them. During their intimate exchange, Matt discreetly slipped into Richie's bedroom, a sense of unease settling in the pit of his stomach. He retrieved the covert camera hidden within the room. As he carefully moved around the room, his eyes darted around. The urgency of the situation intensified as his fingers brushed against the cold metal casing of the hidden camera. Matt's voice trembled as he continued to speak with Nicole, attempting to maintain a semblance of normalcy while his mind raced with uncertainty. His gaze fixated on the camera as he fumbled to access its contents. As the video footage played before his eyes, time seemed to stand still. Shock rippled through his body, as if a jolt of electricity surged through his veins. The secret footage captured on the camera revealed a side of Richie that Matt had never imagined. It exposed a hidden world of deceit, betrayal, and actions that could shatter their lives. The truth unfolded before him, leaving him paralysed with disbelief. The video file clearly capturing Richie holding a handgun and placing it in the wardrobe. Matt turned and moved to the wardrobe. Opened it and looked on the top shelf. Pushing clothing to one side he found the gun. In that moment, Matt's attention snapped back to the ongoing call with Nicole. He could no longer maintain the charade, his voice faltering as he attempted to mask his shock and anguish. With a mixture of guilt and urgency, he stammered out an excuse, abruptly terminating the call before Nicole could sense his distress.

As he stood there, alone in Richie's bedroom, the weight of the newfound knowledge pressed upon him. The camera remained in his hands, a damning witness to the dark secrets that had been lurking beneath the surface. Matt's mind whirled with a whirlwind of emotions, torn between the need for answers and the fear of confronting the painful truth. Matt knew that he had stumbled upon something that would forever change the dynamics. He braced himself for the turbulent journey that lay ahead, aware that the path to the truth would be fraught with consequences and revelations that could not be unseen.

27 Beneath the Veil of Concern

Richie stood outside the bustling train station, observing the rhythmic flow of commuters passing by on this ordinary working day. The air hummed with a sense of purpose and anticipation as people hurriedly made their way to their respective destinations. Bags swung in sync with brisk strides, and the collective energy of the crowd filled the atmosphere. As Richie leaned against a nearby pillar, he became a silent observer in the bustling symphony of city life. Each person seemed encapsulated in their own world, lost in their thoughts, or immersed in the tasks that awaited them. The station became a transient hub of stories, dreams, and responsibilities, where strangers brushed shoulders in fleeting connections. He watched as a young woman in a smart suit expertly juggled her phone and a coffee cup, her determined gaze fixed on the path ahead. A group of friends laughed and chatted animatedly; their camaraderie evident in the way they playfully nudged each other. A weary-looking commuter, laden with bags, hunched forward, their eyes fixed on the ground as if trying to bear the weight of the day.

Richie found solace in the familiarity of this routine, this predictable ebb and flow of humanity. It offered a sense of normalcy, a temporary escape from the complexities and challenges that weighed upon him. As he observed the interactions around him, he realised that everyone had their own stories, their own burdens to carry. A profound realisation washed over Richie, a reminder that amidst the monotony and rush of daily life, there were countless narratives unfolding simultaneously. Each passer-by harboured dreams, hopes, and fears, their lives interwoven in this shared space. The station became a microcosm of the human experience, a mosaic of journeys, and a testament to resilience. Though Richie felt a sense of detachment from the crowd, he also recognised the beauty in their collective existence. Each commuter represented a unique thread in the tapestry of life, contributing to the vibrant mosaic of the area. It was a reminder that among personal struggles, there was a larger tapestry of connection and community, waiting to be explored and embraced.

As the flow of commuters continued Richie could see four huge Billboards lining the streets, advertising a variety of themes "Deluxe chicken sandwiches" to "what's on Netflix." On the corner of the building opposite the train station was a large black sign with a white arrow indicating a 'sandwich shop' fifty yards down the road.

Outside the confines of the station this part of town was a typical working-class area. A good place to move around unnoticed. Dull grey- and magnolia-coloured Victorian semi-detached houses were located on his right as he headed in the direction of the cafe. The homes were not blessed with the best views in town. They seemed devoid of any recent upkeep or exterior maintenance. Opposite was a giant factory painted insipid dull blue which had begun to crack and shed, like the skin of a snake. This factory was situated next to three enormous white storage Silos. All built at this location for its proximity to the railway station. In better economic days workers fetched and carried produce to passing goods trains. A time before modern day haulage companies had put these factories out of business. This Café was situated on the corner of a nearby road junction. Nothing out of the ordinary, just a small-town Café like so many others around the area. It certainly held a different clientele from those who used Elvira's. Entering through the door there was a real noticeable hustle and bustle from customers inside. Commuters and workers in differing attire all focusing on their own conversations. In the far corner Maxim was sitting at a small table tucking into scrambled eggs on toast.

Richie approached a little hesitantly, unsure of the response he would receive. Maxim looked up and smiled, "Hey Richie thanks for meeting me."

Richie felt utterly confused right now. Here he was in a random café, with a guy he had dealt drugs with who was from a country he had no idea about yet been instructed to execute him which he knew he couldn't do. Taking a seat and quickly placing an order for a coffee he went straight to Maxim. "What the fuck did you do to upset Jonesy, he's super mad with you?"

Maxims smile disappeared as he finished his food. "I had to do it; he was threatening me. I've seen what he is doing to Mia, and he is evil. We are just being used and thrown away like a piece of trash, I had to act and get back what's mine." The conversation was interrupted when a young server arrived with Richie's coffee, placing it on the table.

Maxim's voice lowered to a hushed tone as he continued, his frustration palpable. "I connected with the Muslim brothers in Manchester, seeking their assistance. We confronted Jonesy, demanding he return the money he owed us. You see, he stole it from us. It was meant to be a simple retrieval, nothing more." Glancing around the café to ensure privacy, Maxim discreetly slid a bundle of cash across the table to Richie. "Here, take it. This is your share," he asserted, his tone edged with resentment. "Jonesy swindled us out of our earnings. His men ambushed us the other night at Robs place, reclaiming the cash and drugs we had rightfully earned. Now he expects us to foot the bill."

Fury flickered in Maxim's eyes as he clenched his jaw, his words deliberate and charged with emotion. "Jonesy thinks he can push me around, but I won't stand for it. I left my homeland to escape war and build a better life. Yet here I am, dragged back into violence and turmoil. It's unbearable, being forced to fight just to survive."

"You need to watch your back, Maxim," Richie cautioned, his tone laced with concern. "Jonesy's put a price on your head. He's out for blood and he wants his money back."

Maxim's expression hardened as he countered, "Listen, I come from Ukraine, where every day is a battle for survival. I've invested the money with the Muslim brothers to get in on a new market. I plan to work them over too, take their cash, and leave this godforsaken country behind. But we need to stick together, Richie."

His plea tinged with urgency, Maxim continued, "You can do the same with Jonesy. Take what's rightfully yours and cut ties with him. You're bearing all the risk, and he knows it. Let's grab a hefty sum from both gangs and make a clean break for ourselves."

Maxim's demeanour softened into a reassuring smile, leaving Richie to ponder the weight of his words.

"So, let me get this straight," Richie mused, his mind whirring with the implications. "I continue working for Jonesy, dealing his gear, while you do the same for the Muslim brothers. Once we've amassed enough cash from both ends, we vanish to a new city without a trace?"

As Maxim resumed eating his breakfast, Richie forced a strained smile, the turmoil in his life becoming all too apparent. Another roll of the dice, another perilous gamble, was this the way forward? Richie took a long thoughtful sip of his rapidly cooling coffee, "Ok, let's do it, but you need to keep an incredibly low profile around town. Keep out of the way of Jonesy and his associates. You need to send me a clear message to say you have left the country and gone back to Ukraine. That way I can at least convince Jonesy he can't reach you. If Mia gets sight of you, she will snitch so we can't trust her. If you are spotted it will create serious problems, I can't discuss right now. "You get me?"

"Yeah, sure but I'll be back in town hustling so let's use this café and meet here every week. Once we get an idea of our plan, we can work out the finer details." Both men smiled which turned to laughter, fist pumping each other. Maxim produced a small piece of paper from his pocket and read out Iqbal's number for Richie to note, "if you ever need urgent help contact Iqbal. Let's speak soon my friend." Richie stood up, nodded towards Maxim, and walked for the exit leaving Maxim to settle the bill.

****

Matt had been listening to the conversation and was finding it hard to comprehend what these two young men were considering.

Later that afternoon Richie turned up at Jonesy's flat. He was still a little apprehensive but relieved when Mia answered the door. She smiled and invited him in.

"I think he has calmed down a little so you should be Ok," Mia whispered.

Inside Jonesy was sat on the sofa taking sips from a mug. A couple of other intimidating looking men were sat watching football on the TV.

"What's happening then, you seen that dirty Ukrainian fucker yet."

"Nah, mate," Richie began, shaking his head. "I ran into a couple of the regular junkies downtown while I was on the bus. I asked around if they'd seen him, and the word on the street is that he's skedaddled outta town. They're itching for their fix, and if I don't get back out there soon, we'll start losing customers." Richie passed his mobile to Jonesy and remarked, "Got this text from him, says he's skipped the country." Jonesy quickly scanned the message, verifying its authenticity.

Jonesy smiled at Richie. "Ok then," you get back out to 'Robs nest' and set up base. The Cops won't be mixing it there. Mia, you go and sweet talk that Rob fella. Get inside and start serving up tonight. Let me know when you're in and we will get you another delivery. Where's the strap, you still, have it?

"Yeah, it's stashed safe."

"I want you carrying it when you're out at night. Just in case you do see the little fucker and get the opportunity to "Pop him." Keep hold of it for the moment, see it as a little insurance cover for you. Richie felt uncomfortable with this suggestion but didn't show it. He really didn't want to risk wandering around with a loaded handgun shoved down the front of his Jeans.

Jonesy stood up and approached Richie, standing opposite him face to face and smiled. Richie could smell his stale breath and tried not to react.

"Good man Richie, keep doing your shit and your little debt will be paid back in no time." There was a long pause before Jonesy turned and sat back on the sofa. "Go on then what you waiting for, fuck off and take the little tart with you." Mia looked at Richie and they both left without speaking.

28 Unforeseen Guests

Mia approached the front door with cautious steps, while Richie lingered a few paces behind, keeping himself partially concealed. Neither of them wanted to startle Rob, especially after the recent unsettling events at the address.

As Rob made his way to the door, his palms grew clammy, and his heart quickened its pace. The door stood before him like an imposing barrier, amplifying his anxiety with its solid presence. He hadn't been expecting any visitors, and the late hour only heightened his unease. Who could it be at this hour? What if it was something or someone he wasn't prepared to face?

"Who's there?" he called out nervously, his voice tinged with apprehension.

"It's me, darling. Mia," came the reassuring reply from beyond the door. Rob's initial trepidation softened as he recognised Mia's voice. With caution, he unlatched the safety chain, allowing the door to crack open slightly. Peering through the gap, he broke into a smile upon seeing her familiar face.

"Where have you been, Mia?" he asked, a mixture of relief and curiosity colouring his tone. Rob unhooked the chain and stepped into the open doorway to greet her. But his happiness changed to concern when Richie stepped forward out of the shadows, "Alright Rob mate."

"My mum told me I shouldn't let anyone in, especially after that fight and those bad men."

"Don't be daft, you know us, we're your friends and we want to see that you're Ok," Mia assured him.

Rob tried to gather his confused thoughts at by the arrival of his unexpected visitors. Mia walked straight past, kissing him on the cheek as she entered the flat. "We are good friends, and we will both look after you, "won't we

Richie." Nodding at Richie who followed her into the house passing Rob.

"Yeah, we certainly will."

Closing the front door behind him, Rob pushed aside his mother's concerns, his excitement at having Mia and her companions back in his desolate home overriding any lingering worries. The long, dark winter nights had left him feeling isolated and alone, and the mere presence of Mia set his heart aflutter. With each encounter, his affection for her seemed to deepen, her kindness and beauty becoming hopes of light in his otherwise dim existence. Unbeknown to Rob, Mia saw his vulnerability as an opportunity to exploit for her own benefit. His unwavering infatuation blinded him to the warning signs, leaving him defenceless against the heartbreak that loomed on the horizon. For Mia, Rob's adoration was nothing more than a source of validation and power. She revelled in the attention he lavished upon her, manipulating his emotions with calculated precision. To her, Rob was merely a pawn in her game, a means to an end, and she had no qualms about using him to further her own agenda. As their interactions continued, Mia maintained the façade of friendship, all the while plotting her next move. She would flirt with Rob, stringing him along with false hope and promises of reciprocated feelings. To Rob, it was like a dream come true, an affirmation that his love for Mia was requited.

"Where have you been?" Rob's voice quivered with a childlike innocence as he recounted the recent chaos. "Some awful men barged in and started fighting. It was terrifying. The police showed up, and even my mum came by to make sure I was okay. They told me not to let anyone in, but you're safe, right?" His words were filled with the earnestness of a naive child, seeking reassurance during uncertainty. Mia and Richie assuaged Rob's worries and before long he was sat with a hot drink watching TV, happy in the thought he had company to keep. Mia produced a mobile and threw it at Richie. "So, you'd better tell Jonesy we are ready to go. The second mobile is going crazy and the addicts with bad habits are getting desperate to score."

Matt had been monitoring Richie's mobile and was perplexed as to why Richie was doing this. He had watched Mia and Richie hanging around the home before going inside. The occupant who let them inside appeared to have something about him. Odd in that his visible gait and mannerisms didn't quite sit right with Matt.

****

It was dark when the figure of a teenage male on a mountain bike appeared. He wore a black hoodie pulled tightly over his head, obscuring his features from prying eyes. A snood shielded his lower face, hiding any hint of recognition. He pedalled swiftly, his movements fluid and precise, determined to remain unseen. As he glided down the dimly lit streets past Matt, he became one with the shadows, blending seamlessly into the night. The rhythmic sound of his bike wheels turning was the only evidence of his presence, but it was easily masked by the evening breeze. He was focused on what he was doing and like most young drug runners, hyper vigilant of threats. Arriving at the flat, he slowed to a near-silent crawl, in sync with his cautious approach. He dismounted his bike with a practiced ease as the front door opened on his arrival. It was clear they had been expecting him inside. The dealer handed over the package with a precision borne from countless similar encounters, ensuring the exchange was swift and discreet. Transaction completed the door closed he set his foot to the pedal, pushed off and sped away disappearing into the darkness.

Matt's heart sank as he faced the harsh reality that Richie participated in the dangerous world of drug dealing. The weight of disappointment settled heavily on his shoulders, and a sense of betrayal seeped into his very being.

He had always admired Richie, never suspecting that façade concealed such dark secrets. Anger and hurt battled within Matt, wrestling for control of his emotions. He couldn't help but wonder why Richie had chosen this path, why he had succumbed to the allure of easy money and the dangerous world of drugs. Was it desperation? Greed? Or a sense of adventure gone awry? His disappointment mingled with concern, for he knew all too well the destructive power that drugs could wield. He had witnessed lives crumble, dreams fade, and futures collapse under their weight of its violence. The thought of Richie falling victim to the very substances he peddled sent a chill down his spine, a stark reminder of the perilous road he had chosen.

As the weight of disappointment slowly transformed into determination, Matt resolved to confront Richie when the time was right. He watched the address become a hub for those caught in the merciless grip of addiction. Like clockwork, individuals started to arrive at regular intervals, their steps faltering, their eyes glazed with desperation. It was a slick operation they had going. The door would open with a creak to each visitor, they would exchange furtive glances, make a quick transaction and just as they had arrived, would depart, the weight of their purchase becoming an invisible burden on their souls. Each addict would retreat into the night, their steps heavy with a mix of shame, longing, and an insatiable craving that gnawed at their very core. The address would continue to stand, like a silent accomplice, witnessing their departure, the echoes of their footsteps fading into the void. It was a process that seemed endless, an unending procession of souls seeking solace in the darkest recesses of their existence. Matt bore witness to the relentless battle against addiction, the untold stories of lives teetering on the edge, yearning for a way out. Matt had seen enough and slipped away unnoticed.

Richie seemed more focused on making easy illegal drugs money, than coming to terms with his father's death.

How could he be so selfish and insensitive? It infuriated Matt because it was the fast easy money that attracted these young people. Richie had been given every opportunity to do well and achieve something with his young life, but his vulnerability was now leading him in the way of making poor life choices.

As Matt drove back to the house, the weight of his next decision hung heavy in the air. Contemplating the possibility of packing his bags and fleeing back to France, he grappled with the realisation that staying and confronting the looming problem posed far greater risks and consequences. Yet, in the tumult of his thoughts, a small nagging feeling tugged at the back of Matt's mind. He couldn't shake the sense of duty he felt towards Richie, a family member in desperate need of saving from the chaos engulfing them both. As Matt entertained the idea taking shape in his mind, he couldn't ignore the looming spectre of potential consequences. The thought of getting caught sent shivers down his spine, knowing that it could irrevocably alter the course of his life. Provided he planned his ideas, kept calm, and left no trace he believed he would be OK. The biggest issues about being caught by the Police were by becoming the "suspect" in the first place. If he avoided this, then he should be ok. He had done this before and there was no reason why he couldn't do it again.

Matt spent part of the day doing family administration, calling people up to make funeral arrangements and chase insurance companies. He had been made executer of Neil's 'Will' which made things a little easier. He had taken an awkward and confrontational mobile phone call with Sarah. Thankfully, Neil had left a clear 'Will.' Leaving all his estate to his remaining son. Neil did have investments and Matt had avoided mentioning these to Sarah. She seemed to accept that she had already taken what she could from their failed marriage during their divorce settlement. Matt was surprised to have been left twenty-five grand from the estate. This would go a long way in securing his own financial pressures and help him buy a new van to drive back to France. All the rest of his brother's estate which was a significant amount from the property sale would be left to Richie.

29 The Pursuit

Richie made the decision to catch a bus into town, while Mia had slipped away without disclosing her destination, a detail he didn't feel compelled to probe further. Recognising and accepting individual quirks was one thing, but Richie couldn't shake the sensation of being stifled by Mia's presence, finding her increasingly grating. Her drug addiction only exacerbated his doubts, leaving him wary of placing his trust in her. With the profits from the previous night's work securely stashed in a bag hidden within the depths of the sofa, Richie wrestled with a nagging worry. Despite his confidence in the secrecy of his hiding spot, lingering concerns gnawed at him. The unexpected arrival of Rob's mother could spell real trouble, potentially complicating his retrieval of the cash.

To Richie's relief it had been a good night with a steady stream of punters. Jonesy had called earlier asking how business had been doing and seemed content, ensuring the same courier would arrive every evening. Richie reckoned by his calculations he could have twenty grand in the kitty if business continued the way it had. His phone flashed with a missed call from Matt, a reminder of the turmoil waiting for him at home. Despite the urge to confront the mounting issues, Richie opted to bury his head in the sand, delaying the inevitable reckoning with his reality. Ignoring the pressing matters at hand, he resolved to deal with them at a later, more convenient time. Stepping from the bus Richie thought a visit to the Elvira's Café was in order as he was starving. Winding his way through the busy street, his eyes scanned the faces of the passers-by. Something caught his attention, a tall figure with a distinct profile and a strong jawline. It couldn't be, he thought, but there was an uncanny resemblance to, Maxim who had previously suggested he would be coming back into town to deal for the brothers.

Richie's heart raced with a mix of excitement and disbelief. Determined to confirm his suspicions, Richie quickened his pace and followed the figure from a distance. The more he observed, the more convinced he became it was Maxim. The way the person walked, the gestures they made, it was all too familiar. As Richie drew nearer, he mustered his courage and called out, "Maxim?" However, the figure vanished too swiftly for any response to reach his ears. If it truly had been Maxim, he was taking a considerable risk by returning to town while Jonesy was actively hunting him down. Determination surged within Richie as he quickened his pace, intent on confirming the identity of the fleeting figure. Reaching the street corner, he scanned the bustling crowd, searching for any trace of the person among the throngs of shoppers. Suddenly, he felt a firm grip on his arm, causing him to startle. Turning around, he found himself confronted by two individuals who bore the unmistakable aura of plainclothes police officers. Clad in inconspicuous attire of jeans, trainers, and dark coats, their stern expressions betrayed the gravity of the situation. One of the officers thrust a warrant card into Richie's line of sight, signalling that this encounter was far from ordinary.

"Excuse me, sir," one of the officers said in a stern yet composed tone. "We need to ask you a few questions. Can we step aside for a moment?"

Confusion washed over Richie as he complied and followed the officers to a quieter spot on the pavement. His mind raced, wondering what he could have done to attract the attention of the police. He replayed his recent actions, searching for any misstep or unintentional wrongdoing. The officer asked him why he was in town and why he was acting suspiciously. Richie couldn't hide the shock on his face and the officer began to explain that the Police were running an operation to tackle anti-social behaviour, weapon carrying and drug dealing.

Richie immediately adopted a hostile attitude towards the officers, "I aint doing no dealing so why you are stopping me."

The older officer promptly retorted, "What's with the attitude, young fella?" He keenly recognised the defensive demeanour often exhibited by young men when confronted or stopped by the police. This only heightened the officer's concerns, prompting him to further inquire into Richie's identity, purpose in the area, and whether he possessed any illicit items. Each question tightened the noose around him, amplifying the risk of the wraps of coke stashed in his pocket from the previous night being discovered. The prospect of a search filled him with dread; he could find himself in serious trouble if they uncovered the drugs. Faced with a dilemma of "fight or flight," he knew he had to act swiftly. Panic surged within him as the officer continued to grill him, each query adding to his anxiety. Then came the dreaded words: "We are going to search you."

As Richie stood before the officers, a whirlwind of emotions surged within him. An overwhelming sense of anxiety and panic clouded his judgment, leading to a rash and ill-conceived decision. In a moment of irrational impulse, he abruptly shoved through both officers and began running like his life depended on it. As he raced off through the pedestrian precinct people stopped to watch. He heard an officer shouting into his radio that he was in a foot pursuit. Richie had always been good at sport and felt he had a good chance of out running them or at least the older officer. He misjudged it and the younger more athletic officer quickly caught up putting in a quality rugby tackle on the fleeing Richie. Both men came crashing to the floor outside a Charity shop. Pedestrian shoppers watched the melee between Richie and the plain cloth officers assuming it was a fight with a shoplifter and a security guard. Most shoppers avoided the melee preferring to walk on their way, but one person had produced their mobile phone to record the incident, desperate for likes and hits for their social media platforms. Realising that escape was futile, Richie's determination wavered. The reality of his situation began to settle in, overshadowing his initial impulse to flee. The fatigue of his desperate dash mingled with a sense of resignation. Realising that resistance would only worsen his predicament, Richie reluctantly allowed himself to be handcuffed. The officers guided him to his feet and led him into the doorway of a nearby vacant shop, where they began their search. In no time, one of the officers unearthed the small wraps of coke. As the reality of his situation set in, Richie struggled to catch his breath, feeling the weight of impending trouble bearing down on him. The events unfolded in a blur, his young mind struggling to process the gravity of the moment. Amidst the chaos, he heard the damning words: "Arrest, and Possession with intent to supply..." The reality of dealing had hit home and in the eyes of law this was simple he was now a suspected drug dealer, playing in the adult world. His arrest was his new occupational hazard.

The officers quickly established that Richie was under eighteen and needed an appropriate adult at the Police station. When they learned that Richie had recently lost his father, they were taken aback, but they needed someone to step in as his guardian during the proceedings. Richie realised he had no other option. It boiled down to just two choices: his mother or Matt.

After a moment's hesitation, Richie reluctantly provided Matt's contact number and address.

"Is this the address where you're currently residing?" the older officer inquired.

Richie nodded. "Yes, it is."

"Alright then, we'll arrange a search of the premises. You'll be taken to a Manchester Police Station, and while we're there, we'll speak with your uncle to be your appropriate adult," the officer explained. "Is there anything at your home that shouldn't be there, or anything you'd like to disclose to us before we conduct the search? Consider this an opportunity to come clean before we find anything ourselves."

Richie remained silent and without ceremony he was placed into the rear of a Police van. Once seated, the doors to the steel cage slammed shut closing his view of the outside world.

Seated in the back of the van, Richie was overwhelmed by a mix of numbness and shock at how quickly his world had turned upside down. The realisation that the police might discover the handgun hidden in his bedroom struck him like a bolt of lightning. A wave of nausea swept over him, leaving him feeling physically ill as he grappled with the gravity of his predicament. His life was unravelling before his eyes, a consequence of the poor choices he had made. As the van rumbled on, Richie could do nothing but sit in silence, consumed by worry and uncertainty. Mia's words echoed in his mind: "If the police arrest you, say nothing and get a solicitor." It was the only advice he had to cling to in this moment of crisis.

Matt already knew Richie was in custody when the doorbell sounded and did his best to appear shocked when he answered. The officers briefed Matt about Richie's arrest and it was their intention to search the house under section 18 of the Police and Criminal evidence Act. Matt didn't care for the Act or the reasons behind it and happily informed the officers they could do as they wished. Matt informed the officers he was only staying temporarily at the house due to the recent death of his brother and was helping his nephew through this tragic phase in life. The officers felt a little sympathy to the family's situation, but the emotion didn't stop them from conducting their search concentrating their efforts on Richie's bedroom. Matt stood at the doorway and watched the officers go about their very diligent search.

As soon as the officers left the house, Matt wasted no time in dialling Jed's number. It had been years since they had last seen each other during their time in the Royal Marines, but their bond remained strong despite the passage of time. Their shared experiences in the military had forged a connection that transcended distance and time. Jed had always stood out as a remarkable individual, even among their elite group. His intelligence and adaptability were apparent from the outset, traits that served him well in the most challenging of circumstances. Matt admired Jed's ability to navigate complex situations with ease, a skill honed through years of military service and further developed during his studies in law. After leaving the Marines, Jed had carved out a successful career for himself, rising to become a partner in a prestigious law firm in Manchester. It was a testament to his determination and resilience, qualities that had propelled him from his humble beginnings in Belfast. Despite growing up amidst the turmoil of the "troubles," Jed had never allowed his past to dictate his future, a quality that Matt deeply admired. Reflecting on his own life, Matt couldn't help but wonder where he had gone wrong. Compared to Jed, he felt as though he had stumbled at every turn, grappling with emotional setbacks that seemed insurmountable. While they had both endured their fair share of harrowing experiences, Jed had managed to compartmentalise the horrors and move forward with his life, a skill that had eluded Matt at times.

As he waited for Jed to pick up the phone, Matt couldn't shake the feeling of inadequacy that gnawed at him. Life, he realised, was a series of decisions and opportunities, and he couldn't help but feel that Jed had simply been better at seizing them than he had. Yet, even amid his own doubts, Matt found solace in the unwavering friendship and support of his former comrade.

"Not you again," Jed answered sarcastically. There wasn't time for formalities.

"Jed, I need your help. I've got a spot of bother. My obnoxious sixteen-year-old nephew has just managed to get himself 'locked up' for Coke dealing and they need me down the station to function as his appropriate adult. We need a good lawyer, how you fixed?"

"No problem, Matt, which Police Station is your nephew at?"

"Manchester."

Ok give me your nephews name, address, and date of birth. I'll call the station meet you there in an about hour.

"Thanks Jed, appreciate it."

As Richie underwent the booking in process at Police custody, he was taken aback by the sudden entrance of a loud, belligerent individual. Clearly intoxicated and unruly, the man was escorted into the custody suite, shouting obscenities at the officers, and causing a scene. Despite his aggressive demeanour, the officers remained composed and professional, refusing to be provoked by his tirade. Richie observed the officers' calm and collected response to the disruptive individual, impressed by their ability to maintain control in the face of such hostility. Despite their best efforts to calm him down and encourage cooperation, the intoxicated man continued to resist, adamantly proclaiming his innocence amidst the chaos he created.

Alone in his cramped police cell, Richie found himself engulfed in a sea of restless thoughts. Sitting on a thin blue plastic mattress a cold chill washed over him. A musty unventilated body aroma mixed with the scent of disinfectant lingered in the air. God only knew what had been going on in this cell before he occupied it. A cheap metal vandal proof toilet was tucked away in the corner and looked barbaric. He decided he would be going nowhere near it or at least until his body told him otherwise. The sterile walls closed in on him, intensifying the weight of his mistakes. Sleep eluded him, and he was left with nothing but the cacophony of noise echoing from the bustling corridor outside. The sounds of footsteps, distant conversations, slamming doors and clinking keys filled the air, serving as a constant reminder of his current predicament. Each noise intensified the heaviness in his heart, a constant drumbeat of regret and uncertainty. The passing time seemed to stretch on endlessly, amplifying the turmoil within him. As the minutes turned into hours, Richie's mind danced between feelings of remorse and the fear of what the future held. His impulsive actions replayed in his mind like a broken record, the weight of his poor choices weighing him down. But within the confines of his cell, time seemed suspended. The world outside continued its relentless pace, oblivious to Richie's internal turmoil. He felt disconnected from the outside world, isolated within his own thoughts and regrets. The flickering fluorescent lights above cast an eerie bright glow, magnifying the sense of desolation. Unable to find solace in sleep, Richie sat on the hard mattress, his thoughts consumed by the consequences of his actions. The darkness outside his cell window reflected the darkness that had settled within him. It was in this bleak moment thinking about why he had been arrested. Sitting in his cell listening to the chaos outside 'the penny' dropped. Associating with dead legs and dropouts that the worst society could throw he realised he had to stop the direction he was heading, but was it too late for him? He needed to try and get a direction back in his life. In this moment, self-loathing consumed him. He berated himself for his profound foolishness, grappling with the horrifying prospect that this cramped cell could become his permanent reality if the authorities uncovered the firearm. While he had convinced himself that he only possessed nine or ten wraps of cocaine, his mind raced with scenarios of what would unfold if the police conducted a thorough search of his home and stumbled upon the gun.

     After what felt like an eternity, Richie's cell door creaked open, and a police officer informed him that his solicitor and uncle had arrived. Led from his cell, Richie traversed the custody reception area and entered a modest interview room. Inside, a large brown table dominated the space, adorned with recording equipment. Half a dozen plastic chairs were scattered around, two of which were occupied by Matt, and another smartly dressed individual. The officer closed the door behind Richie leaving them in the room. Richie looked at Matt, but his attention was drawn to the other man when he spoke.

"Hello Richie, I'm Jed your solicitor." I'm here to try and help you but I need to understand what happened." Richie sat down and began to retell his account as Jed listened and began to question his account for clarity. "So, you were looking after these nine wraps of coke ok." When we go into interview with the officers, I'm going to advise you to say "no comment" to any questions they put to you in the interview. I will provide the officers with a written statement at the start of the interview, and I'll read it out. All you need to do is sign it and say, 'no comment' to everything they may ask you, ok?"

Richie was still confused by the process, and he looked at Matt to seek affirmation. Matt just nodded in response and Richie confirmed he would do what he had been instructed.

Before he knew it the interview with the Police officers was over, and much to Richie's surprise there had been no mention of the handgun or even one being found. The Police had searched his house, but he was astonished to discover it had not been found. Richie couldn't believe his luck and felt the burden lifting from his shoulders. Jed had provided the officers with a reasonable excuse defence that Richie had been looking after the wraps for a friend and because of the recent death of his father he had not been thinking straight and had simply just panicked when the officers had stopped him. The Police and CPS accepted this excuse and decided to give Richie an official warning as it was his first brush with the law.

Matt understood that Richie had narrowly avoided a disastrous outcome. If Matt hadn't been able to eavesdrop on conversations through Richie's mobile, the handgun would have no doubt been discovered by the Police, leading to dire consequences.

The firearm was safely stowed beneath the driver's seat of Matt's rental car, meticulously concealed to erase any connection to him. He had taken every precaution, donning rubber gloves and sealing it in a fresh freezer bag straight from the kitchen drawer. The knowledge of its whereabouts was his alone. Additionally, he had ensured the covert camera in Richie's room was effectively dealt with to prevent any incriminating evidence from surfacing on the SD card. Reflecting on the infamous case of "Marine A," Matt was acutely aware of the potential repercussions of video evidence resurfacing years down the line and determined to avoid such pitfalls, staying vigilant and maintaining a strategic advantage in this dangerous game.

In the car park outside the Police station both men glanced at each other and smiled before a word was even said. Only a select group would recognise these moments. Two old Royal Marines who had experienced life together at the sharp end of combat but were happy to be back in each other's company without having to worry or be on edge about their safety. Jed still looked physically fit and was dressed in a pair of blue Levi jeans, smart shoes, well pressed crisp white shirt, and clean-cut Jacket. He really did look like the "duty Lawyer" he had now become.

Jed stepped forward and embraced Matt. It was like they had never left each other on the battlefield. They just happened to be in different circumstances but much safer ones. Brothers from different mothers but brothers reuniting all the same.

"Honestly Matt it's not a problem and glad to have been able to help you both out" responded Jed.

Jed took off his jacket and opened the door before getting into his plush Mercedes, waving as he drove off.

Matt turned to Richie and there were seconds before he spoke, "You have dodged a Bullet there Richie" deliberately referring to the gun. Richie stopped and looked at Matt wondering and trying to work out what he meant by the remark.

"Did he actually know about the gun?" This put Richie in an exceedingly difficult position. He wasn't sure if Matt knew about the gun or not. He hoped the Police had just missed it while searching his bedroom and decided to keep quiet until he got home. Matt seethed with anger inside, but he fought to maintain his composure, fully aware of the gravity of Richie's situation. Eyeing his nephew expectantly, Matt waited for a response, but Richie simply shrugged, offering a dismissive "what, I'm sorry," devoid of any genuine remorse or acknowledgment of Matt's assistance. It infuriated Matt to see Richie deflecting responsibility for his actions, revealing a disinterested, resentful, and directionless young man adrift in life. Matt recognised this attitude all too well, having grappled with similar struggles before joining the military. In fact, the Marines had rescued a younger version of Matt from his own self-destructive path. Now, faced with Richie's predicament, Matt questioned whether he could rescue his nephew from a similar fate. Despite his best efforts to provide guidance, Matt understood that true change must come from within Richie himself. Observing Richie's lack of positive male role models in his life, Matt reflected on the absence of strong father figures in young men's lives, a cycle perpetuated by their own fathers' choices or circumstances. Mentoring from older men was essential for shaping the character and behaviour of an aggressive youths like Richie. He believed in challenging young people to question their actions, fostering critical thinking and decision-making skills often lacking today. Matt lamented the decline of traditional family structures and values, noting the pervasive lack of confidence, self-belief, and ambition among today's male youth. He argued that providing young men like Richie with positive male role models could channel their testosterone-fuelled aggression into constructive avenues, offering a much-needed outlet for the pressures and frustrations of modern life.

Charging around assault courses, arduous exercises and teamwork in the Marines was a terrific way for young men like Richie to refocus their minds and burn off life's frustration. Young men who struggled in their teens and early twenties were often reborn in the Military. There was no better way to find out about yourself or learn your limits when undertaking arduous physical challenges. Respect for you and more importantly those around you wasn't a given. It had to be earned side by side with others, facing the same difficulties together. Sadly, for Matt modern society now demanded respect for materialistic items or false lifestyles portrayed on social media. Matt knew this was a shallow social ideology that had formed around young people. A substantial amount broken early by society's expectations on them and why so many young people battled mental health problems. There was no doubt in Matt's mind Richie was close to becoming a "lost cause." He was at a major crossroads in his life, and it was clear the next decisions he took in life could define him. Matt had seen hundreds of young men enter the military. All hoping they could find a form of direction or escapism from what life offered them on the outside in civvy street.

Richie needed something like this to set him on a better course. The easiest thing Matt could to do was go back to France, turn his back on Richie and let him get on with it but Matt was never one for taking the easiest options in life. Richie didn't seem to be upset or have any sorrow for his actions let alone the inconvenience he had caused Matt and Jed. Dragging them out in the middle of the night to bail him out of the situation he had gotten himself involved in.

The, "I couldn't give a shit attitude," angered Matt but he was good at masking out his emotions and keeping control and calmly asked. "You wanna lift home."

"Go on then," Richie responded like Matt was doing him a huge favour.

The drive back to the house was a silent affair. It was clear Richie wasn't in the mood for any conversation when Matt tried to touch on details about Neil's funeral arrangements. Richie showed little interest in the conversation suggesting to Matt he should just speak to his mum.

"You do realise that you are going to inherit a large amount of money from your father's estate? Do you have any idea what you're going to do with it?" Matt asked.

"Nah."

"Your dads' life insurance is going to cover the mortgage on the house and leave you with a good lump sum, of around four hundred thousand pounds. As your Mum and Dad were divorced it's my understanding, she is not entitled to anything now. To be honest she took most before your dad passed away."

To Matts surprise Richie responded. "So, what should I do then."

"Think long and hard about what you see yourself doing in the future. Set yourself short-, medium- and long-term goals in life. Do you want your life to revolve around undesirable individuals who will just use you and discard you once they have no further use for you? Do you have any ambition to join the military or going on to learn a decent trade? Why not use this opportunity of financial stability to run alongside your plans."

"I just don't know," came Richie's honest response.

Matt got the impression he wanted to say something but was holding back for reasons only known to him. Was it embarrassment or was it shock for Richie; it really was hard to tell.

"If you choose to hang around and be led by undesirable people who are happy to break the law for what is often seen as 'Fast money' it will only go one way, I can assure you of that Richie. If you continue down this route there will be only one place you will end up. "I guarantee that!" Tonight, was a flavour of that. You and I both know that you got away with it tonight by the skin of your pants."

Matt pulled up outside the house and switched off the ignition automatically killing the headlights. The interior lights came on enabling Matt to see Richie's face. Richie looked at Matt and responded, "Ok I get what you're saying."

Once inside and having made excuses he was tired Richie went straight to his room ensuring his bedroom door was closed. He turned on the light and went straight to the wardrobe. He frantically pulled out the clothing in the hope the Gun was still located where he had left it. After checking and double checking, he realised it was missing. Who had it!

It could only be two people. Matt or his dead father? He suspected it was Matt, but he couldn't be sure and certainly couldn't ask the question in case it wasn't?

30 Pain of addiction

The next morning Richie diligently checked his voicemails, a mix of urgency and frustration evident in the messages.

"Richie, where are you? You were supposed to lend a hand last night. It's crazy busy, and your absence isn't going unnoticed. Jonesy's not going to be pleased! Rob's incessant pestering is driving me up the wall. You really need to be here to take the heat off me. Call me ASAP!"

Opting to respond via text, Richie composed a message to Mia, aiming for brevity and clarity. "Had a rough time, got caught up with the cops yesterday. Apologies. Just got out this morning. I'll be there by 4 pm today."

Almost immediately, Mia's reply came through. "Ah, gotcha. Figured something was off. See you later."

Moving on to the next voicemail, Richie's ears caught a sense of urgency. "Hey, have you found him yet? If you don't know his whereabouts, I need that item returned... clear!"

Richie's mind spun with the weight of the situation outlined in the voicemail. Collapsing onto his bed, he let out a heavy sigh as his thoughts swirled amidst the chaos. The missing gun, coupled with the mounting pressure to continue dealing at Rob's place, created a suffocating sense of dread. Lying there, he couldn't help but wonder if his late father had stumbled upon the firearm and disposed of it. Had it been tossed carelessly into the outside wheelie bin by his father? The possibilities spurred him to consider checking once Matt had vacated the premises. Pulling himself together, Richie composed another text, striving to reassure and buy himself time. "Apologies for the trouble. Got nabbed last night, but nothing major, just a caution. Still tracking down Maxim, but he's vanished. Will keep you updated. Just need a few more days to sort it out."

As he descended the stairs, his phone buzzed with a response. "Alright, catch up with you over the weekend. Don't let me down," it read, a stark reminder of the expectations resting heavily on his shoulders.

After an exhaustive search of the house, Richie was left with nothing but frustration and confusion regarding the whereabouts of the handgun. Its absence gnawed at his thoughts, fuelling a growing sense of unease. He moved about the rooms, scouring every nook and cranny in a frantic bid to uncover any trace of the weapon. With each fruitless sweep, his anxiety mounted, and his agitation bubbled to the surface. The tension in the air was palpable as he retraced his steps, hoping to stumble upon the missing gun. Yet, despite his efforts, the elusive gun remained stubbornly out of reach. Driven to the brink by his inability to solve the mystery, Richie's frustration boiled over. With a primal scream of exasperation, he hurled an empty milk bottle across the kitchen, the sound of shattering glass punctuating his outburst. Without another word, he stormed out of the room, his mind swirling with unanswered questions and mounting dread.

Mia found herself drifting in and out of sleep, battling the heavy fog of drugs that clung to her consciousness. The day slipped away in a blur, leaving her to grapple with the harsh reality of her escalating addiction. Each passing moment magnified the pull of her cravings, the allure of her next fix growing stronger with every heartbeat. Awareness crept in, casting a harsh light on the chaos that had become her life. The once fleeting escape offered by drugs now shackled her to a relentless cycle of highs and lows, dragging her deeper into the abyss of addiction. Despite the warning signs scattered throughout her existence, Mia had chosen to turn a blind eye, denying the looming precipice that threatened to consume her.

Her gaze wandered across the room, landing on the remnants of her drug-induced haze. What had once been symbols of temporary relief now stood as stark reminders of her downward spiral. Empty pill bottles, crumpled foil, and discarded syringes littered the space, painting a haunting portrait of desperation and dependency. Each object whispered tales of her struggle, serving as a chilling testament to the grip that addiction held over her fragile existence. Her reflection in the cracked mirror offered little solace. Hollow eyes stared back at her, once filled with dreams and aspirations, now haunted by the ghostly spectre of addiction. The vibrant spark that had once defined Mia seemed dimmed, overshadowed by the insatiable hunger that consumed her every waking moment. Days blurred into nights, and nights bled into days as Mia's drug addiction tightened its grip. She recognised that her drug use had become a monster, devouring her hopes, dreams, and aspirations, leaving nothing but a trail of shattered promises in its wake. Her money to finance her habit had dried up. Like so many addicts she had started to steal and take cash that didn't belong to her. She was often surrounded by cash and the temptation to take it or grab a bag of gear was getting stronger by the day. Mia's mind was already plotting, considering the idea of pilfering a small sum later that night to test the waters. Would anyone even detect the absence of a mere tenner here, twenty there, or the occasional bag of gear? In her calculations, it seemed inconsequential, a mere drop in the ocean compared to the substantial windfall Jonesy would undoubtedly secure by week's end. Imagining him awash in a sea of cash brought a sly grin to her lips; surely, he wouldn't even register the disappearance of a few notes amidst his newfound fortune.

Richie arrived at Rob's house with an urgent pace, his worry casting a shadow over his demeanour. Despite knowing he shouldn't let Richie in, Rob's compassionate nature and desire for companionship won over his better judgment.

"Where's your girlfriend?" Richie inquired, a knowing gleam in his eye, aware of Rob's affection for Mia.

Rob's smile faltered slightly at the question; his cheeks tinged with embarrassment. "Mia isn't my girlfriend, you know that," he replied, though his innocence led him to invite Richie back inside, hoping Mia might return in his company.

"Yeah, I know, mate. Just teasing you," Richie reassured, though a hint of mischief danced in his eyes. "But I reckon she's got a soft spot for you. When's your mum coming back?"

"Not sure, maybe this weekend," Rob responded, his tone uncertain.

"Alright, let me know when she's due. It'd be nice to meet her," Richie lied effortlessly, his true intention veiled beneath a facade of politeness. All he truly desired was to ensure he was absent when Rob's mother returned.

As Rob settled into a chair in the kitchen, exhaustion etched into his features, Richie's gaze fell upon a striking crimson mark on the side of Rob's neck. His heart sank as he recognised it for what it was, cigarette burns. Anger boiled within Richie, a blend of protective instinct and disbelief that someone could inflict such cruelty upon a vulnerable soul without reason.

Gently, Richie approached Rob, his voice filled with a mix of empathy and concern. "Rob, what happened? Who did this to you?" His words hung in the air, heavy with a weight that threatened to suffocate the room. Rob averted his gaze, shame and pain mingling in his eyes.

Finally, with a shaky voice, Rob spoke, recounting the events that had transpired, the arrival of Mia, the confrontation, and the violent act that had left its cruel mark. His words carried a sense of betrayal, an unspoken plea for understanding mingled with a desperate desire to protect Mia from the consequences of her actions.

Richie's heart clenched at the sight of Rob's anguished expression, a stark testament to the toll Mias addiction had exacted on him. Amidst the swirl of emotions within Richie, anguish and frustration mingled, his empathy for Rob clashing with his struggle to comprehend Mia's actions.

"What about this brew? It's bloody freezing," Richie remarked, his tone laced with newfound confidence. Even at sixteen he understood the importance of projecting an air of arrogance and assurance on the streets, where survival often hinged on appearing tough and savvy. As Rob busied himself with making tea, Richie discreetly checked on his stash of cash, hidden behind the fabric of the sofa. Satisfied to find it undisturbed, he retrieved it and tucked it securely into his jacket. Just as he finished, the sound of Mia entering through the back door reached his ears, accompanied by a simultaneous knock at the front door.

"Hey, Mia!" Richie called out, before approaching the front door cautiously, his instincts on high alert. Peering through the peephole, he spotted a lad standing outside with his mountain bike, signalling the arrival of another delivery. In a swift and silent transaction, glances were shared, nods exchanged, and the delivery was completed with practiced efficiency. Without a word, the delivery person disappeared into the night, leaving Richie to ponder the intricacies of life in the shadows.

Mia and Rob sat around the kitchen table, Rob sipping on his tea while Mia's dishevelled appearance spoke volumes. Her hair was tangled and greasy, a clear indicator of neglect, and Richie couldn't ignore the signs of her drug use etched on her face. Despite her attempts to appear composed, her speech was still slurred, and her pupils betrayed the effects of the substances coursing through her system. Richie had become adept at recognising the telltale signs of addiction, a skill honed by spending ample time around users like Mia. Meanwhile, she remained oblivious to her deteriorating condition, convinced of her own sobriety even as she battled relentless cravings for her next hit. As they prepared for their evening dealings, she knew she would have to suppress her urges, focusing instead on the task at hand and wondering who would show up to join them in their endeavours.

Desperate for quick cash and trapped in the clutches of his own vices Richie saw a steady stream of punters 'come and go' from the address his moral compass slowly eroding with every transaction. As he opened the door to greet another customer, his heart skipped a beat. Standing before him were a couple of familiar faces, punters seeking their next fix, their eyes hollow and their bodies emaciated. In an instant, memories of their shared past flooded Richie's mind. He recognised them as older pupils from his school days, once filled with youthful dreams and boundless potential. But now, their paths had diverged drastically, veering off into the treacherous terrain of addiction. The sight of his former peers in this state struck a dissonant chord within him. It served as a grim reminder of the paths they had chosen and the choices he himself had made. He felt a pang of guilt, knowing that he was now an enabler, perpetuating the very cycle of destruction that had claimed his former school pals.

As Richie facilitated the exchange, the transaction felt heavy with remorse. With each note changing hands, it was as if fragments of their shared history were slipping away, consumed by the insatiable jaws of addiction. The walls of the room seemed to close in around him, the weight of his complicity pressing down like a suffocating shroud. In that poignant moment, a seed of introspection sprouted within Richie's conscience. He realised the profound influence he held, not merely as a dealer but as a harbinger of change. The faces of his former school mates flashed before his eyes; a sobering reminder of the potential devastation wrought by his actions. The sight of the girl before him, her appearance aged beyond her years, sent a jolt of shock through him. Her frail frame trembled beneath the layers of worn clothing, a stark testament to the ravages of addiction.

"Do I know you?" she slurred; her voice barely audible above the din of their surroundings.

Quick on his feet, Richie deftly deflected her inquiry. "Nah, don't think so," he replied, the weight of deception heavy on his conscience. It was a delicate moment, fraught with the tension of moral ambiguity.

Throughout the night, customers came and went, providing a brief respite from the tumult of Richie's life. Despite the undercurrent of guilt gnawing at him, the allure of easy money drowned out his moments of introspection. The rush of each successful transaction masked his inner turmoil, offering a temporary reprieve from the weight of his conscience.

As the night waned, it became evident that they had amassed a considerable sum. With Rob dozing off to the flickering glow of the television, Mia's restlessness grew palpable as she grappled with her insatiable craving for drugs. Driven by desperation, she slipped away to deal with a couple of regular clients, arranged by Jonesy himself. Richie couldn't shake the suspicion that Mia had indulged in heroin while secluded in the bathroom. Keeping track of the snap-seal bags proved challenging, but he knew he had to ensure he had enough to settle with Jonesy by the weekend. With the stack of cash securely in his grasp, Richie leisurely rolled a joint before stashing the remaining bags of gear at the back of a kitchen drawer. Lighting up, he savoured the first drag, sinking into a chair as he exhaled a plume of smoke and reached for his phone. Among the messages awaited a sombre reminder of his father's impending funeral from Matt, followed by another from Maxim.

"I've got plenty of gear from the brothers and things are moving smoothly. You're still in, right? Let's meet up at the café," Maxim's message read.

As Richie contemplated his next move, he felt the weight of his options bearing down on him. Walking away meant constantly looking over his shoulder, wary of potential repercussions. Continuing to sell drugs meant navigating the volatile terrain with Jonesy, a gamble fraught with uncertainty. Then there was Maxim's offer, promising a different path altogether.

Whichever path he chose, Richie knew it wouldn't be easy, quick, or devoid of risk. Each option held its own set of challenges and consequences, forcing him to confront the complexities of his choices head-on.

31 Abduction

Jonesy gripped the wheel of his sleek black Mercedes as it cruised down Wilmslow Road in Manchester. Though returning to this area always brought a sense of familiarity, it was tinged with an underlying tension. The streets were rife with memories of violence, a reminder that danger lurked around every corner. Even the luxury of his imposing car offered no guarantee of safety. Accompanied by two trusted companions, Jonesy navigated the streets with caution. In an area where threats loomed at every turn, traveling alone was simply not an option. The more pairs of eyes scanning the surroundings, the better the chances of identifying potential dangers. Rumours on the street had linked Maxim to the notorious Mohammed brothers, sparking suspicions of their involvement in the violent incidents that had plagued Jonesy's circle. Armed with this information, Jonesy returned to Manchester with a singular purpose, to gather intel and track down Maxim. If they could locate an associate of the Mohammed brothers, it might lead them to Maxim's whereabouts.

As the Mercedes turned onto Claremont Road, its imposing presence afforded them a strategic advantage. The elevated view provided by the large GLE Mercedes allowed them to scan the streets, peering over the roofs of parked cars for any signs of activity. Approaching the junction with Yew Tree Road, a sudden shout from the front passenger seat pierced the air. "Turn left! I could swear I just spotted Maxim sitting upstairs on that bus!"

Tension crackled in the air as Jonesy's reaction cut through the silence. "Seriously? No messing around with me now!" His voice held an edge of warning, his gaze sharp and unyielding.

"No, I swear. Just follow that bus. We need to get our hands on him," Jonsey urged, his urgency evident as he reached beneath his seat. With practiced precision, he lifted the carpet, revealing a hidden compartment housing a carefully concealed handgun. Swiftly, he retrieved the weapon, deftly chambering a round to ready it for use. Pulling up his bandana to obscure his features, he raised the hood of his jacket, cloaking his identity in shadow. In the back seat, the third member of their group instinctively followed suit, covering his face as instructed.

"Let's tail that bus and see if he gets off," Jonsey commanded, his tone firm as he maneuvered the car into action, determination etched into the set of his jaw and intensity of his gaze.

Maxim, oblivious to being spotted, sat upstairs on the bus as it rumbled through the streets. The late hour had emptied the vehicle of most passengers, leaving only a handful scattered throughout. In this neighbourhood, as darkness descended, confidence in public transportation waned despite the nominal fare of £2 for a single trip to anywhere in the city. No one, not even the mayor, could guarantee safety on these buses, despite the proliferation of CCTV cameras. Each day brought a litany of robberies and petty crimes, many of which went unreported, lost in the shadowy corners of this neglected part of town. The grim reality was that daylight offered little protection against becoming a target; for those like Maxim, without alternative means of transport, relying on the bus was a calculated risk. The threat of theft and robbery loomed over every journey, a constant reminder of the dangers lurking in the shadows. Yet, for Maxim and countless others, it was a risk they had no choice but to take, a grim necessity in navigating the harsh realities of their daily lives.

The bus made three more stops, the monotony broken only by the occasional passenger hopping on or off before it finally reached the junction with Platt Lane. For

Maxim, this was a pivotal moment. He had a meeting planned at Rosford Ave, close to the former Manchester City football ground a stark reminder of the area's decline after the club's departure with the arrival of wealthy new owners years ago, stripping the community of its already dwindling resources. As Maxim rose from his seat at the back of the bus, the harsh glare of the interior lights cast a spotlight on him, catching Jonesy's attention like a light beam in the night.

"That's definitely the dirty fucker," Jonesy shouted excitedly.

Maxim squinted against the blinding glare of light reflecting off the bus's windows, rendering him blind to the world outside. As the bus slowed to a stop and the doors hissed open, he stepped onto the pavement, engulfed by the cool embrace of the night air. Silence descended as he stood alone, the only passenger disembarking into the darkness. With a shiver, Maxim zipped up his jacket, a feeble attempt to ward off the biting chill. He watched as the bus pulled away, its taillights fading into the distance. Lost in his own thoughts, he stepped off the curb, oblivious to the danger lurking nearby.

But fate had other plans. From the corner of his eye, Maxim caught a glimpse of something familiar, a vehicle brimming with malice and intent, poised to strike. As the car revved its engine, a sinister smirk crossed Jonesy's face. Without a second thought, he pressed his foot down on the accelerator, propelling the vehicle forward with a lethal force. The screeching tires echoed through the air, as Maxim's world collided with chaos.

Time stretched thin, each heartbeat a thunderous drumbeat of dread echoing in Maxim's ears. Fear and disbelief surged through his veins, a torrent of panic threatening to overwhelm him. With every fibre of his being, he fought to escape the impending collision, but it was futile. The headlights bore down on him like twin blazing suns, their intensity blinding him to everything but impending doom. In a deafening crescendo of metal and bone, the car struck with merciless force, sending shockwaves of agony rippling through Maxim's body. He was flung through the air like a puppet cut loose from its strings, crashing to the unforgiving pavement below. Pain exploded along his left side; a searing inferno that threatened to consume him whole. Dazed and disoriented, Maxim struggled to make sense of his surroundings. The headlights above him seared his vision, casting the world in stark relief against the cold, damp asphalt. The acrid scent of diesel filled his nostrils, mingling with the metallic tang of blood as he fought to draw breath. As he attempted to rise, the car reversed, a sinister presence looming over him. At first, he thought it was a simple accident, a cruel twist of fate. But the opening of car doors and the harsh commands that followed shattered that illusion.

"Get a grip of him!" the voices commanded, their urgency slicing through the haze of pain and confusion. Two shadowy figures materialised from the darkness, sprinting towards him with predatory intent. Before Maxim could react, a brutal blow sent him reeling, the sharp crack of bone against flesh reverberating in his skull. Blinking through the darkness, Maxim felt a plastic bag envelop his head, suffocating him in a shroud of blackness. Panic clawed at his throat as he struggled for breath, the taste of blood thick on his tongue. His hands were yanked together, the biting sting of plastic ties cutting into his skin as they tightened their grip, binding him in a web of pain and despair.

Maxim's senses reeled as he was hoisted to his feet, the world spinning in a disorienting whirlwind. He felt a sensation of weightlessness, as if unseen hands were lifting him. Shadows flitted at his sides, their presence ominous and foreboding, but he couldn't discern their number or identity. A thick silence enveloped him, broken only by the metallic creak of a car's tailgate being pried open. Without warning, Maxim was propelled forward, his body hurtling through the air until he landed with a bone-jarring thud in the confined space of the vehicle's boot. The heavy lid slammed shut, sealing him in darkness, a suffocating blanket that smothered the sounds of the outside world. Panic surged within him, but his cries for help were swallowed by the suffocating silence. As the car lurched into motion, Maxim was thrown about like a ragdoll, each jolt sending shockwaves of pain reverberating through his battered body. With each violent roll, he collided with the unforgiving metal of the car's interior, his head ringing with the sickening impact of each collision.

32 Lost in the shadows

Mia arrived at Jonesy's flat, her knuckles rapping against the door in anticipation. Silence greeted her, punctuated only by the distant murmur of voices emanating from within. With a sense of trepidation, she inserted her key into the stiff lock, the metal resisting her efforts before finally yielding to her persistence. As she stepped inside, the flicker of the TV in the lounge caught her attention, casting eerie shadows across the empty space. Surveying the deserted flat, Mia's initial anxiety gave way to a sense of relief. "Perfect," she thought, her mind already wandering to the stash of drugs she knew lay hidden within. With a calculated nonchalance, she helped herself to a couple of bags of heroin, convinced that her actions would go unnoticed in the absence of Jonesy and his associates. Alone in the flat, Mia's priorities became clear. She needed to wash, to eat, but to satiate the gnawing cravings that consumed her every waking moment. Seated on the bed in the dimly lit bedroom, she unwrapped the silver foil, revealing the precious powder within. With practiced ease, she heated the substance, watching as it danced and shifted, morphing into a tantalising mirage of relief. Inhaling deeply, Mia chased the dragon, the rush of euphoria washing over her like a tidal wave. For a fleeting moment, she was transported from the squalor of her reality into a world of fleeting happiness, a temporary reprieve from the suffocating weight of her existence.

But as quickly as it had come, the high began to fade, leaving Mia adrift in the stark emptiness of her surroundings. Voices whispered in her ears, distorted and incomprehensible, until finally, they materialised into the form of four men standing over her, their laughter ringing in her ears. Their words, a jumbled mix of languages she couldn't fully grasp, carried a sinister undertone, punctuated by the familiar names of Jonesy and the harsh epithet "slag." As Mia struggled to rise from the bed, the oldest of the four men stepped forward, his movements deliberate and predatory. With chilling determination, he began to undo his jeans, the sound of the belt sliding free filling the room with a sinister echo. Mia's cries for him to stop was ignored as he advanced, his intentions clear and menacing.

A second man materialised behind her, his hands seizing her shoulders with a vice-like grip, muffling her protests as he forced her back onto the bed. Helpless and vulnerable, Mia felt the weight of her assailant pressing down upon her, crushing her spirit along with her body. Desperation flooded Mia's veins as she realised the depth of her predicament. With the other two men closing in, their intentions unmistakable, she knew she had only one chance to fight back. Summoning every ounce of strength within her, she lashed out with all her might, her foot connecting with brutal force against the oldest man's groin. His agonised scream pierced the air, a brief respite amidst the chaos. But before Mia could savour her small victory, her assailants retaliated with savage fury. As they tore away her clothing, exposing her raw vulnerability, Mia refused to submit to their brutality. With a primal instinct for survival, she sank her teeth into the flesh of the man above her, the taste of blood flooding her senses. In response, he delivered a vicious headbutt, the impact sending shockwaves of pain radiating through Mia's shattered world. Through a haze of agony and fear, Mia felt herself slipping into darkness, the warmth of blood mingling with the cold steel of despair. But even as oblivion beckoned, she refused to surrender, her spirit unbroken amidst the storm of violence.

****

Maxim's heart pounded in his chest as he struggled to maintain his composure, his senses on high alert in the suffocating darkness of the car's boot. With every passing moment, the weight of uncertainty pressed down upon him, his mind racing with unanswered questions and escalating fear. The muffled voices and distant music provided little solace, serving only to intensify his sense of isolation and vulnerability. Each laboured breath was a battle against the constricting plastic bag that threatened to suffocate him, the small holes offering scant relief from the encroaching panic. Desperate to assert a semblance of control, Maxim's fingers fumbled in the darkness, searching for his lifeline the mobile phone hidden within his pocket. With painstaking effort, he managed to retrieve it, the cool metal offering a glimmer of hope in the face of impending danger.

As the car veered off the road onto a rougher terrain, Maxim's heart lurched in his chest, his mind reeling with the possibilities of his fate. The sudden stop and the jarring sound of doors opening sent a chill down his spine, each noise a harbinger of the unknown horrors awaiting him. After a short pause he heard steel sliding and grating as if a large shutter door was being opened. His heart was thumping heavily in his chest as he waited for his fate. The boot lid clicked open, and he heard distinct sound of it opening followed by a rush of cool air across his body. In the darkness, Maxim's thoughts raced. He clung to the flickering hope that someone, somewhere, would realise his absence and call the Police. But the walls seemed to close in around him, trapping him in a world devoid of light, hope, and solace.

A chilling voice, unfamiliar and menacing, pierced the darkness. "Listen carefully," it commanded, sending shivers down Maxim's spine. "If you resist, I won't hesitate to end you. Understand?" Maxim's heart hammered in his chest as he nodded frantically, his voice barely a whisper. "Yes, please, just let me go," he pleaded, the fear evident in his trembling words.

With rough hands gripping his ankles, Maxim was forcibly pulled from the confines of the car, his head knocking against the unforgiving metal with each jarring movement. As he tumbled onto the damp ground, a sense of dread enveloped him, his mind racing with terrifying possibilities. He was lifted once more, carried through a disorienting silence that seemed to stretch on endlessly. The air around him shifted, the temperature dropping as he was deposited onto a hard, unforgiving surface before being seated in a plastic chair. Maxim's wrists burned with the tightness of the zip ties, cutting off circulation to his hands. Numbness crept through his limbs, a cruel reminder of his helplessness in the face of his captors' merciless intent.

Choosing to sit quietly in anticipation of what was to come next his heart pounded within his chest, his entire body consumed by a mix of fear and anticipation. Suddenly the plastic bag that had obscured his vision was violently ripped off, blinding lights pierced his eyes, leaving him temporarily disoriented and vulnerable. Blinking rapidly, Maxim tried to adjust to the sudden onslaught of brightness, his eyes struggling to focus. The intensity of the light forced him to squint, obscuring his view of the figures standing before him. He could sense their presence, shadows lurking in his peripheral vision, but their identities remained shrouded in mystery. His mind raced, desperately trying to decipher his captors' intentions. Were they mere pawns in a larger scheme, or were they the masterminds of his ordeal? The unknown sent a chill down his spine, his thoughts oscillating between apprehension and a fervent desire to unmask his captors. Through the haze of confusion, Maxim's instincts kicked in. He recognised the urgency of the situation, the need to regain control over his surroundings. Despite his vulnerable state, he summoned the courage to confront the blinding lights head-on, refusing to succumb to the paralysis of fear. As his eyes slowly adjusted to the assault of brightness, vague shapes and silhouettes began to take form before him. The figures appeared menacing, their intentions obscured by their proximity and the piercing glare that surrounded them. Maxim strained to discern any distinguishing features or clues that might shed light on their identities. But the silence remained oppressive, broken only by the sound of his own ragged breaths. The absence of spoken words amplified the tension in the room, leaving Maxim in a state of heightened vigilance. His captors seemed to revel in his disorientation, their presence an enigma that gnawed at his sanity.

"What do you want?" Maxim shouted in a trembling voice.

There was silence as his eyes slowly focussed back into the brightness ahead of him. Gaining his visual focus, he saw the grinning face of Jonesy glaring at him who snapped, "Listen to me you dirty cheat. I want my money back and you're going to tell me where it is."

Maxim barely had a chance to speak before a deluge of ice-cold water cascaded over him, sending shockwaves of freezing cold through his body. The sudden chill stole his breath, leaving him gasping for air as he struggled to compose himself. Through chattering teeth, Maxim pleaded in desperate gasps, "I swear, I don't have your money! I don't know what you're talking about!" His words were ignored as his captor's voice cut through the icy silence with venomous intensity. "Don't play games with me," the voice growled, dripping with menace. "You know damn well where it is. If you want to live to see another day, you better start talking."

Maxim's mind raced as he grappled with the impossible situation before him. He couldn't betray the Muslim brothers, but admitting to stealing the money was equally unthinkable. Trapped in a perilous game of survival, he knew he had to tread carefully if he had any hope of escaping with his life. Maxim's world spun into a nightmare as his wet jacket and sweatshirt were violently torn from his body, leaving his bare skin exposed and vulnerable. The metallic click of a DIY heat gun echoed through the room, sending chills down Maxim's spine as he realised the horror that awaited him. One of Jonesy's henchmen wielded the menacing tool, its ominous hum filling the air with its fiery tip glowing with malevolent intent. Maxim's heart pounded in his chest as the searing heat drew closer, his breath catching in his throat. With a cruel precision, the captor pressed the scalding nozzle against Maxim's bare flesh, unleashing a wave of excruciating pain that consumed him. A gut-wrenching sizzle filled the room as the searing heat seared deep into his chest, leaving behind a sickening stench of burning flesh. Maxim's agonised screams filled the air, echoing off the walls as he fought against the unbearable pain coursing through his body. He struggled to remain upright, but his tormentors held him firmly in place, their faces twisted with indifference to his suffering.

Jonesy's cold, calculated voice cut through the chaos, his grin a sinister display of his sadistic pleasure. "Where's my money?" he demanded, his words dripping with malice.

"Gag him," he ordered, his eyes glinting with cruel satisfaction.

One of the men lunged forward with a roll of black masking tape, binding Maxim's face so tightly that his tongue was forced back into his mouth, rendering speech impossible. "Who else was in on this with you?" Jonesy's voice boomed, his anger palpable as he whipped out his mobile phone to film the battered Maxim, who could only shake his head weakly in response. With a cruel efficiency, the captor pressed the scorching heat gun into Maxim's back again, holding it there for agonizingly long intervals, inflicting severe burns that sent waves of excruciating pain coursing through his body. Tears streamed down his face involuntarily as he endured the brutal branding.

"Is Richie part of this?" Jonesy demanded; his eyes narrowed with suspicion. Maxim shook his head vehemently in denial, but in his struggle, his mobile slipped from his pocket, its screen flickering with light. Jonesy's gaze fell upon the device, a sinister smirk crossing his face as he snatched it up. "Looks like we hit the jackpot," he sneered, his fingers flying over the screen to uncover Maxim's secrets.

Turning to his accomplice with a dangerous glint in his eyes, Jonesy issued his orders. "Leave him here to stew for a bit. We've got some business to deal with. Make sure this scumbag doesn't go anywhere."

The two men dragged Maxim's chair against the wall, securing him with heavy chains and fastening the chair to a nearby piece of machinery. With a final ominous gesture, they replaced a sack over Maxim's head, plunging him into darkness once more. Trapped and helpless, Maxim struggled to breathe under the suffocating weight of the chains, his fate uncertain as he awaited the cruel judgment of his captors.

****

As Mia gradually regained consciousness, she found herself alone in the room, the echoes of the recent violence still ringing in her ears. With a sickening dread, she realised she was lying half-naked on the bed, her skin sticky with dried blood. Shock and disbelief coursed through her veins, leaving her paralysed with fear and revulsion. Despite the overwhelming urge to flee, she forced herself to her feet, her body trembling with a mixture of adrenaline and trauma. With faltering steps, she made her way to the bathroom, her mind numb with shock as she turned on the shower. Standing beneath the hot water, she scrubbed at her skin with frantic urgency, the memories of the ordeal still fresh in her mind. Each drop of water felt like a painful reminder of the violation she had endured, but she refused to let herself succumb to despair. She stood beneath the relentless stream, her thoughts a whirlwind of confusion and anguish. In that solitary moment, she grappled with the harsh reality of her situation, unsure of where to turn or how to begin to heal the wounds that ran far deeper than the scars on her skin.

33 Racing the shadows.

Matt rose early, the scent of sizzling bacon and frying eggs wafting through the air as he prepared a hearty English breakfast. It had been ages since he last indulged in the ritual of cooking up a traditional morning feast. As Richie strolled into the kitchen, his unkempt hair and relaxed demeanour hinted at a morning just begun. Despite his casual appearance, there was an eagerness in his eyes as he engaged Matt in conversation, inquiring about the upcoming funeral for his father. Matt sensed a hesitation in Richie's demeanour, as if he were wrestling with unspoken thoughts. To keep the conversation flowing, Matt delved into the details of the funeral arrangements. It was to be a modest affair at the local crematorium, reflecting Neil's preference for a Humanist service over religious rituals. With Matt standing as Neil's sole surviving adult relative, the realisation dawned that he and Richie would be the only ones in attendance. It was a poignant reminder of Neil's solitary existence, casting a shadow over the anticipated turnout for his final farewell.

Placing the plates of breakfast onto the kitchen table, both men sat opposite each other. Richie acknowledged with a murmured "thanks" and was soon tucking in. There was a pause before either man tried to speak between mouthfuls. Matt waited in the hope his silence would encourage Richie to say what he had to say. Richie cleared his throat, a hint of uncertainty in his voice as he broached the subject. "Hey, Matt, you haven't happened to tidy up my room, have you?"

Matt shook his head. "Nope, can't say I have. Misplaced something?"

Richie hesitated, his words stumbling out. "Yeah, actually. It's something belonging to a friend, and I can't seem to locate it."

"Ah, tough break. Sorry, mate, can't help you there. What was it?"

"Oh, nothing major," Richie deflected, avoiding specifics.

Changing the subject, Matt suggested, "Got any plans for today? I was thinking of going for a walk to clear my head. Care to join me? We could chat about what your next move might be."

To Matt's surprise, Richie agreed, finishing up his breakfast before they set out of the house.

Four men with a malevolent purpose sat huddled inside the confines of a sleek BMW, their eyes fixed intently on the house. The air within the vehicle was heavy with anticipation, their minds consumed by violent intentions. Each man's face bore the scars of a shadowed past, their expressions hardened and devoid of remorse. Time seemed to stretch as they awaited their prey, their sinister gazes sweeping the surrounding area, ever watchful for any signs of movement. Their patience, a cloak for their dark intentions, was fuelled by a lust for vengeance that coursed through their veins. Inside the car, the atmosphere crackled with tension. Whispers of sinister plans passed between them, the hushed voices betraying their collective determination. Their hands, calloused and marked by the stain of their deeds, rested near concealed weapons, ready to strike at a moment's notice. A rustle of movement from the house caught their attention, and their eyes locked onto the figures emerging from within.

Matt's senses, sharpened by instinct, were attuned to the smallest shifts in his surroundings atmospherics. As he stepped outside, the cool breeze whispered against his skin, a gentle reminder of the world beyond the safety of his home. And then, out of the corner of his eye, he caught a glimpse, a sleek, foreboding presence that sent a jolt of unease through his veins. His glance fixed upon the black BMW, its windows tinted, giving away nothing of the occupants within. It stood there, inconspicuous yet ominous, as if it had materialised out of thin air. It was the only car in the street with its side lights on, a fatal mistake in how to be recognised by an expert. Matt had never been able to let go of his personal hyperawareness from his military training. The principles of "why things were seen" a fundamental piece of his combat training had been drilled into him over the years. Shape, shadow, shine, silhouette, texture, spacing and movement. That was why Matt "clocked" the BMW with a fleeting glance drawing his eye to the male figures occupying the front seats. A flicker of suspicion ignited within Matt's mind. He knew that this was no ordinary vehicle, no mere coincidence. His instincts screamed danger, warning him of an unseen threat lurking just beneath the surface. The hairs on the back of his neck prickled, and a knot tightened in the pit of his stomach. With a surge of caution, he weighed up his options, contemplating the best course of action. Should he alert Richie? Should they retreat inside, seeking refuge from the unknown? A mixture of fear and determination coursed through Matt's veins. He knew he couldn't dismiss this as a mere coincidence. His gut told him that danger loomed, ready to pounce upon them with ruthless intent. As he took one last lingering glance at the BMW, Matt's mind raced. Thoughts of escape and confrontation intertwined, conflicting desires tugging at his every thought. But one thing remained certain, the eerie presence of the car had awoken a primal instinct within him. He was no longer a passive observer but an active participant in a high-stakes game, where the consequences of inaction could be dire. With every fibre of his being on alert, Matt steeled himself for what lay ahead. The encounter with the mysterious car had shattered the illusion of safety, reminding him that danger could lurk in the most unexpected places. The sight of the BMW triggered Matts "ready for action" switch. He had spent years identifying threats and even as a civilian he never really 'switched off.' Richie was oblivious to what Matt had seen and walked from the house.

   The men's faces contorted into twisted smiles, fuelled by the intoxicating rush of their impending pursuit. Their intentions were clear, to hunt their target, to extract their pound of flesh. A predator's instinct took hold, driving their senses into heightened alertness while they meticulously pulled black balaclavas over their heads, concealing their identities with a veil of darkness. It was time to make their presence known, to unleash their malevolence upon their unsuspecting targets. The men's hunger for a fight propelled them forward, they were relentless predators, driven by a twisted sense of loyalty that knew no bounds. Their hearts raced with a mixture of anticipation and sadistic pleasure, their eyes fixated on their prey, the thrill of violence coursing through their veins. With each passing second, the distance between hunter and hunted diminished. Their purpose propelled them forward, unwavering in their pursuit of their intended targets.

Matt strained his ears, picking up the faint rumble of a diesel engine starting nearby. Coupled with Richie's involvement in drug dealing, it was enough to put Matt on high alert. Sensing the imminent danger, he braced himself without needing to glance behind. "How fast can you run, Richie?" Matt asked in a faint voice, his tone serious and urgent.

Perceiving his uncle's inquiry as unexpected, Richie turned to face Matt. "Not too shabby, but what's with the sudden interest?" he queried, his curiosity piqued.

Before Richie could grasp the gravity of the situation, his eyes caught sight of a BMW pulling up beside them. Three figures, their faces concealed by balaclavas, emerged from the vehicle with menacing intent.

"Run, Richie!" Matt's urgent command shattered the air, barely giving Richie a moment to react. As one of the assailants lunged at him from the rear driver's side, Matt's instincts surged into action. Swift and precise, Matt sidestepped the attack, his movements honed by years of experience. With a deft twist of his body, he intercepted the assailant's punch, eliciting a sickening crack as the man's arm was forcibly dislocated. The assailant recoiled in agony; his arm rendered useless by Matt's decisive action. Undeterred, Matt remained steadfast, poised to defend against any further aggression with unwavering resolve.

The sudden onslaught caught Richie off guard, his body flooded with adrenaline as he instinctively sprang into action. With a surge of energy, he pivoted on his heels and bolted down the road, his heart pounding with every stride. His feet pounded against the pavement, the rhythm of his steps echoing in the stillness as he disappeared into the distance, a fleeting blur of motion. Determined to outpace his pursuers, Richie navigated the urban terrain with agile precision, ducking around corners and blending seamlessly into the surroundings. His swift evasion highlighted his youthful agility and primal instinct for survival as he vanished into the safety of the unknown.

Meanwhile, Matt quickly assessed the situation, his eyes darting to the approaching assailants. With a split-second decision, he followed Richie's lead and took off running. After an intense moment of sprinting, Matt halted in a nearby street to catch his breath, his body protesting from the sudden burst of exertion. It had been a narrow escape, but Matt knew it was the right choice. Engaging in a brawl on the street was too risky, especially with uncertain odds and potential consequences. He hadn't anticipated relying on Richie's combat skills and preferred to avoid drawing unwanted attention or involving the Police.

Matt glanced around, his eyes scanning the deserted street as he hastily typed out a text message on his mobile. "What was that about? Are you okay?" he sent to Richie, who was still moving on the tracking app, heading away from the area in the direction of Jonesy's flat.

Richie's reply came instantly, "Yeah, I'm fine. Sorry about that. No idea who they were. Thanks for breakfast. See you tomorrow," he responded.

Matt shook his head in disbelief, muttering to himself in a hushed voice, "What have you gotten yourself into, mate?"

Richie, meanwhile, felt a wave of unease wash over him. He had no clue why the men had targeted him, leaving him shaken and wary of the dangerous world he was entangled in. Trust seemed like a luxury he couldn't afford, realising that betrayal lurked around every corner in the drug-dealing realm. With nerves frayed and adrenaline coursing through his veins, he decided it was best to avoid the streets for the time being, especially now that those men might know where he lived. He anticipated Matt's disapproval and resolved to lay low for a while, giving things a chance to cool off.

34 Lingering impacts of action

Mia opened the door, only to be met with Richie's explosive entrance into the flat. His fury crackled in the air like electricity. "It's insane out there; I swear, they're all out to get me," he spat, his voice seething with pent-up rage. The recent confrontation with his assailants loomed large in his mind, the memory of their threats and violence still fresh and raw. In the grip of his own turmoil, Richie failed to register the distress etched on Mia's face. Oblivious to her silent suffering and distant demeanour, his attention remained squarely fixed on his own turbulent emotions, his senses momentarily dulled to the silent agony unfolding right before him.

Mia had become good at masking her feelings and turned away. Taking a short intake of breath, she composed herself and said, "what's up Richie, have you seen or heard from Maxim?" There was a short pause as Richie stood for a moment realising, she was distressed and upset by something. "No, I haven't heard from him, are you Ok Mia?" he asked with concern written over his face. Mia stared at Richie in the shaded light of the flat. Her usually radiant face masked by an unmistakable veil of sadness. Her eyes, once vibrant and sparkling, were now filled with a haunting emptiness. The corners of her mouth drooped, and lines of worry etched themselves upon her face. Her shoulders slumped, burdened by a weight that defied explanation. Even in the dimly lit room, her distress was palpable, casting a shadow over the space that matched the darkness in her heart. She was visibly upset, her entire being a canvas painted with silent anguish, silently begging for someone to notice and offer solace. Her tough exterior had come crashing down in an instant. Tears formed in her sad blue eyes, no longer able to hide the emotions that hid behind her hard shell. It was clear it wasn't time to talk about why she was upset. Instead, he walked towards her, carefully placing his hand on hers while gently encouraging her to sit down next to him. Her hands were shaking and trembling. She was almost paralysed and unable to talk through her fear and sadness. Unsure what to do Richie placed a comforting arm around her shoulder. He felt her tense slightly but did his best to assure her by saying she was going to be OK. He began to rock he back and forth slightly, like a father cradling an upset child.

    She buried her face in his shoulder, her body trembling with the weight of her emotions. The sobs that escaped her were raw and guttural, resonating with a pain that Richie couldn't comprehend. He held her tightly, his arms enveloping her with a protective warmth, silently urging her to release her anguish. As Mia wept, Richie's heart ached in tandem. He gently stroked her hair, offering whispered reassurances, even though he didn't yet understand the source of her pain. He felt the heaviness of her sorrow seeping into his own being, forging an unspoken connection that transcended words. In that moment, all that mattered was being a comforting presence, an anchor for Mia amidst her stormy sea of emotions. Richie held her, providing a safe space where she could unravel her sadness without fear of judgment. Their shared vulnerability created an unbreakable bond, a testament to the power of empathy and human connection. As the tears subsided, Mia's breathing steadied, and she looked up at Richie with eyes reddened and puffy. A mixture of gratitude and uncertainty lingered in her gaze, as if unsure how to articulate the depths of her pain. Richie locked eyes with Mia, his expression a silent vow of unwavering support. He could sense the weight of her unspoken turmoil, a heavy burden he shared in his own heart. He suspected the source of her distress, but hesitated to address it, fearing it might only deepen her pain. Maxim had often lamented about Jonesy's mistreatment of Mia, likening it to that of an arrogant pimp exploiting her vulnerability and dependence on drugs.

Why me," she wailed, her tears flowing unchecked, a torrent of anguish. "What did I do to deserve this wretched existence, to cross paths with those vile, heartless bastards?" He embraced her fiercely, feeling her pain reverberate through her trembling frame. Words failed him in the face of such raw despair, so he held her not really knowing what else he could do or say.

Jonesy's return to the flat, flanked by his two imposing minders, brought an oppressive tension that hung in the air like a suffocating fog. With each step he took, the atmosphere thickened, his brooding aura casting a shadow over the cramped space. An unsettling unease settled over the room as Jonesy's turbulent energy permeated every corner, disrupting the delicate balance among those gathered. His penetrating gaze fixed upon, filled with suspicion, and veiled threats, causing a hush to descend like a heavy blanket. During the tense silence, Jonesy's voice sliced through the air like a knife, dripping with fury as he demanded answers, leaving no room for evasion or hesitation.

"What have you done with the gun, Richie?" Jonesy's words cut through the air, each syllable carrying a weighty accusation. His words hung there, a palpable threat that echoed in the silence. The intensity of his demand sent a shiver down Riche's spine, a chilling reminder of the dangerous territory he unwittingly stepped into. He shifted uncomfortably, the weight of anxiety settling heavily upon his shoulders. His eyes darted around the room, desperately seeking an escape from the unyielding scrutiny. He knew the stakes were high, and the consequences of his actions could have far-reaching implications. But fear gripped him tightly, leaving him struggling to find the right words, his voice trapped in the grip of a guilty conscience.

Jonesy's impatience grew, his impulsive nature threatening to erupt into a storm of fury. The tension in the room was palpable, a coiled energy ready to explode at any moment. He stepped closer to Richie, his menacing presence dwarfing the room, as if daring him to defy his authority.

In a moment laden with significance, Richie's voice quivered as he confessed, "I've stashed it away safely since my arrest."

Jonesy's response, delivered with an unsettling calmness, caught Richie off guard. "You needn't fret about Maxim anymore," he said, his words hanging in the air like a veiled threat.

The implications swirled in Richie's mind as he met Jonesy's gaze, searching for any hint of what lay beneath his composed facade. Was Maxim disposed of? The silence stretched, amplifying Richie's apprehension.

Summoning his courage, Richie dared to probe further, his voice betraying his naivety. "Where's Maxim?"

Jonesy's stare bore into Richie, sending shivers down his spine. "You know what I despise, Richie?" he asked, his tone dripping with menace. "Betrayal. And Maxim? He's betrayed us. Now, take out your phone and message him. Ask him where he is. Do it now!" he shouted.

Richie fumbled for his phone, fingers trembling as he complied. A faint buzz emanated from Jonesy's pocket, drawing everyone's attention. With a theatrical flourish, he revealed a battered iPhone, its cracked screen a testament to its tumultuous history. As Jonesy scrolled through the messages, his voice rose to a crescendo of anger. "Seems like you and Maxim had quite the scheme, didn't you?" he thundered. Before Richie could react, a minder lunged forward, delivering a punishing blow that left him reeling.

Darkness descended upon Richie's consciousness like a heavy curtain, as the forceful impact of the blow landed squarely on his jaw. In an instant, his world spun out of control, his body losing all sense of balance and stability. Colours blurred, sounds faded into a distant haze, and his body surrendered to the overwhelming force of gravity. Falling backward, he succumbed to the unconscious realm, where time stood still and the world around him faded into oblivion. The pain, the chaos, and the confusion dissolved into nothingness as Richie's mind slipped into an abyss of black, leaving him suspended in an eerie stillness.

35 Lost connection

In the dim light of his garage, the scent of gasoline and grease mingled, adding to the cloak of secrecy enveloping Matt. His tracking app had been buzzing incessantly for the past fifteen minutes, a persistent reminder of the unfolding situation. Straining to listen, he caught fragments of a conversation between Jonesy and Richie, enough to sense danger looming for the latter. Yet uncertainty gnawed at him, did Richie still have his phone? The tracker indicated Richie's phone was moving toward Trafford Park, a sprawling industrial area on the city's fringes, Matt's anxiety spiked. He glanced at the tracker for the Mercedes, but it remained unresponsive, its last known location linked with Richie's phone.

Too soon to involve the police, Matt weighed his options carefully. Drawing the cops into the fray would only complicate matters, potentially jeopardising his own standing. His priority lay in extricating Richie from harm's way, a task that demanded discretion and precision.

With practiced hands, he set about swapping the number plates on his hire car, opting for clones associated with a similar Ford Focus registered in the Northeast. It was a calculated move to evade the omnipresent Automatic Number Plate Recognition (ANPR) cameras saturating the city, a crucial detail in maintaining his anonymity. Though uneasy about resorting to such measures, Matt rationalised his actions as a form of vigilante justice. In his eyes, he wasn't a criminal but rather a guardian of the streets, determined to shield his nephew and others from the clutches of ruthless gangs. In a world where technology could be both ally and adversary, he knew that meticulous planning and pre-emptive measures were his best defence against the encroaching threat.

Under the flickering light of a single bulb, Matt's brow furrowed with determination as he delicately removed the screws securing the original plates. Each twist of the screwdriver echoed in the confined space, a constant reminder of the risk he was taking. Sweat dotted his forehead as he carefully detached the plates, the weight of the task amplifying the weight on his shoulders. Matt affixed the new plates, aligning them exactly right to ensure authenticity. His eyes darted anxiously towards the garage door; his ears attuned to any sound that might signal an unwanted visitor. Every click of the screws tightening brought him one step closer to anonymity, one step further away from detection.

As he worked, a mixture of fear and determination coursed through his veins. He knew the stakes were high, the consequences severe if he was caught. But desperation fuelled his actions, compelling him to take risks he never thought he would need again. The cold metal of the cloned number plates gleamed under the dim light, almost mocking in their deceptive nature. His mind raced with thoughts of the future, of the potential freedom that awaited if his plan succeeded. He knew that every detail had to be flawless, every aspect of his escape meticulously calculated.

As the final screw tightened, Matt took a step back, his breath catching in his throat. The sight of the altered car filled him with a mix of relief and trepidation. He knew that this was just one piece of the puzzle, one step in a much larger plan. But in that moment, as the garage remained cloaked in secrecy, Matt found a glimmer of hope, a flicker of optimism that he could outmanoeuvre the forces that sought to anger him.

Matt carefully placed a pristine "day sack" onto the front seat of his car, its contents crucial for the tasks ahead. With precision, he adjusted the sun visors, obscuring any prying eyes from peeking inside. Positioned neatly beside the pack lay a pair of dark glasses, a rugged olive-green hat, and a striking black and white "Shemagh" scarf, a disguise to cloak his identity amidst Manchester's vigilant surveillance. Drawing a steadying breath, Matt extinguished the flickering light in the garage, shrouding the space once more in darkness. The gravity of his decisions hung heavy upon him as he re-entered the house, steeling himself for the challenges that lay ahead, resolute in his determination to confront the uncertainties head-on.

Armed with determination and a digital map at his fingertips, Matt embarked on a virtual journey to locate the elusive building nestled within the vast expanse of a sprawling industrial estate. He fired up his computer and opened Google Maps, zooming in on the area that held the secrets of his quest.

As he moved the cursor, the screen transformed into an aerial view, revealing the intricate web of roads, buildings, and open spaces. Matt scanned the landscape, searching for tell-tale signs that would lead him to his destination. He zoomed in further, taking in every detail, hoping to spot any recognisable landmarks or distinguishing features. With a few deft clicks and drags of the mouse, he adjusted the view and switched to Google Earth, plunging into a three-dimensional world that brought the industrial estate to life. The immersive imagery allowed him to explore the area from different angles, as if he were flying above it. He surveyed the vast expanse of the industrial estate, its large layout presenting a challenge. Old Trafford Football Ground and the Imperial War Museum were good reference points to use when closing in on his target building. But Matt was undeterred. He utilised the search function, typing in keywords that might lead him closer to the building's whereabouts. Each search narrowed the possibilities, filtering out irrelevant results and homing in on potential matches. His eyes scanned the screen, scrutinising the buildings, their shapes, colours, and sizes. He mentally cross-referenced the imagery with any available information he had about the old garage, hoping for a visual connection that would confirm his findings. There were plenty of other good landmarks in the area and Matt began to familiarise himself with them all. Finally, as if the digital realm conspired to aid his search, Matt's gaze landed upon a structure. Nestled amidst a cluster of industrial buildings, the old garage stood out with its weathered facade and distinctive roofline. It was a serendipitous discovery, a needle in the virtual haystack. With a surge of excitement, Matt captured the coordinates, noting down the address and the best route to access the industrial estate. The digital tools had served their purpose, revealing the hidden gem that had eluded him.

Matt understood the advantage he held in operating across the border of two police districts. However, he also recognised the daunting challenges law enforcement faced in this dynamic landscape. The lack of standardised jurisdictional protocols and varying capabilities among different counties created loopholes eagerly exploited by criminals. Insufficient resources and coordination hindered the exchange of vital information, hampering efforts to track and apprehend offenders. Moreover, the adaptable nature of criminal networks and the ease of transportation further compounded the difficulty in anticipating and intercepting cross-border movements. These obstacles highlighted the urgent need for improved collaboration, intelligence sharing, and targeted strategies to counteract the fluidity of criminal activities spanning county lines. While police forces operated within defined boundaries, criminals operated with impunity across them, an asymmetry Matt was poised to exploit tonight.

Navigating into Trafford Park under the cloak of night seemed a manageable task. Matt anticipated transitioning to a stealthier approach as he neared his target, a two-story workshop with apparent drive-in access from the main road, leading to its rear. Surrounded by warehouse units and shielded by six-foot brick walls, the building epitomised the typical industrial estate layout. Skips scattered in the vicinity offered potential cover points, provided they hadn't been removed since the satellite images were captured. As Matt scrutinised the satellite imagery, a plan began to take shape in his mind, honed by his military expertise. He meticulously identified rendezvous points, potential threats, entry and exit routes, reconnaissance strategies, and contingency plans all while maintaining a covert presence. Detailed examination of the building revealed a roller shutter entrance at the rear of the workshop, secured outside regular working hours. An exterior stairwell ascended to a blue access door situated above the workshop, hinting at an entry point from the rooftop accessible via a small mezzanine balcony. Despite the satellite images being six months old, Matt was startled to observe a Mercedes parked at the rear of the premises. a vehicle matching the colour and model associated with Jonesy. This discovery bolstered Matt's confidence in his connection between Jonesy and the workshop.

  With his analysis of the target building complete, Matt shifted his focus to mapping out his approach. Zooming in on street view, he meticulously scanned for potential threats, eager to acquaint himself with the area's surveillance infrastructure. Contemplating the possibility of rescuing Richie, Matt knew he needed a comprehensive plan. He mulled over his potential responses to various scenarios, how to manage challenges, what to do if stopped by the police, how to react if Richie was injured or incapacitated by his captors. And, critically, he pondered his ability to extract Richie, should the need arise. Matt couldn't take any risks and studied the area of approach relentlessly. What obstacles could he expect to face? Would he have to cross any major roads? If so, did this mean a further risk from a camera? He had to think of every eventuality. If someone ended up dead, then the police would throw their resources into an investigation. Matt needed to make it impossible for them to identify him should anything go wrong. His self-questioning made him think about masking Richie's identity. Richie's recent encounter with the law had left Matt wary, especially considering the possibility of being recognised. The police mug shot, a lingering reminder of that brush with authority, now posed a significant risk of identification. Aware of the rapid advancements in facial recognition and artificial intelligence, Matt couldn't afford to underestimate the potential threat they posed. While not fully comprehending the intricacies of such technology, he understood enough to recognise it as a looming danger. If social media could effectively utilize facial recognition, then it was all but certain that law enforcement agencies possessed the capability as well.

Armed with the newfound knowledge, Matt closed the maps and prepared for the tangible mission that lay ahead. He knew that the digital world was just the beginning, a means to an end. Now, equipped with the information gleaned from his virtual exploration, he was ready to step out into the real world, to track down the old garage building and unlock the secrets it held within its worn walls. Having gone over and over all the possible situations and eventualities Matt decided to grab something to eat, get changed and ready himself. He had carefully selected what he was going to wear which was all designed to reduce his fibre signature. This wasn't a failsafe process, but he was trying hard to mitigate and reduce traces of his presence.

36 In the Clutches of Darkness

Richie eyes fluttered open to the bright glare of lights, the hazy fog of unconsciousness slowly dissipating. As awareness trickled back into his consciousness, confusion clutched at his mind like a vice. The surroundings were unfamiliar, a decrepit garage with an unsettling ambiance, the air thick with a mix of oil and tension. Pain pulsed through his body, a stark reminder of the violence that had transpired. He instinctively tried to move, only to find himself restrained, his hands bound tightly behind his back. Panic welled within him, the realisation of his dire predicament crashing down like a tidal wave. Memories flickered in fragmented flashes, a sudden punch, the sound of scuffling, the suffocating grip of a gloved hand. The gang had taken him, snatched him away from the safety of his own life and thrust him into this nightmarish ordeal. He felt pain at the back of his eye socket. He wasn't sure if this pain came from the lights or his memory of being punch hard in the face. His initial reaction was to face the ground and close his eyes to shield them from the brightness. Richie confused, realised he was seated on a rigid plastic chair and sensed movement from the shadows around him. His hands were bound together behind his back by zip ties which dug mercilessly into his wrists, biting into his flesh with each subtle movement. Every twist and turn sent waves of pain shooting up Richie's arms, a constant reminder of his captivity and powerlessness. Every attempt to find a more comfortable position only resulted in increased discomfort and numbness. His shoes had been removed from his feet and all that remained of his clothing was his Jeans, socks, and T Shirt. He heard metal clanking as if a door had been opened to the outside followed by a chill of a breeze. He started to shiver uncontrollably.

Richie strained against his restraints, assessing their limits with futile resistance. The echoes of his desperate struggles reverberated through the empty garage, a silent cry for help. But the cold reality settled upon him, there was no escape, no immediate rescue. He was alone, trapped in the clutches of his captors. Questions flooded Richie's mind, each one more haunting than the last. Why had he been targeted? What did they want from him? The uncertainty gnawed at his thoughts, amplifying his fear and fire of desperation within him. In the dimness of the garage, Richie's senses strained to gather any clue, any hint of his captors' intentions. The faint scent of diesel lingered in the air, mingling with the tang of fear. The sound of distant footsteps echoed their rhythm a haunting reminder of his captors' presence nearby. He strained to catch fragments of conversation, voices muffled and distorted, yet laced with an undercurrent of menace.

    The first bucket of freezing icy water crashed against Richie's body like a merciless wave, instantaneously robbing him of breath. The shock was immediate and all encompassing, a jarring assault on his senses. The icy tendrils of water penetrated deep into his being, numbing his skin, and sending shivers coursing through his veins. In that split second, time seemed to stand still. His muscles tensed and his heart raced, as if bracing for impact. The frigid water clung to him like a suffocating embrace, penetrating every pore with its icy touch. It felt as though his very essence had been submerged in an arctic abyss. The sudden and extreme temperature shift was an assault on his body, evoking an instinctive reaction to protect himself. Goosebumps erupted across his skin, each hair standing on end in a futile attempt to trap warmth. His teeth chattered uncontrollably, a symphony of involuntary shivers that reverberated through his body.

    As the initial shock subsided, a bone-deep coldness settled in, seeping into his bones, and permeating every fibre of his being. It was an otherworldly sensation, a reminder of vulnerability and the sheer power of icy water. It was as if the freezing water had insinuated itself into his very core, leaving him raw and exposed. The discomfort lingered, an unwelcome guest that refused to leave. His limbs felt heavy and unresponsive, burdened by the weight of the cold. It was a constant reminder of his tormentors' sadistic intent, an attempt to break him, both physically and mentally.

Yet, amidst the torment, Richie fought to maintain his resilience. Each onslaught of freezing water only fuelled his determination to endure the storm with unwavering resolve. Though battered and chilled to the bone, a flicker of defiance burned within him, a refusal to succumb to their cruelty. In the face of the freezing onslaught, Richie drew upon his inner strength. He summoned the embers of his spirit, stoking them to forge a shield against the bitter cold. The icy assault may have chilled his body, but it could not extinguish the fire that burned within his soul.

With each successive drenching, Richie braced himself against the onslaught, steeling his resolve as the icy water tested his endurance. He fought to steady his breathing, striving to regain control after the initial shock of the cold hit. As his eyes adjusted to the dimness of the room, Richie's gaze fell upon the backs of three figures making their exit. The space around him reeked of grime and decay, resembling an abandoned car workshop frozen in time. Silence hung heavy, broken only by the distant rumble of passing cars outside. Refocusing his attention, Richie's heart sank as he took in the scene before him. Across the workshop, bound and gagged to another chair, lay a topless figure, his head bowed and chin resting on his chest. Blood trickled from his face, forming crimson rivulets that pooled at his feet. Deep, weeping burn marks marred his chest and arms, a testament to unspeakable torment. Shock coursed through Richie as he grappled with the horrifying sight before him. The man appeared lifeless, or at the very least, grievously injured a stark reminder of the perilous situation in which Richie found himself.

Richie called out softly, "Hey mate, you Ok."

The man's breaths came in shallow gasps as he lifted his head, locking eyes with Richie. Despite the severity of the bruises and swelling disfiguring his face, Richie sensed a flicker of recognition in the man's gaze. Maxim, once unrecognisable due to the savage beating inflicted upon him by his captors, now bore the marks of their brutality blood and mucus mingling on his battered features. Struggling against the tape that bound his mouth shut, Maxim's eyes widened in alarm at the sight of Richie, his attempts at speech stifled by the constriction. Desperation radiated from him in grunts and snorts, a primal urge to convey a message. Petrified, Richie gazed back, unaware that the injured and disfigured figure before him was his friend. The realisation that Jonesy, known for his erratic behaviour, could stoop to such depths of violence sent a chill down Richie's spine. He watched Maxim's distress escalate, his futile attempts at communication fading into exhausted silence as he struggled to cling to life. The room grew eerily quiet, prompting Richie to strain his ears in hopes of deciphering any sound. Faint murmurs and movements from the adjacent room filtered through the silence, casting a chilling atmosphere over the scene. The callous indifference of those nearby, laughing amidst the agony of a dying man. How could anyone find amusement in such a harrowing situation? Abruptly, the entrance burst open, three figures shrouded in dark masks stormed into the room. One of them, bearing the unmistakable air of authority, strode menacingly towards Richie, demanding answers regarding the whereabouts of the missing money.

 As tension thickened, Jonesy's simmering rage boiled over, culminating in a dramatic unveiling as he ripped off his mask, revealing a face marred by the scars of a tumultuous life a sight that chilled Richie to the core.

 Richie spluttered a response and Jonesy's anger simmered like a volcano on the verge of eruption. His features contorted in fury, his eyes ablaze with an intense fire that seemed to consume his very being. Every muscle in his body tensed, coiled like a tightly wound spring, ready to unleash a storm of rage upon Richie. His brows furrowed into deep creases, etching lines of wrath upon his forehead. The veins in his temples pulsed with every beat of his raging heart, veins that seemed ready to burst with the sheer intensity of his fury. His jaw clenched; teeth gritted in a primal display of his boiling emotions. In his anger, Jonesy exuded an unsettling aura of power. His presence commanded attention, demanding submission from all who dared to cross his path. His body radiated a restless energy, as if the very air around him crackled with the electric charge of his wrath. His voice, usually steady and controlled, now carried the undertones of a thunderous storm. Each word dripped with venom, laced with an unmistakable menace that sent shivers down the spines of those unfortunate enough to be in his presence.

Richie shivered from the cold and fear. He sensed Jonesy was out of control but heard a mobile ringing. Jonesy turned and looked across at a bench where it was located. He casually walked across, picked it up and saw the caller was Mia. "What's up?"

Mia was caught off guard when she recognised Jonesy's voice.

"What do you want, Richie is busy now and can't talk?

"What is happening to him", she pleaded.

Jonesy replied with a smile "nah he's tied up at the moment so won't be with you tonight, so you take care of business at Robs flat and I'll see you right."

Mia felt deflated that she was going to be alone tonight, and that Jonesy expected her to take care of dealing. She let out a deep sigh acknowledging Jonesy, "Ok, see you later."

Jonesy finished the call without ceremony, before reverting his attention back to his victims.

Maxim was slumped in his chair, his body battered and broken. Bruises adorned his face like a grotesque canvas of pain, the hues of purples and blues serving as a haunting reminder of the relentless assault he had endured. Exhaustion weighed heavily upon Maxim's limbs and his muscles trembled with the effort to hold on, to cling to the last shreds of his willpower. The voice of defeat whispered seductively in his ear, tempting him to yield, to relinquish his fight.

Jonesy nodded to his minders and they both approached Maxim. One grabbed Maxims hair and pulled his head back while the second male took out a handgun and proceed to pistol whip Maxim across the face with two sharp excruciating blows. Maxim made small groans after each dreadful blow. The dull thuds were horrific and reverberated across the room. Richie starred in horror watching the brutality. The male let go of Maxim's hair and his head slumped forward with no resistance.

****

Matt drove with purpose, his every move imbued with urgency yet cloaked in a veil of calm. With his cap pulled low to conceal his features, he embraced the mantle of anonymity. In this moment, his entire being was consumed by a singular objective he was a man on a mission.

37 A final Act

Tears streamed down Mia's cheeks as she stumbled out of Jonesy's flat, her body still reeling from the harrowing ordeal she had endured only hours before. Despite the hot water of the shower, she couldn't shake off the lingering sense of despair that clung to her like a suffocating fog. Loneliness weighed heavy on her shoulders, a burden she couldn't seem to shake. In the silence of her own company, Mia felt utterly isolated, as if stranded in a vast ocean of emptiness. Each passing moment magnified her feelings of disconnection, leaving her adrift in a world devoid of solace or companionship. The crushing weight of her emotions threatened to consume her, casting her life into a bleak landscape devoid of joy or warmth. With no one to share her pain or offer a comforting embrace, Mia felt vulnerable and alone, trapped within the confines of her own despair. The walls of loneliness loomed large around her, their impenetrable barrier casting a shadow over even the faintest glimmer of hope. Desperate for a lifeline, Mia longed for a beam of light to guide her through the darkness, a reminder that she was not alone in her struggle.

As Mia trudged through the wintry night to Rob's flat, a bone-deep chill seemed to seep into her very soul. Her trembling intensified, fuelled not only by the biting cold but also by the gnawing craving for another hit of drugs. Though Rob greeted her warmly, his kindness failed to penetrate the fog of despair enveloping her. Offering a perfunctory hello and a forced smile, Mia busied herself with preparing a hot drink, desperate to numb her pain with the familiar haze of intoxication. It was a fleeting escape from the crushing weight of self-pity, agony, and isolation that threatened to engulf her. Surrounded by her own turmoil, Mia's thoughts drifted to Richie, his vulnerability weighing heavily on her mind.

Something about Jonesy's recent behaviour unsettled her, why did he have it in for Richie? The nagging sense of unease grew stronger with each passing moment, a foreboding shadow looming over her already troubled thoughts.

As Mia squeezed a tea bag into her cup, a sharp knock interrupted the quiet of Rob's flat. Before Mia could even register the sound, Rob had swung open the door to reveal a young man in a hoodie, who simply thrust a plastic-wrapped bundle into Rob's hands with the instruction, "Give this to Mia." Rob examined the package with a furrowed brow before closing the door, his expression a mix of confusion and concern. "What's this?" he demanded as he entered the kitchen, his tone heavy with apprehension. Despite his cognitive challenges stemming from past injuries, Rob knew all too well what the bundle contained. "This is drugs, isn't it?"

Without waiting for confirmation, Rob slammed the package onto the table with a forceful gesture. "I can't believe you have this, Mia. Why would it come here?" Mia met Rob's gaze, her voice barely above a whisper as she replied, "I'm sorry, Rob. Someone asked me to hold onto it for them. But don't worry, it's not staying here." Her words were tinged with regret as she attempted to reassure Rob, though the weight of the situation hung heavy between them.

Rob's demeanour shifted as if a sudden realisation dawned upon him. "I don't want you here if you're going to bring that awful stuff with you," he declared, pointing accusatorily at the package. Mia's heart sank at Rob's words. Even her friendship with someone like Rob, with his learning difficulties, seemed to be slipping away. With a heavy heart, she gathered the package and silently exited the house, feeling the weight of disappointment settle upon her shoulders.

****

Dorset Court stood as a testament to the struggles of its time, a typical 1960s council-owned tower block housing a diverse array of tenants. Within its walls resided a spectrum of characters, ranging from the good to the bad, and even the truly terrible. Neglect and decay had etched their marks upon its dilapidated facade, reflecting the economic hardships endured by the community it sheltered. Once vibrant hues had long since surrendered to the relentless march of time, leaving behind a dreary palette of greys and browns. Broken windows punctuated its exterior like jagged scars, bearing witness to the harsh realities unfolding within. The intercom system, a vital link to the outside world, had fallen silent months ago, granting unrestricted access to all who sought entry. The pervasive scent of dampness and neglect hung heavy in the air, seeping into the lives of those who called Dorset Court home. Inside, cramped and poorly maintained living spaces offered little respite from the relentless struggles of poverty. Creaking doors echoed through dimly lit hallways, while flickering lights cast eerie shadows upon worn-out carpets. Residents faced the daily ordeal of navigating countless flights of stairs, the unreliable elevator serving as a cruel reminder of their plight. Dorset Court stood as a sombre symbol of the social inequality and deprivation plaguing inner cities, a stark reminder of the uphill battle for those trapped in its unforgiving embrace.

Mia understood Flat One Hundred and Twenty on the fifteenth floor had become a notorious local crack house, a haven for society's forgotten souls to escape their harsh realities through drugs. The place reeked of squalor and despair, embodying the depths of degradation. To Mia's relief, the flat stood empty, its grim interior a stark reminder of the lives it had consumed. With the front door left insecure, gaining access was a simple task. Though she possessed all of Jonesy's gear, Mia had no intention of peddling it for profit.

It wasn't long before Mia surrendered to the heroin's embrace, swiftly followed by a handful of amphetamine tablets. As the drugs coursed through her veins, she was whisked away from the harsh realities of her conscious world into a hazy, translucent realm. Enveloped in a surreal fog, her senses were heightened, as if she had stepped into a distorted dimension beyond comprehension. Within this altered state, the walls of her surroundings pulsated with vibrant hues, alive with a rhythmic energy that transcended the confines of reality. Colours melded and shifted before her eyes, weaving a mesmerizing tapestry of intricate patterns that defied logic and reason. Time lost all meaning as Mia was swept away on an endless tide of sensations, detached from the constraints of the physical world. Whispers of voices danced in the air, their cryptic messages teasing her consciousness with hidden meanings and revelations. Weightless and untethered, Mia floated on an ethereal current, her body tingling with euphoria and introspection. Among the swirling chaos, moments of profound clarity emerged, offering fleeting glimpses into the depths of her subconscious. In this surreal dreamscape, fictional friends extended hands of friendship, offering solace and companionship in a world fraught with violence and despair. As Mia drifted further from reality, a sense of warmth and peace washed over her, laughter bubbling up from within as she surrendered to the embrace of total happiness.

She could feel herself rising to her feet as wind came rushing over her face making her feel alive. Then there was a moment of utter stillness like her life had been paused. For a moment she heard distant voices of adults shouting "No, No, No." Mia felt safe and in a place of happiness away from the darkness of her life. Wind raced through her hair, and she felt a falling sensation. There was no weight to her body, and she was in a perfect place…… until she smashed onto the concrete pavement outside Dorset court.

The fall proved fatal as Mia plummeted from the 15th-story balcony window, her world shattering in an instant. It was a fall from which she could never hope to survive, another tragic casualty of drug-induced despair. As she tumbled towards her demise, a young man and woman witnessed her perilous descent, their frantic pleas falling on deaf ears as Mia made the fateful decision to leap. In the agonising moments that followed, the couple could only avert their gaze in horror, their hearts heavy with helplessness. With trembling hands, they reached for their phones, dialling emergency services in a desperate bid to summon aid. But despite their efforts, Mia's fate had been sealed, leaving behind only shattered lives and unanswered questions in her wake.

38 Watch and Move

Matt approached the outskirts of Trafford Park, opting for an indirect route through Eccles to evade the watchful gaze of the major motorways and ubiquitous CCTV cameras. The last thing he needed was a curious police officer or a random stop check, which could spell disaster. While explaining his altered car registration plates might be plausible, a thorough search would undoubtedly uncover the fully loaded handgun concealed within his jacket, a scenario he dared not entertain. Hours spent poring over Google Earth had afforded Matt a detailed understanding of the area, allowing him to commit key landmarks to memory. By skirting major hubs like the Trafford Shopping Centre and navigating quieter roads into the estate, he minimized the risk of detection and identification.

Nestled within Trafford Park, the "Ground Works" sprawled as a vast wooded eco area, located approximately one kilometre from the target building. Though not as close as he had hoped, Matt knew the distance afforded a measure of safety, yet posed potential complications in case of injury or urgent retreat. His experience had taught him to expect the unexpected; no operation ever unfolded flawlessly, and improvisation was often required on the fly. Selecting a secluded spot near a grove of trees, Matt brought the car to a halt and silenced the engine. With a quick check of his mobile confirming Richie's presence at the target building, he switched the device to silent mode, allowing his senses to acclimate to the enveloping darkness. Donning his olive hat and "Shemagh" scarf, Matt ensured they obscured the lower part of his face, concealing his identity. With a reassuring pat to the concealed handgun nestled within his jacket, he confirmed its accessibility, should the need arise. Grabbing his daysack, Matt exited the car, pocketing the keys as he stepped onto the cold pavement. The night air was crisp and chilly, punctuated by the distant hum of city traffic, lending an eerie backdrop to his clandestine mission.

With a cautious glance around, Matt set off with a determined stride. Staying close to the building lines, he slipped into the shadows, mindful of the watchful eyes that might be tracking his every move. Each structure he passed boasted sturdy fencing, imposing walls, and vigilant security lights, an arsenal of deterrents tested by Manchester's criminal underworld. Matt had to assume that every corner was monitored, every step scrutinised. Brightly lit units posed a challenge, forcing him to move swiftly through these exposed areas, adopting the guise of a weary worker heading home. He moved with the practiced precision of a seasoned soldier, his steps purposeful and resolute. Every movement was deliberate, every pause calculated as he navigated the estate's labyrinthine pathways. He paused frequently, assessing potential threats, and weighing risks, acutely aware of the consequences of being caught in the wrong place at the wrong time. Matt's eyes scanned the surroundings, attuned to the rhythm of the city, ever vigilant in his quest to blend seamlessly into the urban landscape. Though urgency pulsed through his veins, he resisted the temptation to break into a run, opting instead for a controlled pace that masked his true intentions. His body language spoke of determination, yet it was tempered with a quiet confidence that betrayed no hint of recklessness. As he moved with purpose, Matt remained a shadow in motion, his presence barely registering amidst the hustle and bustle of the estate. His senses were heightened, his focus unwavering as he navigated the maze of streets with practiced ease. Every choice of clothing, every careful step, was a testament to his mastery of subtlety, a skill honed through years of training and experience.

Though driven by urgency, Matt moved with the patience of a hunter stalking his prey, his movements shrouded in secrecy. He was a man on a mission, his determination burning bright beneath a facade of calmness and composure. With each step, he drew closer to his goal, his resolve unwavering as he vanished into the night, a phantom in pursuit of his elusive quarry.

Matt soon warmed from his physical efforts. He knew the risks tonight but felt at home with the adrenaline rush this type of action brought him. The allure of adrenaline surged through Matt's veins, overpowering his senses, and dominating his thoughts. The rush he experienced was like a drug, releasing a surge of endorphins and dopamine that provided him with an intense sense of euphoria. The feeling of his heart racing, the surge of energy coursing through his body, and the heightened state of awareness all combined to create an addictive cocktail that he had missed. Was this the reason why so many veterans struggled after service? Emulating the adrenaline rush experienced during operations proved challenging, impossible to replicate in civilian life.

Matt's steady progress brought him within a mere two hundred meters of the target building. With a cautious eye, he slowed his pace, scanning the vicinity for the optimal approach. His attention was drawn to a modern recruitment building that stood out among the aging architecture of Trafford Park, its sleek facade contrasting sharply with the surrounding decay. Positioned adjacent to a desolate wasteland doubling as a makeshift car park, the recruitment building marked the transition into the older sector of Trafford Park. Here, the modern prefab structures gave way to weathered brick buildings, their worn exteriors a testament to years of neglect. The landscape morphed before Matt's eyes, transforming from orderly streets into a maze of decrepit alleys and scrapyards. Piles of discarded tires and scrap metal littered the terrain, casting eerie shadows in the moonlight. Yet, undeterred by the rugged surroundings, Matt pressed forward, navigating the obstacles with ease. As he approached his target, determination blazed in Matt's eyes. The change in architectural style posed no obstacle to his mission; he moved with purpose, undeterred by the shifting landscape. With every step, he drew closer to his objective, his resolve unshakable amidst the desolation of Trafford Park.

As the ambient lighting dimmed, shadows lengthened, providing Matt with ample cover to advance stealthily. Taking advantage of the growing darkness, he halted beside a heap of weathered car panels, their rusted surfaces blending seamlessly with the night. From this vantage point, he surveyed his surroundings with a keen eye, attuned to even the slightest movement. The scene before him held a palpable tension, every rustle and distant sound magnified in the stillness of the night. Expectantly, Matt strained to discern any signs of activity at the target location. His senses heightened, he listened intently, his ears pricked for any telltale sound that might betray the presence of his adversaries. Despite the cacophony of traffic in the distance, Matt remained focused, his determination unwavering. He knew he had to press on, closing the distance to the target building and uncovering the truth that lay within its walls.

Matt spotted an aged skip nestled within the rear compound. Scaling the wall, he dropped quietly into the yard, seeking cover behind the bulky container. The air was heavy with the pungent scent of old fuel, its lingering presence clinging to the soles of his boots like an unwelcome reminder of the site's neglect. Surveying the surroundings, Matt couldn't shake the feeling of unease that settled over him. The dilapidated yard bore all the hallmarks of neglect, with its dishevelled appearance and lingering odour.

The suspicious nature of the activity unfolding in the yard was not lost on Matt. Manchester's reputation for car theft echoed in his mind, yet the choice of location seemed peculiar. Positioned conspicuously in the heart of an industrial estate, it was a brazen move that defied conventional logic. He mused, their audacity was their greatest asset, hiding in plain sight amidst the chaos of the urban landscape.

On his right were a couple of curtained trailer units adjacent to a wall. To his left was a half-dismantled lorry cab and chassis unit that hadn't been moved in years. The once mighty vehicle now sat forlornly in a desolate compound, its faded paint and rusty exterior telling the story of its abandonment. Tall grass and wild weeds had made their home within its confines, intertwining with the decaying remnants of what was once a bustling truck. The cab, once a symbol of industry and movement, now stood as a relic of a bygone era. Its windows, once clear and transparent, were shattered and covered in a veil of dirt and grime. Nature, with its relentless persistence, had found a way to reclaim this forgotten piece of machinery. Weeds and plants had forced their way through cracks in the cab's metal, their tendrils reaching out like searching fingers, as if trying to bring life back to this abandoned shell. Green shoots and leaves sprouted from every crevice, weaving a tapestry of nature's resilience within this mechanical skeleton.

To Matt this was the ideal spot to monitor the building. Getting right under the nose of a target was often the best means of avoiding detection. An obvious place to hide often became undiscerning to the preoccupied like Jonesy. Matt assumed a position under the empty cab and huddled under his concealed damp observation point, his eyes fixed on the unassuming building across from him. The anticipation coiled within him, fuelling his determination as he focused on the task at hand. In the darkness, Matt strained his eyes, trying to discern the shapes of two vehicles parked near the base of the stairwell. It was difficult to make out details, and he couldn't confirm if one of them was Jonesy's Mercedes. The silhouette bore a striking resemblance, but without his tracker, he couldn't be certain. A sense of frustration prickled at his skin, mingling with the cold sweat that dampened his body. As the chill of the night wrapped around him like a suffocating blanket, Matt felt an icy shiver creep into his bones. Each gust of wind penetrated deeper, stealing the warmth from his body, and leaving him vulnerable to the biting cold. His fingers grew numb and clumsy, a stark reminder of the harsh reality of winter's grip. Despite the discomfort, Matt refused to let the cold deter him. Memories of harsher climates and unforgiving conditions flooded his mind, transporting him back to the desolate landscapes of Afghanistan. Yet, even as doubt whispered in his ear, he remained resolute, unwilling to let the frosty embrace of winter sabotage his mission. With gritted teeth and a steely resolve, Matt pushed through the chill, his determination unwavering. He buried himself deeper into his jacket, bracing himself against the biting wind, focused solely on the task ahead.

    Matt exercised patience, his senses on high alert as he strained to catch any sound in the silence. Gradually, a distant voice pierced through the stillness, faint yet unmistakable. It wasn't a natural noise, and Matt's instincts told him something was amiss. The sporadic nature of the yelling only heightened his concern. The echoes of captivity resonated within him, a grim reminder of his own harrowing experience. He knew all too well the horrors that awaited someone held against their will. The thought of Richie enduring such torment made Matt's blood run cold. In the world of drug dealing, compassion was a rare commodity, and those in power showed no mercy to their victims. Matt harboured no illusions about the ruthless nature of these criminals. To them, it was all about control and dominance, with little regard for the suffering they inflicted upon others. As the distant cries echoed in the night, Matt readied himself for the daunting task ahead, determined to rescue Richie from the clutches of these dangerous individuals.

39 Unseen Death

Jonesy's imposing figure loomed over Richie, his anger palpable in the air. Flanked by his two henchmen, he glared menacingly at the bound figure before him. Richie's eyes darted nervously between Jonesy and the unconscious form of Maxim, slumped forward in his chair. With a menacing tone, Jonesy jabbed his finger towards Maxim. "You see what happens to those who cross me?" he growled, his voice dripping with malice. "If you want to avoid ending up like him, you better start talking. Where is my damn money?"

Richie's heart pounded in his chest as he struggled against his restraints, the fear of Jonesy's wrath coursing through him. But even in the face of danger, he remained defiant, refusing to give in to the demands of his captor.

"I don't know what you are talking about, Richie pleaded.

"Of course, you fucking do, you're his running mate and I don't believe he hasn't said anything to you."

Richie's mind raced as he grappled with the weight of his silence. He knew all too well that the Mohammed brothers had played a role in Maxim's betrayal and the disappearance of the cash. Yet, the grip of fear held him tight, rendering him unable to utter a single word. He understood the consequences of speaking up, more violence, more pain. In the tense silence that followed, Jonesy's gaze bore into Richie, demanding a response that never materialised. The air crackled with tension as Richie's silence spoke volumes, each passing moment fraught with the threat of imminent retribution.

"Come on then, you little shit, whose side are you on. Tell me! Fucking well tell me! If you don't, Mattie fucking bollocks over there is going to lose his."

With hesitation Richie quietly replied, "I don't know."

Jonesy did not want to hear this response and struggled to quell his anger. He turned, stepped away two paces and grabbed a large wooden handled machete, before storming over to Maxim.

Reaching him he pressed the blade against his neck. Maxim was barely conscious and in too much pain to react. He closed his eyes in anticipation of what he thought was to come.

Jonesy turned to Richie and shouted. "Ok it's up to you now. You either tell me where I can get my cash back or you're responsible for what happens next."

It was classic interrogation and intimidation.

Richie was paralysed by fear but managed to whisper. "It's guys in town. I don't know who they are, but they got your cash. I had nothing to do with any of this."

A twisted smile crept across Jonesy's face as he wielded the blade, slicing deep into Maxim's flesh. The sight was horrifying, Maxims' agonised screams echoing through the room before he succumbed to unconsciousness. Richie's stomach churned as he witnessed the brutality, the sight of white fatty tissue oozing from Maxim's cheek turning his blood cold. In that moment, fear gripped Richie like never before, his own mortality flashing before his eyes. If Jonesy could do this to Maxim, what horrors awaited Richie himself? The thought was chilling, leaving him paralysed with dread.

Jonesy turned and calmly spoke like nothing had happened, "Ok, I'm going to give you ten minutes to think about what you say next. Then I'm coming back and if you don't give me some names you can say goodbye to him."

Jonesy nodded to the minders, they released their tight grip on Richie and followed Jonesy out of the door. Richie was trembling with fear and tears were running down his face. He tried to compose his breathing and whispered, "Keep fighting pal, you are going to be alright, we will get out of here I promise." There was no response from Maxim as he remained slumped forward in his seat, blood dripping from his face.

It was evident that Maxim was in a crisis, his body bearing the weight of severe injuries. Suddenly, he lifted his head, locking eyes with Richie. Each breath he took seemed to hang in the air, a fragile thread connecting him to the world. With each exhale, a piece of his essence dissipated into the atmosphere, carried away by the gentle currents of fate. Maxim's gaze drifted beyond the confines of the room, his eyes reflecting a mixture of pain and resignation. In that fleeting moment, a profound silence descended upon the room, as if the universe itself paused to bear witness to the passing of a soul. His eyes, once ablaze with determination, now held a serene acceptance. There was a silent communication in that lingering gaze, a farewell spoken in the language of unspoken understanding. It spoke of a life lived with purpose, of trials faced with unwavering courage, and of a spirit that refused to be extinguished. Maxims eyes, though dimming, held a flicker of defiance, a testament to the indomitable human spirit that persists even in the face of mortality. As the final vestiges of life slipped away, his gaze softened, a gentle surrender embracing his weary countenance. The world around him began to fade, leaving only a profound emptiness in its wake. With one last exhalation, Maxims eyes closed, relinquishing their hold on the mortal realm.

In that fleeting moment, the room was engulfed in a reverent silence, bearing witness to the passing of a soul. Richie had never felt so helpless, and death began to feel inevitable for him. The fragility and transience of life stared back at him through Maxims body, stirring a dormant longing for something greater within his own spirit. In that sacred moment, a resolute determination took hold, and Richie knew that he could no longer tread the treacherous path. Dealing drugs was fast easy money but was thwart with dangers in return. The risk of getting caught by the cops seemed a better option than the risk of getting killed or seriously injured by rivals.

40 Dinner Date

Matt remained steadfast; his focus unwavering as he scanned the surroundings for any hint of movement from within. The biting cold and dampness no longer fazed him; he had long surpassed the threshold of discomfort. His days as a young Commando had forged an iron resolve within him, honing his ability to endure in the face of extreme adversity. It wasn't merely about physical strength and stamina, but about the resilience of the mind. He recalled the gruelling trials of his past, where survival often hinged on one's capacity to overcome the mind's relentless barrage of doubt and fear. Enduring the persistent chill of cold and wet, enduring the indignity of managing bodily functions in the most unforgiving of circumstances, enduring the relentless assault of sleep deprivation on the psyche, enduring the absence of warm sustenance. These were trials that had assessed him to the core, yet they had never broken him. As he lay in his current position, surrounded by discomfort and uncertainty, Matt drew upon the reservoir of strength within him. The wetness seeping into his clothes, the chill creeping into his bones it was a mere inconvenience in comparison to the challenges he had conquered before.

A radiant shaft of light pierced the darkness, emanating from the doorway atop the stairwell. Silhouetted against the luminous backdrop, two figures emerged, their voices muffled yet discernible as they exchanged words. With a firm handshake, they parted ways, one retreating into the shadows of the building while the other descended the stairs with cautious deliberation. As he traversed each step, the dim illumination gradually unveiled his form, unveiling a portrait of determination and resolve. Shadows danced across his countenance, casting an aura of mystery upon his features, revealing a blend of weariness and unwavering resolve etched into his expression. The air hummed with anticipation as each footfall echoed softly, resonating in the empty expanse. At last, he reached the bottom, bathed in the faint glow of distant light. There he stood, a figure shrouded in intrigue, his presence commanding attention as he lingered in the murky embrace of the shadows, his enigmatic nature casting an aura of mystery over the scene. From his pocket, he withdrew an object, and suddenly, the Mercedes sprang to life, its indicators flashing and exterior lights illuminating the surroundings. Bathed in the glow, Matt could discern the registration plate clearly. It was Jonesy's Mercedes and recognised the figure from the café as he slipped into the driver's seat. The powerful engine purred to life, momentarily reversing before roaring off into the night.

    With his night vision momentarily impaired by the sudden burst of light, Matt reached into his day sack, retrieving an untraceable "pay as you go" mobile phone. Carefully dimming the screen's glare, he composed a brief text to Iqbal, recalling the conversation he had overheard between Maxim and Richie in the café near the station. The message read, "In trouble. Maxim said to contact you. Can you meet me at this location now" Matt included a Google link pinpointing the workshop's location.

    Iqbal sat in a friend's restaurant in Rusholme, enjoying the final bites of his Indian meal with his brother Mohammed. As his mobile vibrated, Iqbal's demeanour remained calm and composed, betraying no hint of his identity as a high-end drug dealer to the other diners. Glancing briefly at the message, Iqbal's demeanour shifted subtly, prompting Mohammed to take notice. "What's occupying your thoughts, brother?" Mohammed asked, detecting the subtle change that only he seemed to perceive in Iqbal. Without uttering a word, Iqbal swiftly redialled the number, his mind already ablaze with potential scenarios.

    Matt allowed the incoming call to vibrate a couple of times before declining it. He had no desire to engage in conversation with Iqbal, opting instead to respond with another text message.

"Can't speak, we're in big trouble, and need your help, I'm Maxims close mate and he gave me your number?"

Matt's fingers hovered over the screen, anticipation coursing through him as he pressed send, confident that his message would pique Iqbal's interest. Meanwhile, Iqbal glanced at his brother Mohammed when the call went unanswered, a flicker of uncertainty crossing his features. "I'm not sure," he murmured, voicing his uncertainty to Mohammed. Just then, Matt's text message appeared on Iqbal's mobile, illuminating the screen and cutting through the uncertainty like a bolt of lightning.

After a moment of contemplation, Iqbal glanced at his brother before swiftly typing another text: "Ok, I'll arrange for someone to pay a visit." With a decisive tap, he sent the message, then turned to Mohammed, his expression grave. "Take a few of the lads and head to this location in Trafford Park," he instructed, his voice laced with caution. "It seems Maxim and his friend might be in need of our assistance. But tread carefully we're not entirely sure what's unfolding."

With a satisfied grin, Matt stowed his mobile back into his daysack, patiently waiting for his vision to readjust to the darkness outside. The anticipation of Iqbal taking the bait added an extra layer of excitement to the mission. Before long, the familiar hum of the Mercedes engine filled the air once more. As the vehicle returned, Matt observed the driver hopping out, clutching bags of takeaway food, before hurrying up the stairwell and disappearing through the unlocked door. It was evident that whoever was inside had settled in for an extended stay. Seizing the opportunity, Matt swiftly abandoned his cover and dashed over to the Mercedes. Upon closer inspection, he realised that the tracker had vanished, dislodged, and lost along the way. A wave of relief washed over him at the thought of the tracker now potentially lying unnoticed on the roadside or crushed under passing vehicles.

Jonesy and his two associates pulled up chairs to a table, settling in for the evening. With the voracity of hyenas, they unwrapped and distributed the fast-food feast before them: a medley of cooked kebabs boasting an assortment of meats, accompanied by salad and hot chips. Though hardly a dietary virtue, it satisfied their insatiable hunger, complemented by swigs of full-fat Coca-Cola from the bottles. One of the associates addressed Jonesy, "So, what's the plan with that Maxim guy now? He's not doing us any favours, is he?"

Without a trace of remorse or sympathy, Jonesy replied between mouthfuls, "We'll keep him here tonight and then dump him tomorrow night near the moors. He's not much use to us anymore, but his battered body will serve as a reminder to young Richie that we expect our dues."

Back inside the main workshop, Richie began to feel small muscle cramps creeping into his arms. The awkward position of his bound wrists, tightly secured by plastic zip ties, hindered his blood flow. The initial sensation of pins and needles had given way to a numbing stiffness in his fingers, leaving him worried about any potential long-term effects. His gaze fell upon Maxim's motionless form slouched in the chair, triggering a surge of panic that propelled him to shout out, despite the black tape gagging his mouth. "Hey! Hey! What's going on? What do you want? Let us go! I haven't done anything!" His desperate cries pierced through the air, disturbing the kidnappers as they indulged in their feast.

Jonesy glanced at one of his cohorts, who was stuffing his face with food, and nodded. "Go check on him, and make sure he keeps quiet while we eat."

Matt noticed the muffled and unrecognisable sound of shouting coming from inside. It sounded like the voice of a male in distress. Matt listened hard but couldn't make out what the shouts were saying. Riche's shouting was soon silenced as one of the minders approached and punched him hard in the stomach. The blow knocked the air from Richie's lungs, and he withered in pain.

Outside, Matt, who had stealthily returned to his original position, caught sight of three figures clad in dark attire silently infiltrating the compound from the nearby roadway on foot. They advanced with cautious steps, their forms shrouded in the dim light, casting ominous dark silhouettes against the surroundings. As they drew closer, they remained less than fifteen meters away from where Matt lay concealed. It required nerves of steel to maintain composure in such proximity to potential adversaries. While most individuals would succumb to fear and panic in this perilous scenario, Matt remained composed, his demeanour as cool as ice. Trained as an elite professional, he understood that remaining calm and holding his nerve were paramount to avoiding detection. With the expertise born from countless encounters with the enemy, he possessed a steely resilience and an unwavering resolve that bordered on icy determination.

In the cloak of darkness, the three men struggled to adjust their eyesight, unaware of Matt's vigilant presence. Their intentions seemed clear: infiltrate the building. With quiet determination, one of the figures gestured for the others to follow as they ascended the stairway, their movements calculated and deliberate. Matt's heart raced as he discerned the glint of weapons, a menacing assortment of baseball bat, knife and a gleaming machete clutched tightly in their hands. Reaching the pinnacle of the stairwell, the trio paused, their senses heightened as they tried the doorknob, listening intently for any sign of disturbance. Time seemed to stand still as they lingered in silence, plotting their next move. Then, in a sudden burst of action, they barged through the unlocked door, catching Jonesy and his cohorts off guard as they savoured the remnants of their meal. The intrusion was swift and unforgiving, sending shockwaves through the room.

Though still a couple of strides away from the door, Jonesy reacted with lightning speed, retrieving a handgun concealed within the confines of his jeans.

In his startled haste he pulled the trigger prematurely and the first shot hit the floor by his feet. Bringing his arm to a parallel angle he shot repeated times and all these rounds except one missed their intended targets. One round hit Mohammed in the mouth killing him instantly as he slummed forward like a falling rag doll unable to put his hands out as he crashed face down into the floor. The other two Asian males continued with their forward momentum towards Jonesy and his minders. The Machete struck one of Jonesy's minders across the arm causing a deep gash across his Bicep. The third Asian male managed to swing his baseball bat in the close confines of the room hitting Jonesy on the arm. Unable to take a full swing the blow was ineffective. Jonesy pulled the trigger again hitting the male with the machete in the shoulder causing him to drop the weapon and stagger back in shock and disbelief that he had been shot. In the same instant Jonesy shot again instantly killing the last man standing as the bullet ripped into the side of his head and exiting at the back of his neck. At such close range it was a non-survivable injury.

Like a scene from a tense spaghetti western, the eruption of gunfire shattered the stillness within seconds. Matt's heart pounded in his chest as he registered the unmistakable sound of trouble inside. With swift determination, he seized his day sack, masking his identity with a plastic face mask and slipping into tight-fitting black leather gloves before slinging the bag over his shoulder. Though the gunfire hadn't yet drawn attention from the outside world, Matt knew time was of the essence; the authorities could be alerted at any moment. Bounding up the stairs with urgency, he positioned himself outside the slightly ajar door, adrenaline coursing through his veins. Gripping the Barrette pistol tightly in his right hand, he cautiously peered through the narrow crack, his senses on high alert. Inside, the room crackled with tension as Jonesy and his cohorts grappled with the aftermath of the violent confrontation. Matt's keen eyes noted the shock etched on their faces; the firearm still clutched in Jonesy's trembling hand. With calculated precision, Matt waited, allowing the chaotic energy of the moment to settle. He needed the trio to let their guard down, if only for a fleeting moment, before he could make his move. Every second felt like an eternity as he braced himself for the next decisive action.

Jonesy's two minders flanked him, their expressions a mix of shock and apprehension. One hovered behind Jonesy, inspecting the injury to his arm, while the other surveyed the grim aftermath sprawled across the floor before them. The Asian man, felled by a fatal shot to the side of his head, lay motionless beneath the table, a stark reminder of the violence that had unfolded. In the tense silence that followed, Jonesy and his associates appeared momentarily paralysed by the gravity of the situation thrust upon them. The wounded man, clutching his shoulder where a bullet had torn through flesh, cried out in agony, his pleas echoing in a language foreign to the room. Blood seeped from his wound, a stark contrast against the chaos that surrounded him, yet no one moved to help. The air hung heavy with uncertainty and smell of cordite. Each passing moment amplifying the urgency of the wounded man's plight. Despite the desperate need for medical attention, an unspoken understanding pervaded the room, no one dared to act, the weight of their predicament immobilising them in a state of silent resignation.

Jonesy shouted, "finish him off as we don't need him talking." The larger and uninjured minder stepped forward, picked up the baseball bat from the floor and made three sickening blows to his head. The dull thuds fatally silencing the man from his pain. It was a horrific brutal scene of events, and even Matt with all his war experience found himself flinching from the actions happening in front of him.

Jonesy's tense shoulders visibly relaxed as he gingerly placed his firearm on the table, a flicker of false security crossing his features. It was the opening Matt had been waiting for, an opportunity to strike.

With lightning speed, Matt burst into the room, the deafening shots from his Beretta ringing out like thunder. The two minders, caught off guard, crumpled to the ground with a sickening thud, their bodies falling lifeless at Jonesy's feet. Before Jonesy could comprehend the chaos unfolding before him, Matt's voice pierced through the stunned silence, commanding and forceful.

"Put your fucking hands up and get on your knees!" Matt's voice boomed, dripping with authority and menace, as he trained his weapon on the bewildered Jonesy.

Jonesy, his disbelief palpable, stared wide-eyed at the masked intruder who exuded an air of unwavering determination. With a mix of fear and resignation, he complied, sinking to his knees, and clasping his hands atop his head. As Matt closed in on Jonesy, his movements deliberate and purposeful, a sudden jolt disrupted the tense standoff. One of the dying minders, gasping for breath, reached out in a final act of desperation, his trembling hand grasping Matt's ankle and sending him crashing off balance.

Jonesy, jumped to his feet and sprinted towards the door. Matt reacted by trying to stamp on the hand gripping at his ankle and fired towards the fleeing Jonesy. This time his aim was off, and the round dropped short of Jonesy hitting the wall. Unable to adjust his aim in time Jonesy got to the doorway and disappeared outside. Matt could hear him making his exit down the stairwell. Matt kicked his foot out of the injured male's hand who by now was in no fit state to fight.

Fury boiled within Matt as he cursed himself for allowing Jonesy to slip through his fingers. Like a cunning cat with nine lives, Jonesy had managed to evade capture, leaving Matt seething with frustration. He knew the chase was futile;

Jonesy was slippery and pursuing him now would only waste precious time and energy. Resigned to the fact that Jonesy had slipped away, Matt refocused his attention on the room, his movements deliberate and cautious. He navigated the space with calculated precision, careful to avoid disturbing any telltale blood spatters that could betray his presence. With each step, Matt's mind raced, grappling with the gravity of the situation. The scene before him was a tangled web of violence and deceit, a puzzle that would undoubtedly confound even the most seasoned investigators. As he surveyed the room, he couldn't shake the sinking feeling that this would be a murder scene of unprecedented complexity for the authorities to unravel once they arrived.

With the precision of a seasoned soldier, Matt entered the workshop, his senses attuned to any potential threats lurking in the shadows. As he moved through the space, his eyes swept over every corner, every nook and cranny, searching for signs of danger. Upon reaching the adjoining room, his gaze fell upon the figures of Richie and Maxim, bound, and restrained in their chairs, a stark tableau of vulnerability. Richie's anguish was palpable as he sat upright, his eyes wide with fear. Without hesitation, Matt approached him with practiced ease, deftly concealing the Beretta in his jacket pocket in one fluid motion. With a swift movement, he lifted his face mask, revealing his identity to Richie before lowering it once more. Relief flooded Richie's features as he recognised his Uncle Matt, a ray of hope in the darkness of his captivity. "How did you know I was here?" he asked, his voice tinged with gratitude as a sense of safety washed over him. In that moment, Matt assumed control, his demeanour commanding and unwavering. "I'm in charge now," he asserted firmly, his tone brooking no argument. "Follow my orders without question." Richie, recognising the urgency of the situation, nodded in silent acquiescence, his trust in his uncle unwavering.

With practiced precision, Matt retrieved a small knife from his jeans, his movements deliberate as he approached Richie. The gaffer tape encasing Richie's mouth had been applied with brutal force, its tight grip leaving raw, bloodied marks at the corners of his lips. Matt worked quickly; his focus unwavering despite the urgency of the situation. As he peeled away the tape, a mixture of blood and drying saliva clung to its sticky surface, tugging sharply at Richie's skin with each pull. There was no time for delicacy; the adhesive tore at Richie's face, eliciting a gasp of relief as he finally regained the ability to breathe. Knowing the potential implications of leaving behind such damning evidence, Matt stuffed the gaffer tape into his pocket without hesitation, his mind already calculating the next steps. Turning his attention to the zip ties binding Richie's wrists, he sliced through them in a single fluid motion, the blade of the knife severing the constraints with ease. As the zip ties fell away, revealing angry, blistered marks on Richie's skin, the immediate rush of blood returning to his hands brought a palpable sense of relief. With a swift motion, Matt scooped up the discarded plastic ties, his movements deliberate as he tucked them into his pocket.

    Freed from his restraints, Richie laboriously rose from the chair, his movements tentative and unsteady. Each step he attempted to take was marred by trembling legs, struggling to regain their strength. His head swam in a disorienting haze, his vision blurred, and his senses overwhelmed by the ordeal he had endured. Desperately, he sought stability, reaching out for the nearby table to steady himself and regain his equilibrium. But despite his efforts, the persistent dizziness persisted, washing over him like relentless ocean waves. With each step, he stumbled slightly, his movements hindered by the spinning room. The world seemed to tilt around him, forcing him to lean against the wall for support, lest he lost his balance entirely. Despite blinking furiously to clear his vision, the dizziness refused to abate. Even a deep breath, once a source of solace, only served to intensify his light-headedness, leaving him feeling vulnerable and disoriented.

Though he was determined to regain his composure, he found himself swaying more noticeably on his feet. It was as if the ground beneath him was unsteady, and he struggled to find his footing.

Realising he might need assistance, Richie reached out for Matt to lend a helping hand until this dizziness eased. With a commanding presence, Matt snapped into action, his voice carrying authority as he barked at Richie, "Don't move a muscle until I give the word, understand?"

Richie nodded vigorously, his eyes wide with apprehension. "Yes, yes, I understand," he affirmed, casting a worried glance towards Maxim before turning back to Matt for guidance.

Matt's gaze shifted to where Maxim slouched in the chair, a grim realisation washing over him as he assessed the extent of Maxim's injuries. It was clear that Maxim had lost his fight for survival, succumbing to the brutality inflicted upon him. A heavy weight settled in Matt's chest as he came to terms with the grim reality before him. There was nothing he could do for Maxim now; he would become another grim discovery for the authorities in this house of horrors.

Matt turned towards Richie; his voice low but firm as he instructed him to stay "touch close." They moved back into the other room, where the lifeless bodies lay in grim silence. Matt unslung his day sack; his movements deliberate as he extracted the items he had pilfered from Jonesy's flat. Carefully, he arranged the mugs and cans on the table before meticulously scattering the used cigarette butts into one of the mugs. He knew that Jonesy's DNA would be smeared across these items, providing damning evidence once the police began their investigation. Suddenly, Richie's eyes widened with realisation as he remembered his mobile phone sitting on the side in the workshop. Without a moment's hesitation, he bolted back to retrieve it, his urgency palpable.

"Make sure you turn it off," Matt barked after him, his voice a sharp reminder of the risks they faced.

Their next move was critical: a swift exit with Richie in tow, leaving behind minimal forensic evidence. Matt reassured himself that they had covered their tracks meticulously. Leading up to his arrival, he had taken every precaution to minimize the risk of leaving physical evidence behind. Even the shell casings from the Beretta handgun had been meticulously cleaned. Matt had read about a cutting-edge forensic technique called DART—Direct Ammunition Recovery Treatment, that could extract DNA from shell casings. To mitigate this risk, he had soaked the rounds in bleach before reloading them into the magazine, all while wearing latex gloves. Matt had left nothing to chance, ensuring that their escape would be as clean and untraceable as possible.

Matt turned to Richie; his voice muffled by the mask but commanding, nonetheless. "Stay close, Richie, and listen to my every instruction without fail," he ordered. "Once we're outside, we'll be moving fast on foot. Let's go."

Emerging into the cool night air, they descended the stairwell, scanning their surroundings for any sign of Jonesy. The Mercedes remained ominously parked, its presence a silent testament to the chaos that had unfolded. With a quick test, Matt found the front passenger door unlocked, a stroke of luck in their favour. From his jacket pocket, Matt withdrew a small plastic bag containing white quick firelighters. With practiced efficiency, he ignited the packet and placed the growing ball of fire onto the back seat of the Mercedes. As the flames licked hungrily at the upholstery, he discarded his mask, watching it disappear into the inferno. Leaving the door slightly ajar to fuel the flames, Matt instructed Richie to cover his face with a scarf while he pulled his own up to conceal his identity. "Follow me and stay close," he whispered, his words a quiet reassurance during chaos.

Both men moved swiftly through the deserted industrial estate, the silence amplifying the tension in the air. Richie proved his physical prowess, effortlessly keeping pace with Matt as they navigated their way through the labyrinthine alleys and shadowy corners. Their synchronised movements, punctuated by quick stops to scan their surroundings, evoked memories for Matt of his gruelling "escape and evasion course" during Commando training. As they pressed on, the echoes of his instructors' words reverberated in Matt's mind. "Trust nobody," they had cautioned, instilling a sense of vigilance that now guided his every move. "Expect everything to happen, before it happened, and if it did happen, be ready to react." The mantra, ingrained through days of enduring the hostile terrain of Dartmoor, resonated with renewed significance as they navigated the treacherous landscape of their current predicament. With each step, Matt remained acutely aware of the dangers lurking in the shadows, his senses sharp and alert, ready to respond at a moment's notice. At his side, Richie, wide-eyed and nervous, tried to match Matt's silent steps, his lanky frame hunched forward as if trying to disappear. The scene was cloaked in darkness, broken only by the occasional flickering streetlight casting eerie shadows across the deserted buildings. Their footsteps echoed softly against the tarmac, the sound muffled by the late hour and the desolation that surrounded them.

Matt's eyes darted from one corner to another, scanning for any sign of movement or unwanted attention. Guiding Richie with a reassuring hand on his shoulder, Matt communicated silently, their movements choreographed like a well-rehearsed dance. He signalled Richie to duck behind a row of rusted shipping containers as the distant sound of approaching sirens pierced the night air. The young teenager complied, his heart pounding in his chest.

As they pressed on, Matt's keen eyes detected a small alleyway up ahead, offering a potential escape route. He gestured for Richie to follow him, and together they veered towards the narrow passage, the shadows providing much-needed cover. In this tense game of cat and mouse, Matt's instincts never wavered. His military discipline and acute awareness of his surroundings kept him one step ahead. He remained attuned to the rhythm of the night, detecting the smallest shifts in the environment that could betray their presence. Matt's voice, barely above a whisper, offered steady encouragement to Richie, calming the teenager's frayed nerves. He knew the importance of keeping Richie focused and composed in the chaos surrounding them. With each step, Matt's presence exuded confidence and a sense of protection, instilling trust in the young lad he was leading to safety.

    Matt halted abruptly, his senses on high alert as he scanned the area surrounding his hire car, ensuring it remained undisturbed by prying eyes. Satisfied that they were alone, he motioned for Richie to follow him into the cover of the nearby wooded area. Despite the darkness, cold, and dampness, the dim glow of nearby streetlights provided enough visibility to navigate their surroundings. Turning to Richie, Matt's voice was urgent and commanding. "You need to strip down, completely," he ordered, his tone brooking no argument. From his day sack, he tossed Richie a tightly sealed bag of clothing and a pair of trainers, pilfered from Richie's own bedroom. "Put all your clothing in this bin bag, and keep everything separate," he instructed, his movements swift and decisive.

    Following his own orders, Matt swiftly shed his own clothes, replacing them with the fresh attire he had brought along. In a matter of minutes, both men were dressed anew, their discarded garments neatly packed away in two bin bags and double-bagged for extra security. With a nod of approval, Matt gestured for Richie to make his way to the car.

    While Richie complied, Matt hurried to a nearby pond, disposing of the Beretta with a swift toss into its murky depths. With the weapon disposed of, he raced back to join Richie at the car, a sense of urgency propelling them forward as they prepared to make their escape.

Navigating the back roads from Trafford Park to Manchester, Matt's senses remained heightened, alert to any potential threats or obstacles that might impede their escape. As they neared a desolate layby on the outskirts of Manchester, Matt's eyes caught sight of a large council bin standing sentinel in the darkness. A sense of urgency seized him as he scanned the surroundings for any signs of surveillance. Satisfied that they were undetected, he brought the car to a sudden halt, leaping out with purpose. In swift, practiced movements, he disposed of the bagged clothing into the bin before swiftly returning to the safety of his car. As they sped away from the scene, Matt's mind raced with calculations. Even if the Manchester Police initiated a stop on local council bin collections, it would be a futile effort. They had crossed into a different borough, evading any attempts at detection or interception. With each passing mile, their distance from danger grew, but Matt remained vigilant, knowing that their escape was far from guaranteed.

The journey back in the car was suffocatingly tense, the weight of their actions hanging heavy in the air until Matt's pent-up frustration exploded.

"From now on, you do everything I say," Matt's voice was sharp, laced with urgency. "If I say shit, you shit. If I say stay put, you damn well stay put. Understand?" His words were punctuated by the severity of the situation they found themselves in. "With what went down tonight, there's going to be a full-blown murder investigation," Matt continued, his tone leaving no room for argument. "You won't do anything to jeopardise or risk me getting caught. When we get back to the flat, you'll strip, throw your clothes in the washer, and scrub every damn nail clean. Then, you'll eat, rest, and clear your head with no weed!" His instructions were delivered with a firmness that brooked no defiance.

"When or if questioned about tonight, we were both at home watching 'The Deer Hunter Film,'" Matt instructed, his voice unwavering. "You won't leave the house without my say-so. Our priority now is your father's funeral. We'll play the grieving family, and you'll act like nothing's changed. Got it?"

Richie, stunned into silence, nodded in reluctant acknowledgment.

"And your mobile," Matt demanded, holding out his hand. Richie hesitated, but realising Matt wasn't in the mood for negotiation, reluctantly passed it over.

"Is this a contract or pay as you go?" Matt asked, his tone cutting.

"Pay as you go," Richie replied meekly.

"Good. It's getting binned," Matt declared, his resolve unwavering. "We'll sort out a new one when the time comes."

"But my numbers" Richie began, his anxiety evident.

"Tough luck. You won't need them where you're going," Matt snapped, his patience wearing thin. Richie's anxious expression spoke volumes, confirming the gravity of their situation.

Arriving home, Matt skilfully maneuvered the car into the garage, ensuring they remained unseen. Meanwhile, Richie hurried inside through the internal door, his nerves on edge. Matt swiftly removed the cloned registration plates, revealing the car's identity underneath. With practiced efficiency, he shattered the plates and stowed the fragments in a plastic bag before joining Richie inside.

Drawing on an old military tradition, Matt made his way to the kitchen, his movements purposeful and methodical. He set a kettle to boil for a much-needed cup of tea, the familiar routine serving as a small comfort through the chaos. As the water heated, he retrieved his own mobile phone, meticulously dismantling the tracking app devices he had installed. With each component removed, he felt relieved, knowing they were one step closer to evading detection.

Turning his attention to Richie's mobile, Matt repeated the process, ensuring that every trace of tracking capability was eradicated. He then removed the SIM card and memory card, breaking them into pieces before adding them to the bag containing the shattered number plate. With each action, the tension in the air seemed to dissipate, replaced by a sense of cautious relief as he worked to cover their tracks.

41 House of Horrors

Detective Inspector Jim Layton strode into the familiar confines of Stretford Police Station, his footsteps echoing lightly against the polished linoleum floors. The early morning light filtered in through the blinds, casting long shadows across the desks and filing cabinets. Jim had developed a routine since his promotion to Inspector, a ritual that began with the quiet solitude of the early part of the day. His key turned in the lock with a soft click as he entered his office, the scent of freshly brewed coffee lingering in the air. Jim relished these moments of tranquillity before the hustle and bustle of the day began in earnest. It was during these early hours that he could gather his thoughts, prepare himself for the challenges that lay ahead. With a practiced hand, Jim powered up his computer, the hum of the machine filling the silence of the room. He leaned back in his chair, savouring the first sip of his steaming cup of coffee as he navigated through the internal IT system. As he scanned through the latest updates, Jim's mind began to buzz with possibilities and strategies. There was a certain thrill that came with the anticipation of a new case, a puzzle waiting to be solved. It was what drove him, what fuelled his passion for his work. The weight of his years in service hung heavy upon his shoulders, a testament to the trials and tribulations he had endured throughout his career. Retirement loomed on the horizon like a distant lighthouse, guiding him through the tumultuous waters of his final years in the force. He couldn't help but marvel at the journey that had brought him to this point. The rank of DI had once seemed an unattainable summit, a distant dream in the early days of his career. Yet here he stood, a seasoned veteran on the brink of bidding farewell to the only life he had ever known. There had been moments, of course, when the pressures of police work had threatened to overwhelm him. The long hours, the relentless stress, the constant barrage of violence and crime, they had all taken their toll on Jim's psyche, chipping away at his resolve like waves eroding the shoreline. It was during those dark times that he had turned to the teachings of stoicism, seeking solace and strength in the timeless wisdom of ancient philosophers. The memories of incidents and murders still haunted him, a grim reminder of the fragility of life and the unforgiving nature of the job. One gruesome murder had been a turning point in Jim's life, a catalyst for self-reflection and personal growth. The loss of his partner, DC Terry Smith, had been a harsh lesson in the perils of neglecting one's mental health, a wound that still throbbed with guilt and remorse. But from the ashes of tragedy had risen a newfound sense of purpose for Jim. No longer content to simply endure the rigors of police work, he had resolved to have influence in the lives of those around him. Whether through mentoring younger officers or advocating for better mental health support within the force, Jim had become the light of hope in a world fraught with darkness. And so, as he settled into his office for another day of hard graft, Jim knew that his legacy would extend far beyond the confines of Stretford Police Station.

  As an experienced Detective constable Jim had spent many sleepless nights pondering the idea of pursuing a promotion to Sergeant. It wasn't a decision he had taken lightly. Yet, once he committed himself to the notion, there was no turning back. With characteristic determination, he threw himself into the questionable Police promotion system, navigating its pitfalls and hurdles with grit and resilience. The process, he found, was a painstaking ordeal. Exams, assessment centres, interview panels, each step felt like a trial by fire, testing not only his knowledge and skills but also his patience and fortitude. Jim harboured a deep-seated disdain for the whole affair, viewing it as unavoidable to pad his pension before retirement beckoned. His children, now young adults charting their own courses in teaching and finance, had provided a sense of solace amid the chaos. Their independence had eased the burden on Jim and his loyal wife, affording him the time and space to focus on his own ambitions. Yet, despite his reservations about the promotion process, Jim understood its implications. He knew that success in exams and assessments didn't inherently make him a better leader, it merely demonstrated his ability to navigate the bureaucratic maze. He recognised that there were many talented officers who, for several reasons, chose not to pursue advancement, and he respected their decisions. As an outgoing DI, Jim's focus shifted towards nurturing the potential within his young team. His management style emphasised engagement and praise, seeking to instil confidence and empower his subordinates to excel. For him, true leadership lay not in titles or accolades, but in the ability to inspire greatness in others. With each passing day, Jim worked tirelessly to cultivate a culture of support and encouragement, fostering an environment where his officers could thrive and grow. For him, the measure of success lay not in personal achievements, but in the collective triumphs of his team. And as he approached the twilight of his career, he remained steadfast in his commitment to building a legacy of mentorship and empowerment that would endure long after he handed his warrant card back.

  This approach made Jim a well-liked boss in his office, and he was seen as a breath of fresh air into the once-downtrodden office, infusing it with a sense of purpose and camaraderie that had long been absent. In the wake of years of austerity measures, departmental mergers, and the exodus of talented personnel, morale within the team had plummeted to an all-time low. Jim's arrival had marked a turning point, in a sea of disillusionment. His predecessor, a figure loathed by many for his autocratic style and lack of empathy, had left a bitter legacy. But Jim's approach had been invigorating, a stark contrast to the oppressive atmosphere that had pervaded the office. Officers who had once dreaded the thought of coming to work now found themselves eager to do so, buoyed by the knowledge that they had a leader who would guide, support, and defend them at every turn. The senior detectives, who had withstood the worst of their former boss's tirades and micromanagement, welcomed Jim with open arms. His commitment to fostering a culture of trust and collaboration was a welcome change from the toxic environment they had endured for so long. However, the challenges facing the force extended beyond the confines of their own office. A pervasive sense of apathy and self-interest by senior leaders had infiltrated the upper echelons of the organisation, resulting in a disconnect between management and frontline officers. Budget cuts and increased demands had taken their toll, leaving little room for innovation or improvement. The damning assessment by Her Majesty's Inspectorate of Constabulary and Fire & Rescue Services HMICFRS served as a sobering reminder of the uphill battle that lay ahead. With most areas graded as "requires improvement" or "inadequate," there was no denying the magnitude of the task at hand. Jim and his officers had been hugely upset by the report findings and felt the senior leadership had let him and his colleagues down badly. Although no one was surprised given the direction the force had taken on crime reporting or lack of it. The Stoic inside Jim told him that all he could do was try to improve the HMICFRS concerns and leave a legacy of improvement. So, when the time did come for Jim to step aside, he could hand "the baton of leadership over." Knowing he had done his best and his team were in a much better place to support an ever-demanding public. The absence of the night duty detective who typically would have been present, raised concerns. It hinted at the possibility of something significant having occurred overnight, amplifying Jim's apprehension. Typically, the night detective would be diligently working at their desk, compiling reports on the previous night's incidents.

Seated at his desk, Jim's gaze drifted to a framed photograph capturing moments of joy with his family, a poignant reminder of happier times amidst the challenges of his profession. With a determined click of his mouse, he entered his password, greeted by the glow of his computer screen. Amid the array of notifications, one headline demanded his immediate attention: "Six, multiple fatalities." His pulse quickened as he delved into the grim details unfolding before him. Initial reports spoke of a routine call to a car fire in Trafford Park, nothing alarming on the surface. Yet, as the incident unfolded, the situation morphed into a chilling tableau of tragedy and terror. The aftermath revealed by the officers' updates painted a macabre picture: amidst the ashes of a burnt-out Mercedes, a haunting discovery awaited.

Following the extinguishing of the flames, the revelation of an insecurity at the property's rear sparked a chain of events shrouded in dread. As the officers investigated the scene, they stumbled upon a scene of unimaginable horror. Six lifeless figures lay strewn inside, each bearing the cruel marks of fatal violence. Alongside them, a firearm, silent witness to the unfathomable violence that had transpired. Each detail unveiled painted a harrowing portrait of a night stained by tragedy, leaving Jim grappling with the weight of the responsibility that awaited him.

The scene had been cordoned off, and a specialised murder incident team had been summoned. Jim surveyed the gravity of the incident, recognising the immense challenge it posed for the force. With multiple fatalities involved, he anticipated intense media scrutiny looming over the case. As he delved deeper into the reports, a sense of urgency gripped him. The identities of the deceased remained unknown, adding another layer of complexity to the investigation. Among the flurry of details, one piece of information stood out: a diligent uniformed officer had scoured the vicinity for CCTV footage. A blurry image captured a figure fleeing the scene just before the fire erupted, a potential lead that ignited Jim's investigative instincts.

Already formulating a plan of action, Jim envisioned the meticulous process ahead. Consulting with senior officers, he would orchestrate a strategic approach to unravelling the mystery shrouding the tragedy. The quietude of the office soon dissipated, replaced by the bustling energy of his team's arrival. Footsteps echoed, accompanied by murmured exchanges, signalling the commencement of yet another day in the relentless pursuit of justice.

As the anticipation mounted, Jim sank into his chair, a moment of respite amidst the chaos. With a heavy sigh, Jim reached for his phone, his fingers tracing the familiar contours. He dialled his wife's number, bracing himself for the inevitable disappointment in her voice as he relayed the news of his extended absence. Another weekend planned with his wife dashed by the unforgiving hand of duty.

42 A Restless Night

Matt stirred from his slumber, roused by the persistent buzz of his mobile resting on the bedside cabinet. The soft glow of dawn filtered through the curtains, casting a gentle, golden hue across the room, imbuing it with a sense of warmth and tranquillity. As he reached out to silence the incessant buzzing, a small yawn escaped his lips, a silent greeting to the new day. With a languid stretch, he welcomed the morning, feeling the remnants of stiffness and tension in his muscles from the previous night's activities. A testament to the vigour with which he had pursued his endeavours, a reminder of the physicality of life's journey.

He answered his phone, and the melodic sound of Nicole's voice swept over him like a comforting embrace. Instantly, a wave of warmth flooded his being, dispelling the lingering shadows of the previous night. Nicole's voice, with its calm, measured cadence, had a way of soothing his troubled mind, transporting him to a place of serenity. The gentle lilt of her soft French accent was a balm to his soul, reminding him of the beauty and grace in the world. Despite the turmoil swirling within him, Matt couldn't help but be grateful for Nicole's unwavering concern. Her genuine worry for his well-being, especially in the wake of his brother's tragic passing and the impending funeral, touched him deeply. He knew she would be devastated if she ever learned the truth about his darker deeds. Nicole abhorred violence, always advocating for peaceful resolutions even in the face of familial conflicts. The thought of tarnishing their relationship with the ugliness of his own actions filled Matt with a profound sense of dread. He couldn't bear the idea of losing her, knowing that it would shatter any semblance of normalcy he clung to. For Matt, Nicole was not just a rock in his life but also a lifeline, offering him hope amid chaos. Yet, as much as he valued her principles, Matt couldn't ignore the harsh realities of the world they inhabited. The justice system's sluggishness in addressing modern-day issues, particularly those affecting vulnerable individuals like Richie, left him disillusioned. The rise of phenomena like 'county lines' underscored the system's inadequacy in stemming the tide of violence and exploitation. Despite his reservations, Matt grappled with the notion that sometimes, justice demanded a swifter, more decisive response than the system could provide. The conversation between them meandered, weaving through the threads of their lives separated by distance but united by love. Nicole's joy at the prospect of Matt buying a new van for their rural retreat in France bubbled over the phone lines, infusing the conversation with a palpable sense of anticipation. Matt, too, found solace in the thought of joining Nicole soon after tying up the loose ends following his brother's funeral.

"What about Richie?" Nicole's voice, tinged with curiosity, broke through the pleasant reverie. "Has he figured out what he's going to do?"

Matt hesitated for a moment, grappling with the weight of his unspoken plans for his nephew. "Not entirely," he replied carefully, masking the complexity of his intentions. After professing his love for Nicole and bidding her farewell, Matt ended the call, his heart buoyed by her unwavering support. Energised by their conversation, he leaped out of bed, ready to face the day with renewed purpose.

Already having completed his morning routine, Matt returned home from a brisk walk through the park, his mind buzzing with thoughts of what lay ahead. Upon encountering Richie, who had yet to emerge from his troubled slumber, Matt greeted him with a nod before issuing a directive.

"Grab yourself a drink and a bite to eat," Matt instructed, his tone firm but kind. "Then meet me at the kitchen table. We've got some things to discuss." Richie, his mind clouded with worry and anxiety, complied with Matt's request, the events of the past 48 hours weighing heavily on him. Despite his attempts at sleep, the spectre of the gruesome scene he witnessed refused to release its grip on his consciousness. The memory of Maxim's lifeless form haunted him, mingling with the guilt of leaving him behind in that desolate building. Cut off from the world without his mobile phone, Richie grappled with a torrent of unanswered questions swirling in his mind. How did Matt manage to locate and rescue him? What secrets lay behind Matt's apparent preparedness for the events of the previous night? And most pressingly, what repercussions awaited them at the hands of the authorities? With each question came a surge of apprehension, compounded by Matt's cryptic warnings against divulging any information.

    Seated in silence, Matt and Richie were engulfed by the sombre atmosphere of the morning news, the headlines recounting the grim discovery in Trafford Park. While Matt remained stoic, Richie's shock was palpable as he watched the events unfold before him. Turning to face Richie, Matt's demeanour shifted, his expression grave and unyielding. "Alright, Richie," he began, his tone firm and unwavering. "Listen up. What I'm about to say isn't up for debate. You've seen the news, and I need you to understand the gravity of our situation." With a sense of urgency, Matt outlined his plan, each word laced with determination. "It's clear you've made some serious mistakes," he continued, his gaze piercing. "But I'm going to fix this. We're going to keep you safe and out of prison."

    Addressing the imminent threat, Matt's voice hardened. "Jonesy will want to lay low, but that Asian gang won't rest until they've settled the score. That's why you're staying put, away from prying eyes and potential danger."

    Leaning in closer, Matt revealed his plan for Richie's future. "You're coming with me to France," he declared. "I've arranged everything. The house will be sold, and the funds will be yours in suitable time. We'll sort out your banking, and then we'll start fresh across the channel."

Richie, stunned by the extent of Matt's preparations, could only nod in silent acknowledgment. "But what will I do in France?" he ventured; his voice tinged with uncertainty.

"Don't worry about that," Matt reassured him, a flicker of determination in his eyes. "I've got it all sorted. You'll work hard, and together, we'll make it through this." Richie accepted the gravity of his situation, knowing that Matt's guidance would be his lifeline in the tumultuous days ahead. Richie understood that giving up was not an option, not when his future hung in the balance.

In an instant, the resonating chime of the front doorbell shattered the stillness of the room. Richie's gaze darted to Matt, who motioned for him to remain seated, a silent command in his eyes.

As Matt approached the front door, the silhouette of a man loomed behind the frosted glass. With a practiced hand, Matt engaged the safety latch, a subtle precaution against the unknown. With a wary yet composed demeanour, he swung open the door to confront the visitor.

"Hi, my name's Steve from the car hire company," the man announced, his voice carrying a note of professionalism. "I've come to collect the hire car, which is being off-hired and needs to be returned."

Matt's lips curled into a smirk as he called out to Richie, "It's the car hire company."

Gathering the keys, Matt swiftly made his way to the garage, unlocking the doors to reveal the waiting vehicle. Steve wasted no time, conducting a brisk inspection before finalising the necessary paperwork. With a nod of farewell, he was already driving off into the distance before Matt could even close the garage door.

Returning to the kitchen, Matt's eyes fell upon Richie, who was hunched over the table, his shoulders trembling with silent sobs. Concern etched into his features; Matt approached his nephew with a gentle touch.

"What's the matter, Richie?" he inquired, his voice laced with empathy.

Richie looked up and pointed at the TV. Matt's attention focused on the news story. "A young girl named Mia Arley aged fifteen was found dead at Dorset court in Manchester in a tragic case of suicide. Police said they were not treating it as suspicious, and the matter had been referred to His Majesty's Coroner."

The tragic news had left Richie reeling, his heart heavy with sorrow for Mia whose young life had ended in such a devastating manner. Matt, however, kept his emotions tightly controlled as he grappled with the weight of the situation.

"Richie, we can't dwell on her," Matt began, his voice firm yet tinged with a hint of compassion. "There's little you could have done to prevent it. Right now, you need to focus on yourself. If you let this consume you, it'll only lead to more pain and trouble."

Leaning in closer, Matt's tone grew more intense. "I hate to break it to you, but I'm now involved in this mess," he confessed, his words laden with implication. "You don't have a choice. You'll do as I say whether you like it or not. It's the only way to navigate through this."

43 Cracking the Case

Arriving at the scene in Trafford Park, Jim found himself within a hive of activity. Police tape cordoned off the area, marking it as a zone of investigation. A uniformed officer, determined but clearly weary, stood sentinel at the entrance, dutifully logging visitors in and out, a task assigned through the capriciousness of duty rosters.

Reflecting on his own early experiences, Jim couldn't help but reminisce about his initiation into the grim world of crime scenes. It had been a simpler time, yet equally fraught with the weight of responsibility. In Wythenshawe, a small cul-de-sac had been the stage for his first voyage into the realm of murder investigations. The memory of that fateful day, when a local criminal met his demise at the hands of an unknown assailant, lingered in his mind. Despite their best efforts, the truth remained elusive, shrouded in the shadows of uncertainty.

With a nod of acknowledgment to the young officer, Jim signed the log sheet, offering a word of gratitude for his service. Stepping past the outer cordon, he was greeted by Oliver Walter, the seasoned head of the CSI forensic team a familiar face in the tumult of crime scenes.

"Morning, Boss," Oliver greeted, his tone laced with a mix of professionalism and concern. "This one's a real mess. Looks like it's going to be a real "ball of shit" case. My gut tells me it's more than just a run-of-the-mill hit. Whoever orchestrated this was meticulous and well-prepared. We've got our work cut out for us."

Handing Jim, a pristine white forensic suit, Oliver continued, his voice measured yet resolute. "We've recovered a handgun inside, but I suspect there's more to this than meets the eye. Post-mortems and further analysis will shed light on the weapons used. My gut says we're dealing with at least two different firearms based on the brass cartridge casings."

Struggling to wriggle into his forensic J suit, Jim cursed under his breath, grappling with the stubborn foot holes. With a final tug, he managed to get it on, albeit with a sense of exasperation. Oliver, ever composed, led him up the stairwell to the blue door looming at the top.

"So, no signs of forced entry, and all other doors to the building were locked," Jim observed, his brow furrowed with concern.

"Seems that way," Oliver confirmed, his tone thoughtful. "The team's still trying to untangle the ownership history of this place. It's been dormant for a couple of years, and the ownership records are a mess."

Pausing by the door, Oliver fixed Jim with a grave look. "Be prepared for what you're about to see, boss," he cautioned, the weight of the situation evident in his voice. Jim nodded in acknowledgment, bracing himself for the horrors that awaited inside. As they crossed the threshold, the scene unfolded before them, a tableau of violence and chaos that made Jim's stomach churn. Blood stained the surroundings, evidence of a brutal confrontation that had erupted around the table. The diversity among the victims struck Jim, a stark reminder of the tangled web of crime that enmeshed the city. His gaze lingered on the young white male slumped in the chair, a jarring contrast to the others. Information gleaned from briefings swirled in his mind, painting a grim picture of the victim's association with notorious elements in Rusholme. Jim knew the repercussions of such a high-profile murder, the ripple effect that would send shockwaves through the city's underworld.

Examining the bodies, Jim noted the precise placement of the fatal wounds, a stark departure from the haphazard violence typically associated with gang-related shootings. His mind flashed back to a similar scene from his past at the Grafton Public hours, a cold case that had haunted him for years. Silent contemplation enveloped Jim as he grappled with the gravity of the situation. He knew that unravelling the complexities of this case would demand every ounce of his expertise and resources, a daunting prospect, considering the looming spectre of media scrutiny and public demand for answers.

44 Bon Voyage

It had been a tumultuous few days for Matt and Richie, a whirlwind of emotions and upheaval that now found them hurtling down the M6 motorway, leaving behind the drab, rain-soaked landscape of the Northwest. Despite the dreary weather, Matt's spirits soared as he navigated the sleek contours of his "nearly new" transit van, a purchase that promised reliability and a fresh start in France. In the days leading up to their departure, Matt had orchestrated a flurry of activity, enlisting the help of a house-clearing company to rid Neil's home of its lingering traces. The swift action left them sleeping on makeshift beds in barren rooms, a stark reminder of the void left by Neil's absence. Yet, the busyness had provided a welcome distraction, keeping Matt's mind occupied until the day of Neil's solemn funeral, a quiet affair devoid of fanfare or attendees.

For Richie, the past week had been a trial of nerves, each noise outside the house sending him into a state of heightened alert. The relentless news coverage of the Trafford Park tragedy served as a haunting backdrop to his days, exacerbating his sense of isolation. Cut off from his usual lifelines of social media and mobile communication, Richie grappled with a profound sense of disconnection, the weight of his losses bearing down on him with each passing moment. Unbeknownst to him, Matt watched with growing concern as his nephew wrestled with the emotional toll of their shared ordeal. Sensing Richie's need for closure and a fresh start, Matt gently nudged him to pack essentials for their journey, a silent gesture of support and understanding.

Approaching the channel tunnel's terminal, Matt's nerves danced with anticipation, his mind racing with the possibilities and uncertainties that lay ahead. As they prepared to traverse customs, a small nagging doubt lingered in Matt's mind, a whisper of uncertainty. But for now, all he could do was press forward, his sights set on a new beginning beyond the horizon.

As they approached the check-in area with the revised letter "H" affixed to the rear-view mirror, Matt navigated through the raised barrier, the anticipation of their impending journey coursing through his veins. The drive to the customs booth was brief, and Matt once again presented both passports to the impassive officer seated inside. After a cursory scan, they were waved through, relief flooding over Matt as they continued onward. But their respite was short-lived as a stern-faced female guard motioned them to pull over into a holding compound. Matt complied, guiding the van to a stop amid a flurry of activity. With a practiced efficiency, the guard approached, her appearance unyielding as she swabbed the door handles of the vehicles around them. Matt's pulse quickened, but he maintained his composure, assuring Richie with a reassuring glance. Once the swabbing of vehicles was complete, the guard instructed Matt to switch off the engine and remain inside the vehicle. Matt complied, his mind racing with a mixture of apprehension and determination. As they both waited, tension hung heavy in the air, broken only by the guard's terse questioning. Matt's responses were measured, his confidence unwavering despite the underlying unease.

When instructed to exit the vehicle, Matt and Richie complied without hesitation, moving to the rear of the van as instructed. There, they were met by another customs officer accompanied by an eager Springer Spaniel, ready for duty. Without preamble, Matt opened the rear doors, allowing the dog to begin its search. Moments ticked by in silence, each second stretching into eternity as they waited for the verdict.

To their immense relief, the search yielded no incriminating evidence, and with a nod of approval from the guard, they were swiftly cleared to continue their journey. As they pulled away from the compound, a shared smile passed between Matt and Richie, a silent acknowledgment of their narrow escape. With renewed determination, Matt engaged the gears, propelling them forward toward their awaiting train, leaving behind the tense ordeal of customs behind them.

45 Moving forwards

Jim sat at his desk, engrossed in his investigation notes, when the door swung open, and in stepped Detective Superintendent Laura Holmes, their Senior Investigating Officer (SIO). Laura exuded confidence, a trait she had cultivated despite her working-class upbringing in South Manchester's Woodhouse Park estate. Jim respected Laura immensely; she was a true leader, dedicated to making a difference in the force.

"Hi Jim, can we have a quick team meeting to run over everything we have to date?" Laura's smile was warm and inviting.

"Of course, Mam. I'll gather everyone in the briefing room in ten minutes," Jim replied, already mentally preparing for the discussion ahead.

Jim had worked with Laura on previous homicide investigations, and her guidance had been invaluable. She had supported him through his journey to Inspector, offering advice and encouragement every step of the way. Jim knew he owed much of his success to her mentorship.

Soon, Laura, Jim, Oliver, and a handful of specialist officers convened around the briefing table, ready to delve into the complexities of the homicide investigation. Detective Sergeant Keith Butler began by detailing the findings of the pathologist's examinations. As he spoke, Jim couldn't help but wince at the brutality of the victims' deaths. Keith's thoroughness and expertise shone through, his former military background lending an air of discipline to his approach.

"Four gunshot wounds, blunt trauma... it's a grim scene," Keith acknowledged, his tone solemn yet resolute. Laura listened intently; her focus unwavering as Keith outlined the forensic evidence. The discovery of a fingerprint on the handgun left at the scene piqued everyone's interest, particularly when Oliver revealed it belonged to Kyle Jones, a notorious figure in the city's drug scene.

"Kyle Jones... we finally have a suspect," Laura remarked, a glimmer of satisfaction in her eyes. "Let's mobilise a team to track him down."

The room buzzed with a renewed sense of purpose as they discussed their next steps. Jim couldn't help but feel a surge of optimism; they were one step closer to bringing justice to the victims and their families.

****

Richie sat in the passenger seat, watching the unfamiliar sights of Paris pass by. He couldn't shake the feeling of apprehension that had settled in his gut since they left England. The mid-afternoon traffic grew denser as they approached the outskirts of Paris, a city teeming with life and activity.

"Hey Matt, where are we heading?" Richie finally broke the silence, his curiosity getting the better of him. Matt glanced back at Richie, his expression unreadable for a moment before he replied, "We're heading into the East side of the city. I've got an old friend there who might be able to help you out."

Richie raised an eyebrow, scepticism evident in his voice. "And how exactly is some stranger in East Paris supposed to help me?"

Matt sighed, preparing himself for the conversation ahead. "He's an old military buddy who's been through some tough times himself. Trust me, he'll have valuable advice to offer. We could all use a fresh perspective sometimes."

Richie mulled over Matt's words, still unsure but willing to entertain the idea. "Does this guy have a name?"

Matt chuckled, evading the question. "You'll find out soon enough."

As they navigated through the streets of Paris, Richie couldn't help but feel a sense of unease. The towering apartment blocks and foreign streets felt alien compared to home and where he was used to.

Eventually, they reached their destination, a nondescript area with rows of apartment buildings. However, one feature stood out, a towering stone wall that encircled a secluded area, its purpose shrouded in mystery.

Matt parked the van, breaking the silence. "Alright, grab your bag. We're here."

Richie complied, curiosity mingling with apprehension as they approached the enigmatic stone wall, unsure of what lay beyond its imposing facade.

Once they reached the roadside, Richie set his bag down beside him, his curiosity piqued by the sight before them. Matt gestured toward an imposing structure with a grand stone entrance. "Welcome to the Groupement de Recrutement de la Légion Etrangère," Matt explained, pointing to the fort. "This is Fort de Nogent, the preselection center for the French Foreign Legion."

As Matt spoke, a smartly dressed legionnaire soldier emerged from the entrance, his presence commanding attention. Dressed in impeccable military attire, adorned with bright red epaulettes and the iconic white kepi hat, he exuded an aura of authority. Matt waved in recognition, a warm smile gracing his lips as the soldier approached.

"Bonjour Matt, Hello Matt," the soldier greeted in a distinctive Southern English accent. "Alright Paul, good to see you in fine form. It's been far too long," Matt responded, reciprocating Paul's greeting with a handshake and a heartfelt embrace.

"This is my nephew Richie," Matt introduced, his tone earnest as he gestured towards Richie. "Paul Robinson, meet Richie. We were comrades in the Royal Marines, but Paul chose a different path, as you'll learn in time. He found his way to the Legion here in Paris."

Paul nodded in acknowledgment; a sense of camaraderie evident in his gaze as he extended a hand to Richie. "Good to meet you, Richie. Matts told me a bit about you."

Matt's gaze softened as he addressed Richie directly, his words carrying weight.

"Richie, I know you've been at a crossroads. The way I see it, you've got two paths ahead. You're on your own now, lad. You can carve out your own future, or you can give the French Foreign Legion a shot. It's a chance to start anew, to give it everything you've got. If you commit, they'll take care of you. And when your service is done, you'll have options: stay in France, start afresh, or return home. Your inheritance will wait until you've proven you're ready to manage it responsibly."

Richie listened intently, absorbing Matt's words with a mix of apprehension and hope.

Paul chimed in, his voice steady and reassuring. "Listen, Richie. You've got nothing to lose by giving it a shot. I came here with nothing but trouble behind me, and the Legion gave me a purpose. They'll do the same for you if you show them, you're serious. Trust me."

The weight of the decision hung heavy in the air as Richie processed his options.

Finally, he nodded, a sense of resolve dawning in his eyes. "Thank you, Matt. I appreciate it," he said, his voice tinged with gratitude and determination. With a heartfelt embrace, Richie conveyed his gratitude before picking up his bag, ready to embark on this new chapter.

As Richie and Paul made their way towards the fort, Matt watched them go, a mixture of pride and relief washing over him. With a silent nod to Paul, Matt turned and began the long journey home, knowing he had given his nephew a chance at a fresh start.

THE END

Thank you for taking the time to read my book. If you found it enjoyable, I would appreciate it if you could leave a review on Amazon.co.uk. Your feedback is invaluable to me as an author and helps other readers discover and appreciate my work.

Printed in Great Britain
by Amazon